Demon of Oakhaven

Demon of Oakhaven

Painted in Death

Some monsters hide in the dark. Others paint their work in daylight.

W Mark Harrington

Disclaimer

This is a work of fiction. While the streets, towns, and landmarks of South Carolina may feel real, the people who walk them in these pages are creations of the author's imagination. Any resemblance to actual persons, living or dead, or to actual events, is purely coincidental.

Content Warning

This story pulls no punches. It contains graphic depictions of violence, sexual assault, abduction, and murder, along with strong language and themes that may be disturbing. It's intended for mature readers who can handle the darker corners of human nature.

Dedication

To my crew of M's—my built-in chaos and cheerleaders.

Through the calm days, the loud ones, and the moments only we could ever understand, you've been my constant inspiration. We each think and act in our own way, but somehow that mix is exactly what makes us work. Thanks for believing in me, even when you thought I was gaming instead of writing. Turns out, the final boss wasn't on a console... it was in my word count. And to those who kept pushing me to finish what I started years ago—this one's for you.

P.S. Don't worry—no M's were harmed in the making of *Demon of Oakhaven*.

Table of Contents

Table of Contents

ACKNOWLEDGMENTS

Thanks to my mentors from before and during my law enforcement days—those who taught me the right way to do the job, and those who told me I was too smart for it.

And to the one lady who's had my six since day one—you know who you are. Thanks, Mom.

"The only thing necessary for the triumph of evil is for good men to do nothing."
— Edmund Burke

In Oakhaven, doing nothing isn't an option — because evil doesn't wait

Prologue: Circle of Evidence

Morning sun crept over the stone buildings and old-growth oaks of Ravenwood University, a prestigious private institution located in the heart of South Carolina, nestled along the serene northern shores of Lake Murray in the picturesque town of Oakhaven. Known for its lush, tree-lined campus and a rich blend of Southern charm and academic excellence, Ravenwood offers a tranquil yet vibrant setting for higher learning.

The university's Gothic-inspired architecture and red-brick pathways wind through sprawling greens and magnolia groves. At the same time, its lakeside promenade provides stunning sunset views that have become a signature feature of campus life. With a strong emphasis on liberal arts, criminal justice, environmental sciences, and business leadership, Ravenwood attracts students from across the Southeast and beyond.

Despite its idyllic setting, Ravenwood remains closely connected to real-world issues through strong community partnerships, a nationally recognized law enforcement program, and cutting-edge research initiatives.

Oakhaven itself, once a quiet lakeside town, has grown into a thriving university community, where historic charm meets modern convenience. Yet beneath its peaceful exterior, both town and gown share a history full of secrets... and stories that don't always stay buried.

That morning, the sun bathed the quad in soft gold, casting long shadows that stretched across the courtyard like reaching fingers.

Crime scene tape fluttered in the breeze, a stark slash of yellow slicing through the calm, marking off a patch of once-pristine grass that now belonged to the dead

Detective Will Anderson stood within the cordon, motionless, the faint murmurs of the growing crowd—students, professors, campus security—blurring into background noise.

He didn't hear them.

His eyes were locked on the body. The latest victim.

And the brutal, unmistakable signature left behind by the killer who'd been haunting his thoughts, and his nightmares, for weeks.

The victim was a young woman, late teens or early twenties, nude except for the chilling arrangement of her underwear and bra, laid atop her body... The positioning reminded Will of an unsolved case from years back — a jogger found off a lakeside park path, arms and legs deliberately arranged, no signs of a fight. The scene had haunted him, even though the file was eventually closed as inconclusive.

She was on her back, arms stretched above her head in a perfect Y, ankles crossed. Her entire body was painted white, the artificial pallor almost luminous in the morning light. On her stomach, a large red "O" had been drawn—crude, defiant, and unmistakable.

Will crouched, studying the edges of the mark. The color. The texture. The brushstrokes—no, not brush, fingers. A child's smear of pigment. But this wasn't paint.

Blood.

Not hers.

And that was when it finally locked into place in his mind—the "O" wasn't random. It wasn't just part of the killer's theatrics. It was his calling card. The missing piece in the pattern Will had been chasing, hidden in plain sight. Every scene before this had carried its echo: a circle in a chalk outline, a round smear on a wall, a bottle cap placed just so. Now the truth stared back at him in screaming scarlet.

This wasn't just another murder.

This was the work of him.

3

Enter Murphy

A ripple moved through the crowd as Detective Casey Murphy arrived, ducking under the tape with a crisp nod to the patrolman. Red hair pulled back in a tight ponytail, street clothes instead of uniform, badge clipped to her belt — she scanned the scene, her second in as many weeks.

Will met her inside the tape, jaw set. The exhaustion of the first case, still unsolved, hung between them, but there was something else now: grim recognition. "Word is that this is the missing 23-year-old Leslie Nance, reported missing 2 days ago?"

"It's definitely him," Will said, voice clipped. "Same posing, same paint, same calling card. He's not changing his pattern. Not yet."

Casey's eyes flicked from the victim to Will. "Then he's not finished, either."

Will's phone vibrated. Captain Dan Rogers' name lit the screen. Will stepped a few paces away before answering.

"Talk to me," Rogers barked. "The mayor's breathing down my neck. Two murders in two weeks — at the university. I need something I can take upstairs."

"Same signature as before," Will said. "No physical evidence. Same staging, same red 'O.' Not the victim's blood."

Demon of Oakhaven

A long exhale from Rogers. "Then get me answers, Detective. Fast. Whatever it takes. Call me the second you have something. Understood?"

"Understood," Will said, ending the call.

He met Casey's gaze, the pressure on both of them sharp as a knife.

"Command wants answers," he muttered.

Casey gave a dry, determined smile. "Good thing we weren't planning to sleep."

Will nodded toward the crowd. "Let's get to work."

Somewhere, he knew, the killer was watching — waiting for them to play their next move.

The Killer Speaks

The next morning, Will hunched over a mug of black coffee at Jack'd Up, the local paper spread across the counter. Casey slid into the seat across from him, messenger bag thumping to the floor.

"You see this?" she asked, nodding at the front page.

The lead editorial stared back at him:

INVISIBLE BORDERS

In a town built on tradition, we tell ourselves the world is safe if we keep our rituals, lock the doors, mind our own, look away at the right moment.

But what if the darkness is always waiting inside the circle, clever enough to wear the right face?

Some guardians watch the gates. Some only stare at their reflections. And sometimes, the ones meant to keep us safe are only chasing ghosts, never the real thing.

The real monster always slips through.

– A Watchful Neighbor

Casey's voice was barely above a whisper. "It's him. It has to be. He's watching us, taunting us. He knows exactly how close we are—or how lost."

Will traced the words with his finger, the phrase *inside the circle* catching in his mind. Circle. Ritual. The red O, painted on each victim's stomach. Was it a message? A mark? Or the center of some pattern they hadn't cracked yet?

"Feels like he's reading our case file," Will said. "Like he's already in the room."

"Or he just wants us to think he is," Casey replied, though her jaw was tight.

Will folded the paper, the ritual, and the O still grinding in his thoughts. Kelly Vance, painted white, posed in a perfect K. Leslie Nance, a letter Y, the crimson O like a brand. Different parks. Different days. Same precision. Same staging. Both had vanished in broad daylight from high-traffic spots — just like two other women, years ago, whose disappearances were written off as a coincidence— and not a single witness.

Not luck. Method. And if the pattern held, the clock was already ticking toward the next body.

Julien Cain, the sharp-eyed barista, appeared with the pot, refilling Will's cup. His gaze lingered on the folded paper. "Rough morning, Detective?"

Will glanced at him. "You see a lot working this counter, don't you, Julien?"

The man hesitated, lowering his voice. "Yeah. And... I probably should've called this in sooner, but I wasn't sure it mattered."

Casey leaned in. "What'd you see?"

Julien glanced around, then back to Will. "Your latest victim—she was here yesterday morning. Back corner. Arguing with some older guy. It got heated."

"What about?" Will asked.

"Money. She told him the money was enough, that she was done. Kept saying, 'I'm out. I'm done.'"

Will's eyes narrowed. "Describe him."

"Older, maybe late forties, fifties. Dressy, country club type. Nice car—silver. Not sure the make."

Casey jotted notes. "Anything else?"

"She left first. He hung around, made a few calls, then drove off."

Will nodded, his voice low. "If you remember anything, you call me."

"Of course," Julien said, stepping back, his expression uneasy.

When he was gone, Will and Casey locked eyes. Another piece in the puzzle. Another step closer—not just to the truth, but maybe to the center of the circle the killer was drawing around them.

Type O Theory

Back at the precinct, Will and Casey sat side by side in the cramped squad room, case files spread between them. Will stared at the crime scene photos, his eyes lingering on the crude red "O" painted on each victim's stomach.

He tapped the image with his pen. "The O... It's got to mean something. It's not just a calling card. It's symbolic to him."

Casey swiveled in her chair, lips twisting into a wry smile. "You know, he never leaves a trace, no DNA, no footprints, nothing. It's like he's a ghost. You have to know this area inside and out to move that smoothly."

Will nodded. "He's local, or at least he's spent a lot of time here. These are high-traffic places, campus quads, golf greens, always somewhere that should be impossible to escape unnoticed."

Casey smirked, raising an eyebrow at the photos. "Maybe the O's just his way of overcompensating. Like... maybe the guy's impotent. Can't give a girl an O, so he paints one on just to make a point."

Will actually cracked a tired smile at that. "Morbid, Murphy, but you might be onto something. Obsession with control, performance, humiliation... It's all about leaving his mark."

Casey's face grew serious again. "Whatever it is, he's escalating. The way he taunts us? He wants us chasing him. He wants to be in our heads."

Will leaned back, eyes narrowing. "He's already there."

A moment of heavy silence passed before Casey spoke, her voice soft but determined. "We'll get him, Will. I promise."

Will nodded, gathering the files, determination hardening his features. "Let's start with the car. Someone around here has to know who our guy is."

And with that, they were off, one step closer to the truth, and to the killer who watched from the shadows.

Follow That Lead

In the unmarked cruiser outside the university coffee shop, Casey hunched over her tablet, scrubbing through campus security footage. Will watched the steady stream of morning traffic, his mind running loops of possibilities.

"Julien said silver, something fancy," Casey murmured. "Not a lot of those hanging around here."

"Check the last three mornings," Will said. "Focus on the side street by the exit ramp. If he's careful, he won't risk the main gate."

Casey fast-forwarded through clips, then froze. "Wait— there." She enlarged the frame: a silver sedan easing away from the curb, sunlight glinting off polished chrome. A dark-suited man sat at the wheel.

Will leaned in. "Zoom the plates."

She adjusted, squinting. "Partial: JNZ-something. That's enough for DMV to chew on."

Will studied the silhouette. "Older. Dress shirt, tie. Matches Julien's description."

"That's no student ride," Casey said. "That's country club money."

Will's eyes narrowed. "Pull traffic cam footage from the country club road. If he's a regular, we'll see him again."

Casey's fingers flew. "And I'll have dispatch check for silver sedan stops in the last month. If he slipped once, we'll find it."

Will's phone buzzed — forensics: Blood on victim's abdomen is human. Type AB negative. Not the victim's blood (O positive). Running database now.

He passed the screen to Casey. "Less than one percent of the population. That's rare enough to matter."

Her eyes sharpened. "A rare mark for a killer obsessed with leaving his own. If it's in the system, we've got him."

Will hesitated. "Unless... it's from someone else entirely. Could be a trophy. Could be a victim we haven't found yet."

The thought chilled them both, but Casey's gaze didn't waver. "Either way, we run it. Every lead."

For the first time that day, hope cracked through Will's guarded expression. "Let's go hunting."

The cruiser rolled out, each clue tightening the net — or maybe, drawing them deeper into the circle the killer had been building all along.

Wrong Type of Nervous

Later that afternoon, Will and Casey eased the unmarked cruiser to a stop in front of an immaculate brick townhouse not far from Eagle's View Country Club. The silver sedan from the security footage sat gleaming in the driveway, plate JNZ 481.

Casey scanned the DMV record on her phone. "Howard Ellison. Fifty-two. Retired from finance. Long-time club member. Lives here alone—wife's got a condo in Florida."

Will straightened his jacket as they walked up the path. "Let's see if he's the kind of careful we're looking for."

The door opened to reveal a tall, silver-haired man in pressed khakis and a golf shirt, posture sharp as a tee-off stance. His eyes flicked to their badges, his expression cooling by a few degrees.

"Yes?" The clipped tone fit the wardrobe.

"Mr. Ellison," Will began, "were you at the Jack'd Up coffee shop yesterday morning?"

A brief pause. Then: "I stop there most mornings on my way to the club. Why?"

Casey kept her tone light but direct. "We're looking into an altercation between a young woman—college-aged, brunette—and an older gentleman. Witnesses described a silver sedan, similar to yours, leaving the scene."

Ellison's face flushed. "Excuse me? I was there alone. I don't know any college girls, and I certainly wasn't having an argument. Are you insinuating—" He cut himself off, jaw tight.

Will held up a hand. "We have to follow every lead. Sometimes witnesses get it wrong."

Ellison's grip on the doorframe whitened. "My routine's simple: coffee, paper, club. If your witnesses are so sure, maybe they should get their eyes checked."

Casey gave him a courteous smile. "We appreciate your cooperation, Mr. Ellison. Sorry to intrude."

The door shut with measured force. "See that you are."

Back on the sidewalk, Casey exhaled. "Fits the profile, but not the attitude."

Will shook his head. "Wrong type of nervous. That's embarrassment. Not guilt."

Casey glanced back at the spotless sedan. "So the real driver's still out there."

As they drove off, Will's eyes lingered on the rearview mirror. Somewhere, the right kind of nervous was waiting – and it wouldn't be embarrassment. It would be the thrill of the game.

All Jack'd Up

Will planned to meet his son, Billy Anderson, and Billy's girlfriend, Julia Weeks, at Jack'd Up, the coffeehouse just off the square. It was supposed to be casual — catch up on life, check in on Billy's lacrosse progress, and split a dessert.

Julia slid into the booth first, skirt brushing her knees as she crossed her legs. Her chestnut curls caught the café's warm light, subtle crimson accents in her outfit echoing the streaks in her hair. A small silver crescent moon pendant rested against her collarbone, catching the light each time she moved.

Billy sat opposite her; Will took the seat beside his son. Conversation was easy — classes, training schedules, the occasional father-son jab. Julia laughed readily, her hand drifting to her knee when she shifted in her seat, the pendant swaying gently with the motion.

Halfway through, Julia's phone buzzed, slipped from her lap, and vanished under the table.

"Of course," she muttered with a small laugh, half-laying across the booth to reach it. As she stretched, her skirt — already caught on the booth's seatback — shifted higher, revealing a flash of lace-trimmed crimson beneath tan lines.

15

Will's gaze caught before he could stop it. He turned away sharply, jaw tight.

Twenty years old, he reminded himself. Barely out of her teens. Still just a kid. And his son's girlfriend.

He took a slow breath, forcing his focus onto the rim of his coffee mug, the rising steam. Across the table, Billy was grinning at something Julia said, oblivious.

Julia popped upright with her phone, smiling as if nothing had happened. She was still all youth and unawareness, taking up space without realizing how the world bent around her. The crescent moon pendant glinted as she leaned forward to rejoin the conversation.

Will smiled back, but the knot in his chest stayed.

They finished their desserts, standing to leave. As Billy and Julia stepped outside, Will lingered at the counter.

Julien Cain was wiping mugs, his eyes flicking toward the door. "Nice seeing you, Will," he said.

"You too. Keep an eye on those two," Will replied with a faint smile.

"She's a striking one, that Julia," Julien said, almost casually — but his gaze lingered a second too long, the way Will had seen crowds fixate at crime scenes.

Will's smile thinned. "Most of the young women around here are."

Julien nodded, mouth curling faintly before returning to his mugs.

Will stepped into the fading afternoon light, the comment echoing in his mind, and watching, always watching. He'd heard those words before — in the killer's taunts — and now they followed him down the sidewalk like a shadow.

What Happened to Julia?

Two days after the quiet café meeting, the nightmare began.

Billy Anderson walked into the station looking like he hadn't slept in a day. His hoodie hung loose, eyes red-rimmed, voice cracking as he said the words: "Julia didn't come home."

She was supposed to meet him after lacrosse practice for dinner. She never showed. At first, he'd told himself she was just late, maybe stuck somewhere. But when she didn't answer his texts or the five voicemails he left — and no one had seen her — panic took over.

Will took the initial report, keeping his face steady while his insides clenched. Every instinct told him this wasn't a delay or a misunderstanding. It was too close to the others — the time of day, the public place, the sudden silence. Kelly Vance. Leslie Nance. And now Julia. The killer was accelerating, and he'd taken it personal.

Billy was quickly under the magnifying glass. No solid alibi. Last to see her. Standard procedure, but no easier to watch.

Casey Murphy requested the interview — she knew Will was too close. She also knew Billy from department gatherings, but none of that mattered now.

Billy sat in the metal chair, shoulders hunched, arms locked across his chest like a barricade. His eyes were swollen from crying, but his face was stone.

From behind the one-way glass, Will folded his arms, jaw tight. Beneath the grief in Billy's posture, he saw it — a hard glint of rage.

"Where were you after practice?" Casey asked, calm and even.

"Gym. Then home. I waited for her at The Grille for over an hour. She never showed."

Will's chest ached. Julia was supposed to be safe.

"Did Julia ever mention anyone bothering her?" Casey asked.

"Someone watching her, maybe following her? Did she say anything out of place?"

Billy's head snapped toward her. "Bothering her? Yeah — probably whoever took her while we're in here talking."

Casey didn't flinch. "Watch it, Billy."

Will's shoulders tensed. He'd seen Billy fight like this before — cornered, hurting — but never with this edge.

Then Billy leaned back, eyes sharp. "Maybe if you weren't so busy eye-fucking my dad every time he walks into a room, you'd be better at your job."

Will's stomach dropped.

Casey froze. The flicker in her eyes could have been fury, or hurt, or both, but she set her pen down carefully and folded her hands.

On the other side of the glass, Will's heartbeat thudded in his ears.

Billy stared past her, voice colder now.

"Your move, Detective lady."

Casey's gaze didn't waver. "Cute. You always deflect when you're scared?"

Billy's mask cracked — lip trembling, breath unsteady. "No. I deflect when I feel like I'm falling apart, and no one believes me."

Casey's tone softened just enough. "I believe you're upset. And I believe you care about Julia. But this is about facts. Help me with them."

He rubbed at his face. "I'm telling you everything I know. I didn't do anything to her."

"I know," she murmured, barely audible. But the interview had to go on. And Will knew — no matter what Billy said — the shadow of the killer's ritual had already closed over her, and suspicion would linger until they either found Julia... or her body.

A Ghost in the Trees

When the hikers found Julia's body two days later, the forest went still.

They hadn't meant to stumble onto anything — just a shortcut back to their car after a long day on the trail. But there she was.

Suspended. Displayed.

She hung between two pine trees, arms and legs pulled into a taut X, ankles bound to saplings that bowed under the strain, wrists lashed high to thick limbs. Her head slumped forward, caught between prayer and surrender.

Her skin was ghostly white, every inch painted as if the killer had stripped away her humanity. A crescent moon pendant dangled from her right ear on a slender silver chain — its presence deliberate, its meaning unreadable.

On her stomach, the bloody crimson O — thick, uneven, pressed in with fingers. Not paint. Not hers.

One hiker vomited into the brush. The other backed away, phone shaking in his hand as he called 911.

By the time Will got the call, he already knew.

Billy hadn't spoken since the night she vanished. Neighbors said he sat on the porch in the same clothes, shoes untied, hands dangling between his knees, staring at the concrete as if it might open beneath him.

When Will arrived, Billy didn't look up. Didn't blink. Just whispered, hoarse and dry, "She was so scared of the woods."

Will swallowed hard and crossed the walkway.

At first, Billy didn't react when Will's hand settled on his back. Didn't move when Will's arms went around him. But then, slowly, like a wall crumbling after too much silence, Billy leaned in — trembling without sound, the quiet quake of a boy breaking under grief too big for words.

Will held him tighter, as if he could shield him from the ruin.

"I'll get him," Will whispered, low and raw. "For her. For Julia. For every girl he's taken."

Billy's gaze lifted, red-rimmed and blazing with grief and rage.

"This ends with him," Will said, jaw set. "No more victims."

And in that moment, the promise wasn't just between a father and a son.

It was a vow.

A reckoning.

Later, at the crime scene...

Casey stood beneath the pines, the late afternoon sun knifing through the branches in narrow beams. The forensic techs worked in silence, their movements deliberate.

She crouched near Julia's left ankle, studying the way the sapling bent under the strain. "No knots," she

murmured to herself. The bindings were looped, not tied —
a slip method, fast to apply, faster to remove.

Her gaze moved up the body to the pendant.

The crescent moon's silver surface was scratched, a
series of tiny, deliberate marks etched along the inside
curve. At first, they looked random. Then she saw it — three
short, shallow lines, a gap, and then a single vertical slash.

It wasn't part of his usual staging.

It was new.

She straightened, scanning the tree line, the shadows
shifting with the wind. The killer was still refining his
message, and now he'd added something — a code, maybe,
or a number.

Whatever it was, she knew it wasn't meant for the
press.

It was meant for them.

Pressure from the Brass

The pressure was building, and not just from the public.

Inside the department walls, the atmosphere turned cold. Whispers in the hall, late-night calls left unanswered, and paperwork that used to get cleared in hours now sat in limbo for days. Every move Will and Casey made on the serial murder case seemed to be met with skepticism or outright resistance, mostly from one man: Captain Dan Rogers.

Rogers had always carried himself like a company man. Slick smile, polished shoes, and a knack for politics that made him more administrator than cop. But lately, his scrutiny had turned sharp, almost personal. He called Will and Casey into his office regularly, grilling them not for updates but for missteps.

"You're chasing ghosts," Rogers said during one tense meeting, fingers steepled over a pristine desk. "No suspects. No motive. Just more bodies and bad press."

"We have leads," Will said firmly. "We're closing in."

"Then close faster." Rogers's voice dropped. "Or I'll hand it over to someone who can."

Casey clenched her jaw beside Will. "Someone who'll sweep it under the rug, you mean?"

Rogers smirked. "Careful, Detective. That badge doesn't come with immunity."

The implication hung in the air like rot.

Outside those meetings, their investigation hit wall after wall. Requests for surveillance footage were delayed. Evidence logs came back with gaps. Lab reports were "misfiled." Informants dried up. A few officers who had once been cooperative now avoided eye contact entirely.

And then things got darker.

In the department's archaic digital archives, Casey unearthed a heavily censored internal affairs file. Its fragmented data hinted at a conspiracy: several high-ranking officers were implicated in the disappearance of funds tied to confiscated narcotics.

Meanwhile, Will dug into cold homicide files and found something worse — three cases, spread over a decade, where young women had vanished in broad daylight from high-traffic public spaces. The locations were eerily similar to the current victims: a busy lakeside park, a campus quad, a golf course. No witnesses. No signs of struggle. And in two of those cases, the bodies had been found days later in staged positions that, while not identical to the killer's current displays, carried the same hallmarks — public spectacle, symbolic placement, deliberate posing, were those his too?.

One of those cases had been hidden in the records due to a "clerical error," its evidence destroyed in a purge. Another had been closed as a "runaway" despite physical details suggesting otherwise. All three had quietly faded from departmental memory.

The coincidences were too precise. Too suspicious.

The deeper they dug, the more threads they pulled, and the more they realized something was seriously wrong inside their own house.

Rogers's next warning was less subtle.

"One more screw-up, and I'll pull the plug. You're too close to this, Will. And Casey — don't think being a rising star gives you immunity from transfer."

Neither backed down.

They started meeting outside the station: quiet booths in diner corners, locked office doors, burner phones when necessary. They compared notes, flagged names, and cross-checked timelines. And each time they did, it became clearer — this wasn't just about a killer.

It was about a department built on secrets.

And someone wanted those secrets to remain buried.

They weren't sure who they could trust, but one thing was certain.

They could depend on each other and trust each other.

The Photo

The envelope waited at the front desk as it belonged there.

Plain manila, legal-sized. No return address. Will's name written in block letters—neat, deliberate, unmistakably intentional.

"Who brought this in?" Will asked.

The desk sergeant shook his head. "Nobody saw it. It was just... there. Between shift change."

That was answer enough.

Will didn't open it right away. He took it back to Homicide, shut his office door, and sat down. The room felt smaller than usual, the air thick with the sense that something bad was already happening.

He slid a finger under the flap.

One photograph.

Glossy. High quality. Recent.

Julia.

Alive.

For half a second, his brain rejected it outright—refused to accept what his eyes were seeing. She stood against a dark, indistinct background, bare skin pale against the shadows. Her face was turned slightly toward the camera, eyes open, unfocused but conscious. Not posed like the bodies they'd found. Not staged for death.

Not yet.

A man stood behind her, his face cropped out of the frame. One arm wrapped across her chest, forearm covering one breast, his hand deliberately placed over the other—possessive, claiming, obscene in its restraint. Dangling over Julia's shoulder was a dark crimson pendant: an ouroboros, the serpent devouring its own tail, polished until it caught the light.

Around Julia's neck—still there, impossibly normal—hung her silver crescent moon pendant.

The same one.

Will's hand tightened until the photo bent.

His chest hollowed out, something hot and furious burning its way up through the grief. Regret hit first—sharp and merciless. Every missed lead. Every moment, he'd gone home instead of staying. Every second, he'd believed he still had time.

Then came the anger.

Cold. Focused. Absolute.

This wasn't evidence.

It was a message.

The door creaked softly.

Casey had stopped short just inside the threshold. She took one look at Will's face and knew—whatever he was holding had crossed a line.

"Will?" she said quietly.

He didn't answer. He just held the photo out.

She stepped closer, took it from him, and her breath caught despite herself. Her jaw set, eyes hardening as she took in the details—the pendant, the positioning, the deliberate cruelty of proof without mercy.

"He wanted you to know," she said. "That you were close. And not close enough."

Will nodded once. "He wanted me to see her alive."

Casey handed the photo back carefully, like it might cut. "We'll get him."

Before Will could respond, Casey's phone buzzed. Then she frowned and looked past him toward her desk.

A yellow notepad sat dead center on her blotter. It hadn't been there an hour ago.

No envelope this time. Just a single page written on the tip line reporting form.

Check the old hardware store.

Edge of downtown.

River road

You're running out of time

Casey looked at Will. "That wasn't there this morning."

Will stared at the note, then back down at the photograph in his hand.

"This is him," he said. "Still controlling the board."

Casey grabbed her jacket. "Then we stop reacting."

Will stood, the photo already sliding back into the envelope like a wound being sealed. Turned over on his desk.

"We move," he said. "Now."

And somewhere in Oakhaven, the killer already knew they would.

The Set Up in the Alley

Night pressed down on Oakhaven like a lid, trapping the late summer humidity and the quiet tension of a town unraveling under an unsolved string of killings.

The tip had been vague — rushed, almost too convenient — but urgent enough to drag Will and Casey from their desks to the boarded-up hardware store on the edge of downtown.

"This feels wrong," Will said. "I have a bad feeling about this," Casey murmured as they moved into the alley.

It stank of mildew, wet concrete, and something older, sourer — a place the town pretended didn't exist.

Will took point, Casey a step behind.

Then the dark erupted.

Two figures burst from the shadows, muzzle flashes lighting brick. The gunfire cracked and rolled in the narrow space, the echoes tripping over each other like thunderclaps.

Casey spun for cover, but the first volley caught her mid-stride. Pain flared across her upper back, just under the shoulder blade, hot and searing. She stumbled, half-turning before crashing behind a rusted bin.

"Casey!" Will barked, returning fire. The recoil slammed into his palms; brick dust puffed where rounds hit walls.

The shooters moved with precision — no wasted motion, no blind panic.

One bolted for the street. The other sprinted to Casey's unmarked cruiser. In seconds, the engine roared, tires screaming as the car fishtailed out of sight.

The second suspect vaulted a fence and was gone before Will could draw a bead.

Silence seeped back into the alley, leaving only the hiss of Casey's breath and the metallic tang of gunpowder.

She pressed a shaking hand to her back, wincing. "Graze," she gritted out, "but deep enough to hurt like hell."

Will stepped to her, scanning the wound — a long, bloody streak where the bullet had skimmed her. She stayed upright, but just barely.

Then something caught his eye near the dumpster — a glint of metal.

He picked it up. A heavy-duty flashlight. Fresh scratches on the casing. The engraving was clear:

OAKHAVEN POLICE DEPT.

Casey's expression hardened. "They knew we'd be here."

Will turned the flashlight over in his palm, his voice low. "And they moved like they were trained to leave without a trace."

Both suspects are gone. No injuries. No names.

Casey bleeding.

Now they knew for certain — this wasn't just a killer.

It was a conspiracy.

And the rot in the department wasn't just deep.

It was armed.

Will helped her toward the street, one arm bracing her weight. She gave him a pained smirk.

"You know," she said through gritted teeth, "this is exactly why Han shot first."

Will glanced at her, one eyebrow up. "You're bleeding and making Star Wars jokes?"

"Priorities," she said, wincing as they kept moving.

Some Wounds Heal

Back at Casey's apartment, the reality of the evening's violence set in. Casey winced as she shrugged off her jacket, feeling fresh blood trickle from her back.

"I need a hand," she admitted, voice tight.

Will set his go bag on the counter, his expression grave. "Let's see it."

Casey hesitated, one hand clutching the hem of her shirt, her face flushed with pain and something else — uncertainty.

"I, uh... I'll need to take this off," she said, low but steady. "And... the bra too. The cut's high."

She kept her face turned away from Will, jaw clenched, doing her best to hold onto control over a moment that had already cost her enough. With careful, deliberate movements, she slid her arms out of her shirt, flinching as the fabric pulled against the raw edge of the graze. Her fingers fumbled slightly at the bra clasp, but she didn't ask for help.

Will averted his gaze, busying himself with the med kit, giving her the dignity of space without having to be told.

Casey pressed a clean towel against her chest with one arm, holding it in place as she let the bra slide off and fall to the side. She stood there, back exposed, the angry red line of the graze stretching just below her shoulder blade, shallow but long, still faintly oozing.

"Ready," she muttered.

Will turned back, professional and silent, gloves already on. Antiseptic, closure strips, wound glue — everything ready in his hands.

Whatever else existed between them, this moment wasn't about that. It was about trust, pain, and the quiet courage required not to break under either.

He worked quickly, cleaning the wound with a firm but gentle touch. The antiseptic stung sharply; she inhaled through her teeth but remained quiet. The chemical scent of the glue lingered in the air as he sealed the strip in place.

"All done," Will said, voice steady. "Keep it clean. No lifting, at least tonight."

Casey nodded and reached for a clean T-shirt from her laundry basket. Still holding the towel to her chest, she shifted into it without losing coverage. Only then did she face him, a shaky smirk curling at her lips.

"Well," she said, "that's a hell of a team-building exercise. Even better than my Han Shot First theory."

Will managed a small laugh. "I'll put it on your eval."

Outside, the sirens had faded into nothing. Inside, the flashlight marked **OAKHAVEN POLICE DEPT.** sat on the kitchen table, a fresh dent along its rim catching Will's eye. Someone had dropped it recently. Someone who'd been in that alley with them.

The only people they could trust were in that room.

Off the Books

Will didn't take the cruiser. He left Casey's building on foot, flashlight wrapped in the towel under his arm, the night air heavy with the lingering taste of summer rain. Two blocks over, he slid behind the wheel of his own car and headed for the industrial district.

The meeting spot was an old machine shop with a "For Lease" sign, half-rotten in the window. Only one light burned inside — a single bulb over a workbench stacked with tools and jars of screws.

A tall man in a faded Army jacket looked up as Will stepped in. His beard was trimmed short, his eyes alert and tired all at once.

"Jesus, Anderson," the man said. "You don't call for months, then you show up with that look? What happened?"

"Got something that needs a print and DNA run," Will said, placing the wrapped towel on the bench. "Quietly."

The man — Vince Carrow, a former crime lab tech turned private consultant — peeled back the towel. His brow furrowed when he saw the engraving.

"Oakhaven PD? You finally start robbing your own evidence locker?"

Will didn't smile. "Found it at an active scene. Alley ambush. Whoever left it knew exactly where we'd be — and how to leave without being seen."

Vince turned the flashlight over, running a thumb over the fresh dent in the rim. "That's a new mark. Looks like it hit concrete. I'll dust it now."

He worked with steady, practiced motions, brushing powder along the grip and barrel. A faint print bloomed under the light — partial but distinct enough to chart.

"Not bad," Vince murmured. "Glove smudge on the rim, but this one here? Bare skin. And—" He stopped, leaning closer. "Looks like it's been worn down on one side. This grip's been handled a lot, same exact spot every time. That's muscle memory."

"Meaning?" Will asked.

"Meaning the person who carried this didn't just grab it once. They've used it for years. That's not patrol work either — too clean. My guess? Former SWAT or special detail. Somebody trained to keep their gear immaculate and ready."

Will's jaw tightened. "That narrows it."

Vince slid the flashlight into an evidence bag. "I'll run the print against my private database. Won't show up in official records, but if they've worked a private security contract, military, or freelance gig in the last ten years, we might get a hit."

Will nodded once. "Call me direct when you do. No messages. No email."

Vince smirked faintly. "And if I find out it's one of your golden boys from the department?"

Will's voice was flat. "Then I know exactly where to aim next."

The Latest Headline

The next morning, all of Oakhaven buzzed over the Oakhaven Herald's front page. The anonymous editorial—almost certainly from the killer—read like a gleeful confession. It mocked the chaos in the alley, describing in unnerving detail how detectives had been lured by a tip, gunfire sparking off brick, and bullets chasing them into cover while two masked suspects vanished... in a stolen police detective's own car.

The detail was so precise, it was clear the author hadn't just heard about the ambush. They'd seen it—or planned it.

Rumors spread like wildfire, fueled by the killer's own words.

At the station, Captain Dan Rogers waited behind his closed office door, newspaper in hand, the front page crumpled where his grip had tightened. He slapped it onto the desk with a sharp *smack*.

"Care to explain," he said, voice cold, "why I'm reading about your little firefight in the *morning paper* instead of in your incident reports?" His glare shifted between Will and Casey like a metronome.

Will spoke first, steady but firm. "It was an ambush. Whoever set it up knew exactly what they were doing. The suspects got away in Casey's car."

Rogers cut him off with a hand slice. "And you didn't call it in? You didn't notify me or command? Do you have *any* idea how this makes the department look?"

Casey stepped forward. "We found a flashlight. Department property. Dropped by one of the shooters. We think—"

Will's voice dropped. "—someone inside helped them."

The room went still. Rogers leaned forward, his stare hardening. "Accusing your own brothers and sisters in blue is a big step. Got proof? A name? Anything I can take to the mayor or IA?"

Casey shook her head. "Not yet. Just a dirty flashlight and too many questions."

Rogers' palm slammed the desk. "Then keep it to yourselves. You hear me? No more wild accusations. You want to keep your badges, you play it *by the book*. Find something real—or drop it."

When they left his office, the unspoken truth followed them down the hall: the killer wasn't the only threat in Oakhaven. And from here on out, the only thing they could trust was each other—and whatever truth they could dig up before the brass shut them down.

A New University Art Display

Late in the morning, Oakhaven University's campus was buzzing — students streaming between buildings, cutting across green lawns, voices rising over the hum of cicadas. But today, all eyes were locked on the heart of the quad.

An unmarked black sedan idled in the middle of a wide brick walkway near the student union, hazard lights blinking in perfect rhythm. Blue and red LEDs pulsed inside, bathing the empty seats in alternating washes of cold light.

Campus security had gotten there first. By the time Will and Casey arrived, yellow tape ringed the car, and a knot of students had gathered just beyond. Some whispered, some took pictures, a few laughed.

Casey froze. It was her car.

The suspects hadn't abandoned it quietly — they'd parked it dead center in the busiest part of campus. A trophy. A warning.

As Will circled the vehicle, eyes scanning for anything left behind, Casey forced herself closer. The doors were locked, but the hazard lights and blue LEDs flashed in alternating bursts, a beacon to anyone within sight. Inside, the dashcam bracket sat empty. The radio was unplugged. The on-board laptop gone.

From the trunk and glovebox, her first aid kit, extra cuffs, and case notes — all gone. She checked each compartment anyway, jaw locked, cheeks burning under the students' stares.

"Couldn't just dump it quietly, could they?" Will muttered.

The real message sat in the center console: a single folded piece of paper, block letters sharp against the white page.

NICE TRY, DETECTIVES. BETTER LUCK NEXT TIME.

Beneath it, drawn in thick crimson marker — the crude outline of an O.

Casey stared at it for a beat, then stuffed it into her pocket, knuckles white.

The car was eventually towed, blue and red LEDs still pulsing as it rolled away. Students filmed every moment, their voices carrying: *"Was that a cop car?" "What the hell happened?" "Think it's a prank?"*

Someone near the front of the crowd yelled, loud enough to cut through the noise, "Hey! That's not even a parking spot!"

A few students laughed. Others kept filming, phones held high, hungry for spectacle.

As Casey scanned the crowd, her gaze snagged on a girl near the front — chestnut hair, backpack slung low, a slender crescent moon pendant glinting against her T-shirt. For a half-second, Casey's breath caught. Julia's pendant had been almost identical.

Will's voice drew her back. "They wanted a show," he said, placing a steady hand on her shoulder. "They wanted you rattled."

Casey's jaw tightened. "This isn't just about rattling me. They had time to strip it clean after the alley ambush, pick through my gear, then park it here without anyone stopping them. That's planning. That's access."

Will's eyes narrowed. "Inside help."

She nodded once. "Same people who set us up in that alley are still running the play. And now the whole damn campus just got front-row seats."

They both knew — the killer, or whoever was helping him, had just proved nowhere was off-limits. And everyone in Oakhaven had just seen how close danger could get.

Friday Night and Old Connections

Friday night draped Councilman Renfrow's estate in warm golden light. Beneath chandeliers and over the polished hardwood, Oakhaven's elite traded laughter and champagne.

Will, in a suit for once, felt like a foreign coin in the wrong currency. Kristen, though — she belonged. She glided through the crowd in a shimmering ruched blue silk slit dress that caught the light like water. Her dark hair was twisted up, wisps curling at her neck, and heads turned when she passed.

As they mingled, Kristen lit up at the sight of an old acquaintance. Will's stomach tightened when he recognized him — Steve Creegan. Tall, well-dressed, a smile just this side of smug. Kristen's college ex.

Creegan greeted her with smooth charm, and she laughed at something he said — but Will caught the tiny eye roll she hid in the next breath. Once, she'd told him "Creegan" was short for "CreepMan," and nothing had happened between them for a reason.

Will drifted toward the bar for drinks, but his phone buzzed. Dispatch. The serial killer had struck again.

He turned to Kristen, voice tight. "I have to go. They need me."

Kristen didn't miss a beat. She kissed his cheek and squeezed his hand. "Go. Save the world, Detective."

From over her shoulder, Creegan said lightly, "If you need a ride home, Kristen, I'm leaving later."

Will kept his eyes on her. "If you can't get a car, the Uber app's ready on your phone."

Kristen smiled. "I'll be fine."

Will nodded once and left, badge taking over. On the way to his car, he called home. Emily answered on the second ring.

"Everything okay, Dad?"

"Yeah. I'll be late. Mom's at the party. You good?"

"Good. Just finishing the polish on my toes. Ellie's at a sleepover. Already locked up now, right after you guys left."

"Alright. Love you, kiddo."

By 11:03, the party had thinned to a handful of lingerers. Kristen stepped outside to order an Uber — no drivers anywhere nearby. The air was cooler now, a faint mist creeping off the lawns. She rubbed her bare arms.

On the porch, Creegan jingled his keys. "Need a lift?"

She hesitated a beat longer than she meant to. He was safe... probably. "Yeah, thanks. Before I get cornered again."

As they walked toward his car, Kristen noticed the driveway beyond the estate lights was swallowed in shadow. The last of the guests' taillights disappeared down the road.

Inside the car, she texted Will: *No Ubers. Getting a ride home with Mr. Wannabe Steve Creeper. Love you.*

They pulled away, the glow of the estate fading fast behind them. The road was empty, the kind of rural stretch where the trees on either side pressed in like walls.

Creegan talked — something about golf, about work — but Kristen found herself glancing at the side mirrors more than listening. Once, she thought she saw headlights far back, low and steady, but when she looked again, the road was black.

Her phone buzzed with a reply from Will: *Be careful.*

She smiled faintly and typed back, *Always.* But the tiny knot in her stomach didn't ease.

Fun House of Horrors

Emily had spent the night alone.

The house felt different after dark — too still, too quiet. Every creak in the walls made her flinch. She pulled the blanket tighter, scrolling on her phone until her eyelids sagged and sleep finally took her.

It wasn't restful.

Somewhere after midnight, she stirred again, pulled from half-formed dreams by voices. Low. Muffled. Unfamiliar.

At first, she thought it was just the TV in her parents' room. That happened sometimes when her mom came home late. But this was... different. Laughter. A man's voice she didn't recognize.

Footsteps overheard.

Her heart gave a small flutter. *Mom must be home,* she told herself. Probably just talking to a friend.

She swung her legs over the bed, padding barefoot into the hallway. Halfway down the stairs, she paused.

Through the front hallway blinds, she caught sight of a car in the driveway. Sleek. Dark. Low to the ground. A sports car. Definitely not her dad's. Not her mom's either.

It looked expensive and out of place.

The kitchen lights were still on — strange. Her mother always switched them off before bed.

Then she saw the blue silk dress from the party crumpled on the floor, one heel tipped near the entryway, the other halfway into the living room. On the counter, a half-empty bottle of wine, two glasses — one upright, the other tipped, a red stain bleeding down the edge.

Emily frowned. Messy. Careless. Not impossible... but off.

She moved toward the bedroom hallway. On the carpet lay her mom's new blush-pink sheer lace strapless bra — the one they'd picked out together. The sight of it discarded here sent a sharp, cold ripple through her.

The bedroom door was cracked, light spilling into the hall. Her mother never left the lights on at night.

Emily's chest tightened as she stepped closer, every nerve on edge.

Inside — her mother, sprawled across the bed, hair tangled, eyes half-closed, a man beside her. Naked. Not her father.

The man shifted, and Emily's stomach dropped. She recognized him. but where.

Kristen mumbled a name, slurred and blurred: "Will?"

The man's voice came back low and sure: "No... but you know my name, Kristen. It's Steve."

Emily's mind spun — confusion, disgust, betrayal all crashing at once. She took a step back, desperate to retreat.

The floorboard under her heel groaned.

Dazed and Confused

A violent crash erupted from her mother's room — something heavy hitting the floor hard enough to make the walls shiver. Emily froze mid-step, her pulse ratcheting up until she could hear it in her ears.

A silhouette appeared in the spill of light from the bedroom. Steve filled the hallway like a blockade, bare-chested, wearing some chest rig with a blinking red light that looked unsettlingly like a camera.

His gaze locked on hers. "You," he spat, voice low and sharp. Then, with an edge of disbelief, "Where did you come from?"

Emily stepped back until her spine pressed into the wall, the picture frames behind her rattling. Move. Run. But her legs refused.

He closed the distance fast, his hand suddenly on her jaw — too tight, cold. She caught the scent of her mother's lavender perfume clinging to him and her stomach turned.

"Well, hey there," he said, the words slow, casual, wrong. He gripped her under her chin, examining her. "You look just like her... back when she was your age."

Her skin prickled. Her voice wouldn't come.

Steve tilted his head, his smile widening. "Do you like games?"

Her throat tightened. Every instinct screamed for distance. She sidestepped, but his shadow followed.

The moment blurred — his forearm pinning her to the wall, his bulk crowding her space. She tried to twist away, her elbow clipping a vase on the table. It tipped and rattled to the floor, water spilling across the tile in a sudden sheet. Trying to plant, her bare feet slid out from under her, and she hit the ground hard.

He laughed — a short, cruel sound — and caught her ankles before she could scramble away. Water soaked the hem of her underwear and shirt as he dragged her back toward him.

Her hands clawed for purchase, nails skidding on the slick floor. "Not so fast," he jeered. "You're getting ahead of yourself, lying down. Nobody said endgame yet!"

He wrapped his arm around her and hauled her upright, spun her to face him. "Stand up," he ordered, releasing her as if daring her to try something. "Hit me, woman!" She did. She swung at him — wild, fueled by panic and fury. Her knuckles cracked against his cheekbone, and the pain reverberated back into her wrist."

He barely flinched. "Nice one, Wildcat. My turn."

The punch to her stomach knocked the air out of her in a choking gasp. She folded over, clutching her midsection, lungs refusing to work. The room swayed. She heard the drip of water from the table to the floor.

That's when she felt it — a sudden, humiliating tug at her underwear, fabric biting into her skin before sliding halfway down her thighs. Cold air hit the exposed skin like a slap.

Emily froze. Her lungs seized, caught in her throat, and no relief was coming.

Steve's hand lingered at her hip for a beat too long before pulling away — not gone, but circling. Watching her reaction.

She stumbled backward, heart pounding. Her underwear, pale lavender with a small cartoon leopard and a pink bow on the waistband, stuck damply to her legs from the spilled water.

He smiled faintly, eyes flicking downward as if memorizing it. "That's better," he murmured, almost to himself.

Just as a whisp of air crossed her lips, the second hammering blow recoiled her back into the choking void. Still reeling, trying to catch her breath as the world sounded as if she was underwater, trying to keep from falling, her hand finds the wall again.

That's when she felt it — the heat of his hands gripping at her thighs, rough and insistent, the sudden tug that sent her underwear sliding down in a humiliating collapse around her ankles. Before she could move, his foot came down on the fabric, pinning it to the floor like crude shackles, rooting her in place.

The elastic stretched with a faint snap before going slack. The cold tile pressed against her bare feet, and above it all hung the scent of his sweat – sharp, sour – tangled with her mother's lingering lavender perfume.

Her mind shattered, bouncing between humiliation, fury, confusion, and fear, each one crashing into the next until her thoughts blurred. She grabbed at anything to pull herself away from the moment, holding onto something absurd, something small: her toes.

Freshly polished just that afternoon, a soft lavender that matched the dress she planned to wear tomorrow. The glossy color looked almost unreal against the pale floor and his shadow looming over her. The more she focused on them, the more the rest of the world seemed to blur, as if the tiny swirls of polish could keep her from drowning in what was happening.

Then came the pressure – his body too close, pressing into her space, radiating the uninvited, unconsented presence that set every nerve on fire. Then it was gone, but his laugh still echoed, loud and menacing. Then he was back, toying and teasing her with the inevitable line about to be crossed, her mind wondering why the horror hadn't come with each tug and pull, like a puppet on a string. The air between them seemed to shrink until she could barely breathe. Her body shivered with anticipation, as if... NO! In her mind, she silently screamed, confused once again by her body. She felt the heat and the tease of the monster puppeteer controlling her. She prepared once more to accept her fate.

Then, from the hallway, a voice: "Em... is that you?"

Kristen stood in the bedroom doorway, one hand on the frame for balance, eyes glassy, hair mussed.

Steve turned toward Kristen, stumbling against the doorframe, just for a second.

Emily moved. She shoved past him, feet slipping in the water, legs barely holding her up, but she ran. Down the hall, through the blur of the living room, toward anywhere that wasn't here, up the stairs away from the monster in her house.

She didn't look back.

Kristen Stirs, Steve Plots

Steve watches Emily stumble and vanish down the hall, wheezing, broken, and lets out a low, mocking laugh.

"Guess we'll have to revisit this wildcat another time—when we've got more time to play, folks!" he calls to no one but himself, his voice dripping with cruelty.

His attention shifts to Kristen, now swaying unsteadily in the bedroom doorway. She leans against the frame, barely upright. Her eyes roll lazily, unfocused, her tangled hair glowing wild in the lamp's backlight.

"Stev?" she murmurs, voice thick with wine. "Is tha.. you, St..eve?"

Steve grins. "Of course it's me. I just dropped you off from the party, remember?" His tone is smooth, practiced. "You really went overboard, sweetheart. Let's get you to bed."

He moves toward her, taking her gently by the arm and waist, guiding her toward the mattress. Kristen stumbles, limp in his hold, and his fingers take the opportunity to wander over her hips, claiming without consent.

"You good guy... " You god... good driver you here," she slurs, mumbling praise that barely makes sense as he gives her a slight push forward, and against the bed she lowers herself face down.

"That's right," he whispers near the back of her head. "I am a god... and you're going to be my beautiful star."

His hand trails down her body in one final, deliberate caress. "One last touch from a god... for now," he says quietly, savoring it. His fingers slide under her, a violation disguised as intimacy. He grunts, "One for the road for me, a surprise later for you."

Then he begins gathering his things—pulling on his pants, pocketing Kristen's panties, removing his phone from the tripod still standing by the bed.

As he heads for the door, a glow catches his eye—Kristen's phone lighting up on the nightstand. A message from Will flashes: *On my way.*

Steve pauses, smirks, picks up her phone, crouches beside her, and lifts her limp hand. Her thumb trembles slightly, but it's enough. He presses it to the sensor—*click*—unlocked.

"Perfect," he mutters.

In seconds, he's added his own number to her contacts, sent himself a single-word message to log it, deleted the thread, then repeated the process in her messages app. Everything is precise and clean. He places the phone back beside her as if it had never been touched.

Before leaving, he rolls Kristen over, holds her phone above her, and snaps a crotch shot from her perspective—then hits send. Kristen's breathing is shallow, the wine having dragged her into a heavy, unresponsive state.

Steve pockets his device, muttering under his breath, "That's for calling me Will," before driving his fist into her abdomen. Kristen lets out a deep, involuntary sound, her body shifting slightly before going still again.

He unstraps his recording harness, folds it neatly, and tucks it into a pillowcase. Then, as he exits the bedroom, he picks up Emily's underwear from the floor—cartoon leopard print—and holds it between two fingers with a smirk.

Fitting, he thinks—a wildcat to the end.

On his way out, his shoe splashes in the thin sheet of water from the vase Emily knocked over earlier. The puddle splash fans outward, catching the dim light in tiny glints. He pauses, glances toward the hallway, and chuckles to himself before stepping through it, tracking faint wet footprints toward the stairs.

At the bottom, he calls out, voice slow and mocking:

"I'm leaving now, Wildcat. You can come out."

A pause. Then darker:

"Tell anyone... and I won't be so nice next time. I know where you sleep. I know where they sleep."

His voice sharpens, cruel:

"Maybe next time, your mom or sister joins in. Or that pathetic excuse for a father of yours." A low, mocking laugh. "Hell, we'll make it a family affair."

Another pause, then a twisted singsong:

"Your mom loves affairs..."

Emily doesn't move. Frozen. Every word sears into her memory.

Then, the front door opened.

An engine roaring to life.

Gravel spitting against the siding like a rain of stone and sand.

And silence.

The terror is gone.

But the fear? That stays.

It's just gone quiet.

Erase Everything

Emily drifted through the house like a ghost—numb, hollow, her body moving on instinct alone. She gently closed the front door and turned the lock, but the gesture now felt meaningless. Her hands trembled. The sticky sweat on her skin still clung to her like a stain she couldn't wash away, a cruel reminder of what had just happened.

The house was quiet once more, but it still didn't feel safe.

She moved instinctively, heading back toward the bedroom. When she turned on the light, the scene struck her hard—Kristen sprawled across the bed, snoring softly, limbs everywhere, sheets on the floor, completely unaware. Peaceful. Untouched. Not a care in the world.

Emily's chest tightened, heat stinging her eyes. She wanted to scream at her, shake her awake, make her see. The betrayal echoed in her mind, demanding to be shouted. But when she finally spoke, it was barely more than a cracked whisper.

Fuck you, Kristen.

She entered the bathroom to splash water on her face. As she moved the towel, a crinkling sound caught her attention, a small foil wrapper fell onto the tile. She froze, staring at it. Disgust tightened her stomach. Grabbing a

58

tissue, she pinched it up and flushed it, watching it swirl away. No plan. Just erasing.

Back in the hallway, she saw it—the thin sheen of water she had slipped in earlier, still pooled on the floor from the toppled vase. She crouched and started mopping it with a towel, her movements slow and automatic. Then she gathered her mother's scattered belongings: the crumpled blue silk dress, a single heel near the entryway, the other tilted toward the living room, and the bra they'd bought together, delicate blush sheer pink lace.

And there she took off and added her own ripped, oddly stretched T-shirt, limp and wet. She placed it in the pile in the laundry room washer, poured in detergent until it spilled over her fingers, dropped the flooded cap, and shut the lid. Wiping the detergent on her side and flicking the rest away haphazardly. Wash it all away. Wash him away.

In the kitchen, the wine glasses waited, one upright, the other knocked over, the red trail still staining the counter's edge. She poured both out, rinsed, and scrubbed until her knuckles ached. The half-empty bottle followed, but this time she hesitated. One sip. Another. Then a long, steady pull. The burn made her cough, but she didn't stop until the last drop was gone—the empty bottle clanged into the sink, glass against glass.

Each act was erasing evidence, though she didn't think of it that way. She was trying to restore the house to its original state. Trying to make *herself* feel like she had before. But nothing she touched felt clean.

She slowly climbed the stairs, her body aching in ways she couldn't explain. The shower scorched her skin, yet she remained under it until the steam obscured the mirror. Her sobs began softly, then shook her so fiercely that she had to grip the wall to stay on her feet.

When the water finally stopped, she walked dripping to her bed, pulled the covers over herself, and curled into a tight ball. Downstairs, the low rumble of her dad's Tahoe pulling into the driveway made her breath catch. Relief washed over her—he was here. But Steve's threat still echoed: *I know where you sleep. I know where they sleep.*

She stayed still, pretending to sleep, afraid that moving toward her dad would shatter the fragile safety his presence brought.

That's when it started.

Her mind replayed the hallway, the grip on her underwear, the heat of his hands, the way the red recording light blinked in her peripheral vision. And then—out of nowhere—a warm, rolling sensation spread through her chest and stomach. A soft wave that made her muscles loosen. No... no... I don't want this.

It happened again, stronger this time, pulling her into a hazy, almost weightless feeling she didn't understand. Why is this happening? Why now? Did I... like that? What didn't he do? No. No, I didn't. I couldn't. Another warm, comforting wave. What is wrong with me?

The confusion felt worse than the fear. She hated her body for betraying her, reacting to him against her wishes.

She hated that she didn't have control over it, even now, safe in her bed.

Another wave rolled over her—euphoric, terrifying— and she squeezed her eyes shut, willing it away. But the harder she fought it, the better the haze felt, the heavier her eyelids became. The warmth blurred into darkness, her mind slipping under before she could make sense of any of it.

Will's Discovery

The garage door thumped shut behind him, cutting off the sticky night air. Will set his keys on the counter with a tired clink. The house was dim, quiet — just the soft, steady churn of the washing machine coming from deeper inside. Odd. Kristen wasn't in the habit of doing laundry after midnight.

In the sink, a wine bottle lay on its side, its neck pressed against a single rinsed glass. Kristen never left anything messy for long. Faint red streaks trickled down the steel basin like the remnants of a toast no one remembered.

He almost lingered on it, but Wendi Baylor's face shouldered its way to the front of his mind.

Twenty-two. Nursing student. Found posed at home plate on the high school baseball diamond. Arms raised like a referee signaling a touchdown, though the bold scrawl of "HOME RUN" across her chest made the gesture cruel, mocking. The other details came unbidden — the obvious barbaric assault, the removal of her pubic hair causing skin burns, the familiar red O. Will could still see Casey's face at the scene, set and pale, the horror visible even through her professional armor.

He forced a breath out and moved down the hall.

Kristen's snoring reached him before he reached the bedroom. Low, steady, unfamiliar. She rarely snored.

She was sprawled diagonally across the mattress, her bare skin exposed, tangled hair, and rumpled sheets off the bed, limbs splayed as if she'd collapsed there mid-motion. A faint sheen of sweat along her shoulder caught the thin glow of the streetlight filtering through the blinds. It wasn't her usual sleeping style, but... she'd had her share of wild nights. Will had come home before to find her and her old college friends still laughing on the pool deck at 2 a.m., clothes scattered everywhere, margarita pitchers empty. He'd seen bras and panties sailing through the air as they sang about tequila making their clothes fall off.

A smile ghosted at the edge of his mouth, but the image of Wendi Baylor — posed, humiliated — chased it away.

He bent to lift Kristen, sliding his arms under her shoulders. She was heavy in the way deep sleep makes a body, head lolling as he shifted her toward her side of the bed. A sharp, musky scent rose from the sheets — not her perfume, not exactly alcohol. He frowned faintly but didn't linger on it.

"Come on," he murmured, pulling the sheet over her.

Kristen gave a soft, awkward snort. Will gently rolled her onto her side, the medic in him ensuring she wouldn't choke if the wine caught up with her during the night. Will noticed her hair was all matted strangely against her face. "Good thing it's Saturday," he said quietly.

The washing machine cycled in the background, a muted hum under the stillness.

He would lie down beside her, exhaustion settling in. The scent lingered faintly, but Wendi Baylor's lifeless eyes were all he could focus on when he closed his own. The killer was escalating and running out of time.

The house was quiet.

Too quiet.

But Will didn't notice.

Not tonight.

Dazed Duo Darlings

The next morning, sunlight slid across the floorboards in thin, warm lines. Will blinked awake, stretching against the mattress. The house was still quiet — too quiet for a Saturday with two teenage girls under its roof, even if one was away for the night.

Beside him, Kristen lay on her stomach, one leg kicked free of the sheet, hair a chaotic tangle glued to her cheek. She looked like she'd gone a few rounds with a bottle and lost, the kind of "morning after" posture that only came from overestimating your tolerance.

What the hell did you get into? he thought, lips twitching into a faint smirk.

The sharp memory of Wendi Baylor's crime scene cut through the domestic calm — the heat of the floodlights on the baseball diamond, the sick joke of her body's positioning, the thick scrawl of "HOME RUN" across her chest. He forced the image back down, pushing himself upright. Coffee. He needed coffee.

On the way to the kitchen, he passed the spot where he'd dropped his keys the night before. His socks whispered over the hardwood, and he caught the faint, clean scent of detergent — oddly fresh for this hour — and noticed a darker streak on the floor near the hallway. He stepped over it without a thought.

At the sink, something made him pause. Two wine glasses now, not one.

Huh. His brows knit for half a second before he shrugged it off. Guess Steve had one for the road.

The coffee maker sputtered and gurgled to life, the smell filling the kitchen in seconds. Will poured himself a mug, took a long, satisfying sip, and leaned against the counter, letting the caffeine start its slow magic.

The morning stayed still, the kind of still that made him glance toward the hallway to make sure the world hadn't stopped. Kristen was still out cold. Neither she nor Emily had stirred, both in the bed asleep long before him.

10:30 a.m., and not a soul is moving.

Will took another sip, telling himself to enjoy the rare quiet — even if something about it didn't sit quite right.

The Toasted Daughter

Will headed upstairs, coffee forgotten in his hand, and stopped outside Emily's door. He gave it a light knock.

"Emily?"

No answer.

He tried the handle — locked. That made him pause. Emily never locked her door. Not once in sixteen years.

Concern growing, he crossed the hall, reached above Ellie's doorframe for the small emergency key, and returned. The lock clicked open with a soft turn.

"Emily?" he called again, easing the door inward.

The room was dim, with curtains pulled tight. Emily lay curled up under her covers, her back turned to him. Her breathing was steady but shallow — not quite snoring, but close enough to remind him of Kristen's drunken wheeze last night.

She gets it honest, Will thought with a faint smirk.

"Hey, kiddo, you planning to sleep all day?"

Emily stirred, rolled toward him, eyes barely open.

"I drank... I..." she mumbled, her voice thick and unfocused.

Before he could respond, she rolled too far and tumbled off the bed with a soft thud.

"Whoa—easy!"

He stepped forward but froze halfway. Emily was tangled in blankets, clearly not dressed beneath them, her body a disoriented heap on the floor. Instinct told him to help; another voice in his mind told him to look away. He glanced toward the ceiling, then the floor — anywhere but directly at her.

Some things a father shouldn't witness.

She tried to get up, her legs unsteady. When she stumbled toward him, he caught her, guiding her upright without looking directly at her. She was warm, groggy, heavier than she looked — and there was a faint, sharp scent clinging to the blanket around her. Detergent. Fresh, like laundry just pulled from the machine.

That's when he saw it — a faint purplish bruise just below her ribs. His stomach clenched.

"Emily... are you okay?"

"I... drank... dr...ank..." she slurred, head lolling.

Will eased her back into bed, pulled the covers off the floor, and over her. She was out again instantly, breathing slow and heavy.

"Wine..." she murmured, eyes fluttering shut.

He stood over her a moment, taking in what he'd seen: the locked door, the bruise, the scratch along her waist, another on her thigh, her hair matted in places as if she'd slept hard.

So they drank together? he wondered. *Kristen and Emily? Is that why Kristen was passed out?*

The red mark at her waist caught his mind's eye again. It wasn't deep, but it looked fresh. His jaw flexed.

Maybe she slipped in the shower. Perhaps it was nothing.

But the unease lingered.

Will pulled the covers higher around her, the faint detergent smell brushing his nose again, then quietly backed out of the room and closed the door. Downstairs, his coffee sat cooling on the counter — untouched.

Fuzzy Memory

Will came back downstairs and stopped in the doorway. Kristen was sitting up in bed, looking dazed, her hair a tangled mess, eyes puffy, skin pale.

"Long night, I take it," Will said, leaning against the doorframe.

Kristen glanced at him and groaned. "Not really... but I feel awful," she said, one hand clutching her stomach. "I'm so sore, and I don't even know why. It's like I've been doing medicine ball crunches for an hour."

She winced as her fingers pressed into her side. "I'm actually bruised. Will, I don't even remember how."

Will crossed his arms. "So... how drunk did you get last night? And our daughter? What's going on there?"

Kristen blinked, clearly confused. "I... I didn't get that drunk. I barely drank anything. I left the party not long after you did."

Will's tone sharpened. "Well, Emily is still half passed out upstairs, stumbling drunk." She told me she drank wine, and it looks like she didn't even dry off after her shower before getting in bed.

Kristen looked at him, eyes wide.

"There's a wine bottle and two glasses in the sink, Kristen." Will looked at her, voice low and serious. "Put two and two together, you got our teenage daughter drunk."

Kristen looked at Will, groggy and confused. "Seriously, I don't know... I don't remember. Weren't you here with me?"

Will raised an eyebrow. "No, Kristen. I came home to you sprawled out on the bed, snoring like a drunken sailor. No covers, no clothes. You're usually buried ten layers deep in blankets."

He leaned in for a kiss, then paused and sniffed. "Well, Captain Morgan, you still reek of something I can't quite identify. Definitely time for a shower. And you've got something crusty on the side of your head; your hair looks like Medusa."

Kristen squinted at him. "Well, you're partly to blame for my glamorous look this morning. You should've kept your hands to yourself. Taking advantage of your drunken sailor wife, you ought to be ashamed. I'm a respectable captain."

Will chuckled. "Oh, don't blame me. All I did was roll you to your side and tuck you in. You were already in La-La Land, snoring like Paul Bunyan."

Kristen scowled, still unsure. "Stop it. I know what we did. Don't mess with me, we had sex last night."

"In your dreams, maybe," Will said with a grin. "Glad to know I'm still the man of your dreams."

Kristen rubbed her temples. "Maybe it was a dream... It was pretty foggy. But you were there, Loverboy."

Will turned toward the kitchen. "Well, coffee's ready. I'm getting another cup. Hop in the shower and meet me on the deck."

Kristen slid out of bed, every movement stiff from soreness, and headed toward the bathroom. As she reached for the light, her phone buzzed on the nightstand.

Ding.

She turned, grabbed the phone, and unlocked it. Her vision was still slightly blurry from sleep and dehydration, but the sender's name was clear.

Steve

The name alone twisted her stomach into a knot. Her breath caught in her throat as she tapped the message open.

"That's where I hid the surprise."

Above the message was a photo—a close-up of a woman's vagina. A small daisy tattoo sat just above the crease of the hip.

Her tattoo.

Kristen's hand flew to her mouth. Her phone nearly slipped from her grasp as a cold wave of nausea surged through her. She was shaking, with full-body tremors, and the room tilted around her.

With a trembling thumb, she scrolled up.

The first message at the top was from her number.

To Steve.

Kristen scrolled up through the thread, her fingers barely steady enough to control the phone.

Kristen: *"I've never been satisfied like I was tonight!"*

Steve: *"I aim to please."*

Kristen: *"Better than anything I've ever experienced."*

Steve:*" Thank you for the wild ride!!!"*

Then came the photo. Her photo. A close-up of her crotch, unmistakably her daisy tattoo in plain view. Sent from her phone.

And finally, the message she'd just seen:

Steve: "That's where I hid the surprise."

Kristen stared, frozen. Her mind reeled, trying to make sense of what she was seeing.

This has to be a joke. A prank. Deepfake? Something. But no... the texts... the photo... The voice in her head whispered what she didn't want to admit: That was me. I was there. It was Steve, not Will.

A wave of nausea rolled over her. Her stomach churned. She stumbled backward onto the bed, breathing fast and shallow.

What did I do? What am I going to do?

She wanted to scream, to run, to tear the past twelve hours out of her memory, but the proof was in her hand. She had crossed a line she didn't even remember stepping up to.

Kristen stepped into the bathroom, still clutching her phone, with the weight of the last message lingering in her mind like poison.

"That's where I hid the surprise."

The words echoed, chilling her to the bone. Her thoughts spiraled. Did he... not use protection? Could I be pregnant?

Panic surged through her. *No. I can't get pregnant, No! not possible. Will had a vasectomy after the twins... how will I...* her mind raced.

But this wasn't Will.

No. No. No. Dear God, not now.

Desperation gnawed at her chest. She reopened the text thread, her fingers trembling, and typed:

"What is the surprise?"

A moment later, Steve replied.

"Dig for treasure, silly!!!"

Her stomach flipped. The nausea rose so fast she nearly collapsed, catching herself on the bathroom counter.

This can't be happening. This isn't real. This is some sick game.

But it was real.

With dread pulsing through her veins, Kristen hesitated, then, driven by horror and the need to know, she reached down with trembling fingers, exploring cautiously, praying there was nothing.

What kind of twisted mind leaves something behind like that? What is he playing at?

She paused, breath hitched.

This was no longer about a night she couldn't remember. This was turning into something far more disturbing.

74

That's when she felt it.

A thin, rubbery ridge.

Kristen scissored it gently between her fingertips and pulled, her breath caught in her throat. Her body tensed.

A condom.

Removed from inside her.

She stood frozen, staring at it in disbelief, horror washing over her in a tidal wave. Her mind fractured into chaos, thoughts colliding and splintering.

How? When? Why don't I remember this? What have I done? That had to be Will.

Her world was no longer what it had been just one day ago.

Ding.

The sharp buzz of her phone yanked Kristen out of her haze.

Another message lit up the screen.

Steve: *Sorry again about the condom. And the hair. You were... wild last night. Wish we'd figured this out back in college. Round 4 soon? I'll come prepared this time. Easier when your man's always gone.*

She didn't have time to process before the final message arrived.

A photo.

Taken from above. Her eyes half-closed, mouth open, Steve's body unmistakably framed in the shot.

Her phone buzzed one more time.

Steve: *Glad we reconnected. The fun's just getting started.*

Kristen's stomach churned. Her skin prickled with revulsion.

She turned the shower on full blast, scalding hot, but didn't wait for it to warm. She stepped straight into a freezing deluge, icy needles pounding her skin and stealing her breath. But no amount of cold or heat could wash away what she was feeling. Within seconds, she doubled over and vomited into the drain.

The water poured over her, but it didn't wash away anything.

Steve's words kept echoing—the image of that condom in her hand, the photos, the bruises.

Her body had betrayed her. Her mind had locked away the truth.

And now, the weight of it all crashed down on her.

Shame. Disgust. Terror. Helplessness.

How could I have let this happen?

But most of all, how am I going to face Will?

Emily Stirs

Emily emerged late, her steps slow and heavy, hoodie zipped to her chin, pajama pants bunched at her ankles. The Oakhaven Cheer Squad logo across her chest felt like armor.

Will looked up from the kitchen table. "Well, look who's up and dressed for the day," he said with a teasing grin. "Did you enjoy your mom's wine a little too much last night?"

Emily froze halfway down the stairs. A flicker of memory — her lips on the bottle, the sweet rush, the burn — slammed into her chest. Her pulse spiked. *How does he know?*

She forced a half-smile. "Maybe?"

Will's brow lifted. He nodded toward the sink. "At least your mother wasn't drinking alone."

Two wine glasses sat side by side in the basin.

Emily's stomach turned. A wave of dread pressed down on her chest. She wanted to run to him, bury herself in his arms, confess everything — what happened, what she saw, what she couldn't unsee. But she couldn't. She saw the fallout before it happened — his face, his rage, the way their family would break under it. *I can't tell him.*

Her throat tightened. Without another word, she slipped into the laundry room.

The washing machine's lid was up. Inside: her mother's blue silk dress, Emily's own ripped t-shirt, Kristen's bra, all twisted together in damp knots.

The sight triggered the fragments from last night — the spill of water on the floor, the tearing sound, the rough grip, the smothering heat. And then... her toes. Painted lavender. She could see them in her mind, absurdly clear in the chaos, her polish almost glowing against the tile.

The memory brought something else with it — the sudden awareness now, in daylight, that the underwear she'd been wearing in that moment was gone. Not just any pair, but the cartoon leopard panties she'd begged her mom to buy last summer as a joke. She remembered laughing about them in the store aisle, saying they made her look like "a wildcat."

The joke no longer felt funny, but made her nauseated.

Her hands shook as she yanked the clothes out and stuffed them into a black garbage bag.

Erase.

The wine bottle went in next.

She stepped outside, the cool air biting her skin, and dropped the bag into the bin at the curb. The lid shut with a dull thud, but nothing felt lighter. If anything, the weight on her chest grew heavier.

Back upstairs, she closed her bedroom door softly, as if the sound alone might shatter her.

The loop resumed — flashes of the night, the hands, the voice, the overwhelming closeness. And worse than the violation was her betrayal by her own body.

Heat. Tension. That uninvited flutter that made her want to crawl out of her skin. Every instinct had screamed *no*, but her body hadn't listened.

She pressed her forehead into her knees. *Why did I feel that? Why didn't I stop it?*

It wasn't want. It wasn't consent. But the whisper of doubt still clawed at her, cruel and insistent.

And then came the deeper wound—her mother. Kristen had let him in, had been right there, and done nothing.

How could she not have heard? Have you not seen? How could she choose him — even for just one night — over me?

Emily bit the inside of her cheek until she tasted blood, trying to hold back the flood. But the silence in her room only made the memories louder.

She felt alone.

And nothing could erase the weight of what she could no longer unfeel.

Collectables

"Letter to the Editor: On Justice, Beauty, and the Hunt"

Submitted anonymously. Published under editorial review.

To the fine people of our proud little city,

The recent surge in law enforcement activity has been... admirable. Watching Detective Will Anderson run in circles has been the most satisfying entertainment I've had since my last creation. For a fleeting moment, you almost had me worried. Almost.

But let's speak plainly.

Justice is a noble concept, isn't it? Clear. Righteous. Unyielding. Much like our respected District Attorney, Kristen Anderson. A commanding figure in the courtroom, yes, but I wonder... is she as resolute when the robe is off? She seems to know exactly when to exercise her authority— and when to surrender it.

And then there's Detective Casey Murphy—red hair like a flare in the dark, eyes sharp enough to cut glass, and a mouth that has never learned the discipline of silence. Such a pity. She exudes strength and fire, yet doesn't realize she's already in my sights. I suspect she burns in more ways than one.

You see, I collect things that fascinate me. Things that shine. Things that stand out. Things that defy the rules—until I make them mine.

Even the untamed have a place in my gallery. And as I've learned recently, every Wildcat can be tamed... with the right patience, the right tools, and the right audience.

How poetic, don't you think, if justice herself were preserved? Frozen. Eternal. Displayed with the same reverence I've shown my other pieces.

Tick-tock, Detective Anderson.
Keep chasing.
I'm not done yet.

Yours,
—X

Jack'd Up Coffee Shop

Will sat across from Casey, the morning paper spread flat between them, the headline and taunting letter staring back. The espresso machine hissed in the background, steam curling in the air like a slow exhale.

Casey tapped the column with one neatly chewed fingernail. "This isn't just a taunt. This is him laying out his menu, and I'm on it."

Will's eyes stayed on the page. "Why you?"

Casey leaned in, voice low. "Because guys like this don't just kill—they break. They want to take women who don't bow, who don't shut up, and grind them down until they're quiet, compliant, and looking up at them like they're a god." Her lip curled. "That's not me. And that pisses him off."

Will sipped his coffee, saying nothing.

She smirked without humor. "I'm the kind of woman they dream about wrecking. They want to rip the fight out of me, make me their little trophy. But I've got news— nobody puts me on a shelf."

Will finally looked up. "You're not exactly the quiet type."

Casey's grin sharpened. "I'm about as quiet as a blaster fight in the Death Star's garbage compactor."

Will gave her a sideways look. "Star Wars?"

"Exactly. He's Palpatine with a thesaurus. And I'm not Leia in my bikini waiting to be rescued. I'm the one who strangles him with the damn chain."

Will's phone buzzed against the table. He glanced down, saw the time, and thumbed through his contacts until Kristen's name came up.

"Gonna call her?" Casey asked, draining the last of her latte.

"Yeah," Will said. "She needs to see this before it blindsides her."

The phone rang... and rang... then dropped to voicemail.

"She's probably in court," Casey said, shrugging. "Your DA wife's busy putting away bad guys while we drink overpriced caffeine."

Will hung up, opened his messages, and started typing.

Will: Read the paper as soon as you can. This isn't a joke.

He hesitated, then added another line.

Also, open the top drawer of your desk. Happy birthday, keep it with you.

Casey raised an eyebrow. "You bought her a gun for her birthday?"

"Better than flowers," Will said, sliding his phone back in his pocket. "A SIG 365 will last longer."

"Nice choice, have one myself, just tricked out a little." Casey patted her side.

They sat silently for a moment, with the background noise of the coffee shop filling the silence. Will was scanning the letter again when Casey's earlier words echoed in his mind. I'm not Leia in some bikini...

He frowned, looking at her over the paper. "Hold up— did you say 'my bikini'?"

Casey didn't even blink. "Yeah."

"As in... you own a Leia bikini?"

Her grin was all teeth. "Don't act so shocked, Detective Will Anderson. Some of us are prepared for Comic-Con and a fight to the death."

Will shook his head, muttering, "I can't unhear that now."

Kristen's Discovery

Kristen's hands trembled as she stared at her monitor. The office was still, sunlight spilling across a neat stack of case files, the courthouse hum muted behind her closed door. But inside her chest, something was pounding—wild, uneven, panicked.

The email sat open. One attachment. A video file.

She clicked.

It was grainy, cropped, jumpy, and edited just enough to make it look deliberate. Consensual. Even inviting.

Her stomach twisted. She remembered nothing—just broken shards of sensation—heat, weight, disorientation—and now they were rearranged into something damning.

Beneath the video, the message was short and cold:

Comply, or this goes public.

Her fingers hovered over the keyboard, but no words came.

Another notification pinged. Second email. No text this time—just a single image.

Kristen's breath caught.

A pair of cartoon leopard-print panties.

Emily's.

The edges of her vision blurred. This wasn't just blackmail. It was a warning. Steve told her that he had been in her home with her daughter and was willing to use Emily as leverage.

Her phone vibrated. The third message. One encrypted link. And below it, a single line that made her skin crawl:

Here's a look at the other girls I've helped find new homes. Some scream. Some don't.

She didn't need to click. She knew exactly what she'd see—what kind of depraved trade Steve was involved in. Girls turned into commodities. Pain as entertainment.

They wouldn't be actresses. They'd be women like her. Like Emily.

Kristen's throat tightened until she could barely breathe. The blackmail wasn't just about her career anymore. This was bigger. Darker. And now Steve's attention was locked squarely on her.

Kristen's phone buzzed again. She jumped. This time, it wasn't Steve.

Will – 10:47 a.m.

You need to read the paper. Page five, "Letter to the Editor."

Also, open the top drawer of your desk. Happy birthday, keep it with you.

Her eyes flicked toward the bottom drawer of her desk. The one she never locked. She hesitated, her pulse hammering in her ears. Will had been talking about getting her something practical this year, "something for peace of mind," he'd said.

She pulled it open. Nestled inside, still in the case, was a sleek Sig Sauer P365. Her fingers hovered over it but didn't touch.

Her phone buzzed again—same thread.

Will – 10:49 a.m.

Please don't leave the courthouse without it.

Kristen's gaze stayed fixed on the pistol. The earlier emails still glared at her from the monitor, the leopard-print photo burned into her mind.

Will's warning about the letter. Steve's threats. The gun in the drawer.

The worlds she'd been trying to keep separate—her courtroom battles and the shadows bleeding into her home—were about to collide.

She closed the drawer slowly, her hand trembling as she reached for her phone again. She didn't respond to Will. She couldn't. Not yet.

She sat frozen in her chair, the weight of it all pressing down on her chest like poured concrete. The room tilted. Her throat tightened.

He had her cornered.

Professionally. Personally. As a mother.

Sick. Filthy. Afraid. Powerless.

She didn't know how to tell Will. She didn't even know if she could.

If she did... what would he think? What would he do? Could she risk that spiral? Could she risk Emily?

Right now, there was only one truth Kristen could hold onto:

She would do anything to protect her daughter.

Even if it meant sinking beneath the weight of a monster.

A Flash of Information

Will's phone buzzed across the desk.

Vince Carrow's name flashed on the screen.

Will glanced around the office, then at Casey. He mouthed, *"Flashlight."*

Her brows lifted—finally, their first real lead in days.

Recovered near the ambush site in the alley, the flashlight had been standard-issue, military-grade, its casing dented and scuffed, the knurled grip tacky with dried blood. It was the kind of thing that could've cracked the whole case open—if it talked.

Will answered. "Carrow."

"No joy," Vince said, voice flat. "Nothing on the flashlight was usable. I'll bring it to you. You're gonna have to do this old school."

Will's eyes dropped to the cluttered desk. "Copy."

He hung up and set the phone down slowly. Casey was already reading him.

"No prints, no DNA?" she asked.

"Nothing clean enough to stick," Will said. "Our only play now is running it through the PD's issued-equipment database."

Casey frowned. "And let half the department know we found it? Might as well take out a billboard."

89

"Exactly," Will muttered. "One leak and whoever owns that flashlight will be gone before we get within ten miles."

She leaned back in her chair, arms crossed. "So we either risk it... or find another way to trace it without the brass breathing down our necks."

Will's gaze sharpened. "We do it quietly. We keep it off the books."

Casey's grin was small but feral. "Now you're still speaking my language."

Casey tapped her pen against the desk. "Technically, Carrow was our first trip off the books with this thing. You handed it to him after the alley, remember? To keep it out of evidence."

Will nodded slowly. "Yeah. Now we need it back—quiet."

She leaned forward, lowering her voice even though the door was closed. "We call Carrow. Tell him we need another look. He won't ask why if we keep it vague."

Will's brow furrowed. "And when we have it?"

Casey's grin tilted sharply. "Then I work my magic."

"You're talking about hacking the PD database?"

"Not hacking," she said innocently. "Strategically accessing."

"Which is?"

"Mask my IP, slip into the issued-equipment registry, pull the assignment record for that flashlight... and make sure it can't be traced back to us. If the leak's as bad as we think, this is the only way we get an honest answer."

Will leaned back in his chair, skeptical. "And how exactly are you getting into that part of the system without tripping alarms?"

Casey smirked. "Eddie."

Will groaned. "The geeky IT guy who's got a crush on you?"

She shrugged. "Crush, admiration, unhealthy devotion... semantics. I just need a reason to sit down at his terminal for a few minutes."

Will's eyes narrowed. "What kind of reason?"

"I'll think of something," she said, already pulling out her phone. "Something that'll make him feel like a hero."

Will shook his head, half amused, half wary. "You're gonna owe him forever."

"Please," Casey said with a wicked little grin. "I already do."

She started dialing. "Let's get the flashlight first."

The meet was set for the back lot of an old storage facility on the edge of town—neutral ground. No cameras. No curious uniforms.

Carrow's battered gray SUV rolled in first, its windows tinted darker than department regs would have allowed when he still wore the badge. Will and Casey pulled up a minute later, their unmarked idling just long enough for Carrow to clock them before stepping out.

The man looked older than the last time Casey had seen him—more silver in the beard, deeper lines around the eyes—but his presence still carried that quiet weight of someone who'd spent decades walking into rooms most people ran from.

"You brought it?" Will asked.

Carrow didn't answer right away. His gaze swept the lot, then the rooftops, as if he expected someone to be watching. Only when he seemed satisfied did he pop his trunk.

The flashlight lay inside, tucked into a beat-up evidence bag.

"Here," Carrow said, passing it over. "Clean enough to keep it off anyone's radar. But if you're thinking of running it through the PD's issued-equipment database..." His voice dropped. "...be smart about it. The leaks upstairs are worse than you think."

Casey glanced at Will. "We know."

Carrow shifted his weight, lowering his voice even more. "If you're going in through IT, don't make it look like it's coming from your buddy Eddie's desk. That'll burn him fast. You want it to stick? Make it look like it came from one of the admin terminals upstairs—brass level."

Casey's brow lifted. "You mean fake the point of origin?"

Carrow smirked faintly. "Not fake. Borrow. Every machine leaves a footprint. You need to make it look like it walked in their shoes."

Will frowned. "And if they trace it?"

"They'll be chasing ghosts through their own offices while you're already ten steps ahead. Carrow reached into a bag, pulled out a few USB drives, looked at them carefully, and then handed one to Casey. 'This will do the trick," Carrow said. "I'll give you the lowdown on it."

Casey slipped the evidence bag into her tote like it was nothing more than a coffee order. "Appreciate the tip, Carrow, and the magic drive."

He gave her a look that was half warning, half old habit. "You two didn't get this from me. And if anyone asks where I was tonight..."

Will finished for him. "You were home, watching the game."

Carrow nodded once. "Good luck. You're gonna need it."

He got back in his SUV, engine rumbling low as he pulled away, leaving Will and Casey standing in the lot, the flashlight now feeling heavier than it had when they'd first found it.

Oakhaven PD's IT bullpen always smelled faintly of burnt coffee, overheated servers, and that particular brand of anxiety only sysadmins carried. Casey walked in as she belonged there, which, technically, she didn't. She'd timed it for mid-morning—peak chaos—when Eddie would be juggling network tickets and trying to keep three captains happy at once.

She found him hunched over two monitors, a Yoda bobblehead nodding judgmentally from his desk. His "Millennium Falcon Parking Only" sign hung slightly crooked on the cubicle wall.

Perfect.

"Hey, Jedi Master," Casey said, leaning casually against the cubicle opening. "Got a sec? I'm having a little... connectivity issue."

Eddie glanced up, blinking behind smudged glasses. "Uh, connectivity? Like... internet?"

"Like my laptop's not talking to the upstairs network the way it should," she said, lowering her voice as if she was confessing something classified. "And the brass needs this file. Today."

Eddie straightened a little at "the brass." "I mean, I can remote in—"

Casey stepped in closer, close enough for the subtle brush of her arm against his shoulder as she "leaned to see" his monitors. "Honestly, I'd rather you work your magic in person. I know how good you are with... complicated systems."

The corner of Eddie's mouth twitched into a nervous half-smile. "Uh... sure. Let me just... uh..."

As he clicked through menus, Casey let her gaze drift over his desk, spotting the admin workstation login he'd been using to push an update. She slipped her phone from her pocket, tilted it just enough to snap a casual photo.

"So," she said, "if this were Star Wars, what would you be right now—Obi-Wan in the Jedi Archives, or Lando sweet-talking the Falcon's nav computer?"

Eddie chuckled awkwardly. "Uh... definitely Obi-Wan. I mean, the archives... they're... everything."

"That's what I thought," Casey said, smiling as he'd just passed a test.

When he turned to grab his coffee mug, she slid the USB drive Carrow had given her into the side of the admin machine. Two quick keystrokes—thanks to the spoofing script Carrow had tipped her toward—and the flashlight's serial query was routed to look like it originated from upstairs. No trail to Eddie. No trail to her.

Eddie turned back, oblivious. "Okay, your laptop should be talking to the network now."

"You're a lifesaver," Casey said, pulling the USB free with a subtle flick and palming it. "And for the record? Lando's got nothing on you."

She left him sitting there, cheeks slightly flushed, Yoda bobblehead nodding in her wake.

Back in her desk, she slotted the USB into her own laptop. The query results were already there—one name, one badge number.

Their next lead.

Her eyes scanned the results, and then she froze.

"You've got to be kidding me," she whispered.

Will stood. "What?"

Casey turned the laptop around to Will. "According to equipment logs, that flashlight was last assigned to Captain Dan Rogers, part of the donated equipment the department received."

Silence stretched between them.

Will's expression hardened. Rogers had been his mentor. His commanding officer.

"We're not bringing him in yet," Will said after a moment. "Not until we know more."

Casey nodded. "So what's the plan?"

"We track him. Quietly. If he's involved, we can't give him a reason to disappear or cover his tracks."

They both looked at the window, beyond it, the parking lot where Rogers' cruiser was parked, as if everything was normal.

Casey pulled open a drawer and retrieved a small GPS tracker, the size of a matchbox.

"I'll take care of the install tonight," she said. "We'll keep an eye on him. Every place he goes. Every move he makes."

Will nodded, but his jaw was tight.

If Rogers was involved... it meant something much worse than a killer on the loose.

It meant corruption, deep and personal.

And it meant the next moves would have to be played very, very carefully.

Another Chilling Photo

He was replaying every detail of what he had just learned and feared inside the department. Is this how the killer stays a step ahead? Is Rogers involved? Is he being set up? Then he shifted focus as he approached his SUV, only to spot a plain envelope tucked under the wiper. His name was printed on the front, nothing else.

Will's pulse quickened as he pulled it out. Even before he opened it, he knew: another photo

Will's mind flashed back to Wendi Baylor—the nursing student left posed like a grotesque trophy at home plate, "Home Run" scrawled across her chest, arms raised as if she'd just scored. The memory was burned into his mind: the brutal assault, the humiliation, the killer burning off her pubic hair, the shallow scrapes of the letters, the familiar red O smeared by hand, the calculated cruelty. Even Casey, usually unflappable, had been shaken.

In the photo, the victim was alive, naked, her hands bound tightly behind her head, hair pulled back and forced into a pose of helpless surrender. The terror in her eyes was unmistakable, the evidence of torment already etched across her face. Behind her, a man pressed in close, his own body bare, the cruel intimacy leaving no doubt about the threat he posed. No doubt the reason her hands were posed for that spot in the photo was another sick message.

One chilling detail stood out: an ouroboros tattoo wrapped in crimson and black along the man's ribs, more precise and more intricate than the pendant. The message was deliberate, taunting.

Though the man's face was hidden from view, Will could sense the perverse satisfaction behind the image, the killer's need for control, for power, for spectacle. It was another challenge, and the game was nowhere near over.

Another message from the killer. The nightmare wasn't finished with him yet.

Private Eyes

Ellie was packing for a sleepover when something caught her eye in the shared bathroom she and Emily used. Reaching under the sink for her travel bag, she glanced up and froze.

A small, metallic glint winked from inside the vent above the mirror.

She frowned, stepped onto the edge of the bathtub, and leaned closer. Through the slats—barely visible—was a tiny black lens.

A camera.

Her stomach lurched. She scrambled down and rushed to find her father.

Will looked up from the kitchen table as Ellie came in, pale and breathless.

"There's a camera," she blurted. "In our bathroom."

Will was on his feet instantly.

"Show me."

Minutes later, the vent cover lay on the counter, and Will held the small, concealed camera in his hand. Rage tightened in his chest like a vice.

He didn't say a word—just started searching.

Emily's room. Ellie's room. The upstairs hallway.

Another camera behind the molding above Emily's vanity mirror. A third tucked so subtly into the baseboard that he almost missed it.

Then two more—hidden in the vents of his own bedroom and bathroom.

Five cameras.

All professionally placed. All wired into the house.

He called Casey.

She arrived fast, laptop bag slung over her shoulder, expression grim.

Casey didn't need to ask why—Will's tone on the phone had been enough to tell her this was bad.

She set the bag on the kitchen island and powered up her machine.

"By the way," she said as her fingers moved, "the GPS tracker's up and running. No hitches."

Will gave a short nod but kept his eyes on the five black cameras lined up on the counter like trophies from a hunt.

"Good. We might need it sooner than we thought."

Casey glanced at the pile, her jaw tightening. "Let's see who's been watching."

"I'm in the home security system," she said. "Remote access has been active for weeks. Whoever did this had full control—door locks, internal feeds, motion logs. Will... this wasn't just spying. This was systematic."

"Where's the feed going?" he asked, voice low.

"Still tracing it. It's masked behind multiple layers of encryption, but I'll get there."

Will's eyes swept the walls, the vents, the shadows. "They've seen everything," he muttered.

His gaze lifted toward the stairwell, where the girls' rooms sat beyond the landing.

"I'm getting them out. Tonight."

Casey nodded. "Do it. I'll stay here and keep digging."

Later, Ellie and Emily sat in the back seat of Will's Tahoe, overnight bags at their feet. The silence was heavy. Will drove one-handed, the other clenched tight against his thigh.

He didn't know who had done this. Or how long it had been going on.

But someone had crossed into his home and watched his family.

That was war.

And if Rogers had anything to do with it?

Will would find out.

Will's phone lit up on the console—Casey's name.

He answered on the second ring.

"Talk to me."

"Rogers is on the move," she said without preamble. "Figured you'd want eyes on him."

Will's grip tightened on the wheel. "I'll swing by and pick you up."

By the time he turned down his long driveway, the house was dark behind him, the twins already settled at his sisters-in-law's for the night. At the far end, silhouetted against the streetlight, Casey stood like a Roman soldier waiting.

She had her laptop bag slung crosswise, one hand in her jacket pocket, the other holding her phone, which was still warm from the call. Her hair whipped lightly in the evening breeze, but her expression was all business.

Will slowed, headlights washing over her. She stepped forward, pulling the passenger door open before he'd even come to a full stop.

"Let's go," she said, sliding in.

Will hit the road and was on a mission, filled with many thoughts and perspectives.

The Random Witness

Will adjusted the rearview mirror, gaze fixed on the entrance of the Copper Barrel—a low-lit dive just off campus, always packed with students and the occasional off-duty cop who wanted to forget about work for a while. Tonight, the place seemed to hum with energy, neon lights flickering over a shifting sea of college kids.

Captain Dan Rogers had been inside for over an hour now. No sign of a patrol car, no radio check-ins, nothing to suggest he was there on official business. Just his own sedan, parked a few spots down, windows tinted. The whole setup sent up red flags, the kind that Will had learned to trust.

"Still inside," Casey murmured, glancing at her phone where the GPS tracker's blue dot hadn't budged. "Not moving."

Will nodded, lips pressed tight. He scanned the sidewalk out front, watching as clusters of rowdy students spilled out into the parking lot, laughing and shouting over the thump of bass from inside. Then something caught his eye.

"Wait," he said, sitting forward, tension prickling down his spine.

A young woman, barely steady on her feet, teetered off the curb. She wore a short black dress and impossibly high heels, mascara streaked from tears or maybe the weather, Will couldn't tell. She blinked blearily at the row of parked cars, completely unaware of the three frat boys trailing behind her, their laughter turning mean as they closed the distance.

Will's stomach dropped. He recognized the girl instantly.

"That's Tiffany Sinclaire," he muttered. "Julia's roommate."

Casey looked up, eyes narrowing. The atmosphere in the car changed—no longer just surveillance, but now something urgent and dangerous. Will watched Tiffany head toward the wrong car, with the boys gaining speed behind her, and a cold wave of dread hit him. This was about to go bad, fast.

Casey followed his gaze. "You sure?"

"Positive."

Casey cursed under her breath. "We blow our cover if we step in. Rogers sees us, this whole surveillance is, "

"I know," Will cut in, voice sharp. He watched as one of the guys reached for Tiffany's arm.

Another popped the back door of their car open.

"Hell with it." Will shoved open the driver's door and stepped out.

Casey followed instantly.

"Hey!" Will barked, flashing his badge low at his waist. "Step away from her. Now."

The three boys froze, surprise flickering across their faces as their cocky bravado crumbled. They looked at one another, weighing whether to push back, but the glint of Will's badge and the edge in his voice made up their minds.

"We're just helping her get home, man," one protested, trying for innocence but coming off shaky.

Casey moved in, stepping firmly between Tiffany and the open car door, her posture unyielding. "That wasn't a request. Back off." Her tone was all steel.

The boys hesitated, eyes darting between the detectives. Then, like a pack of dogs called off a meal, they slunk away into the crowd, muttering curses and excuses that trailed off into the night.

Tiffany swayed, her shoulder pressing hard into Will as if gravity had turned up just for her. Her mascara was smudged, her eyes were glassy and unfocused. "I'm fiiiine, I swear," she slurred, trying to muster a smile. "You're... you're Detective Anderson, right? Julia's Billy's boyfriend's dad detective?"

Will caught her before she could slide down the side of the car, steadying her with gentle hands. "Yeah, that's right. Let's get you somewhere safe, okay?"

Tiffany nodded, but the motion nearly toppled her. She blinked, trying to focus, and for a split second her gaze cleared, sharp with something like fear or memory.

"I... I remembered something," she mumbled, voice soft. "From the day she went missing. Something weird.

But I... I can't..." She trailed off, words dissolving in the thick fog of whatever she'd been drinking.

Will glanced at Casey, concern written in the lines around his eyes. Casey gave him a subtle nod, her own face set with quiet resolve.

"We'll take her home," Casey said, guiding Tiffany toward the sidewalk. "We can talk more in the morning, when you're feeling better."

Tiffany mumbled something that might have been gratitude, her head lolling against Will's shoulder as they steered her toward the waiting cruiser. The night around them seemed to close in a little tighter, as if it too was holding its breath, waiting to see what she would remember when the fog finally lifted.

By the time they returned to the parking lot, Captain Rogers was gone.

Will climbed back into the driver's seat, jaw tight. "Damn it."

Casey checked the tracker. "He left while we were dealing with the frat boys. Drove to Jack'd Up, the coffee place over on Ashbury. Then straight home."

Will exhaled slowly, gripping the wheel.

Jack'd Up.

Owned by Jack Upshaw.

The all-too-familiar small-town coffee shop with too many late-night regulars and plenty of back-alley rumors, Will's usual haunt. The last place he saw Julia Weeks alive.

"Alright," Will said. "Tomorrow, we talk to Tiffany. Then we find out what Rogers is doing at that damn coffee shop after midnight.

Casey nodded. "And if it connects to Julia?"

Will stared through the windshield, eyes narrowing. "Then Rogers doesn't walk away again."

Coffee House Confessions

Kristen sat in her car, staring at the text.

Meet me. Now. Or everything goes public. You know where. – S.

Her hands trembled as she pulled into Jack'd Up Coffee. The shop looked normal — laptops glowing, baristas laughing, the smell of espresso hanging in the air — but it all felt foreign now.

Another buzz.

Skip the line—booth in the back. Privacy, remember?

She found him in the corner, already sliding into the booth beside her, boxing her in. He set down two coffees as if it were a date.

"Good choice, Counselor," he said with a smirk. "Skirts. Style and strategy in one."

Her jaw tightened. "What do you want?"

Steve didn't answer right away. Instead, he pulled out his phone. One swipe revealed a draft email — subject line with her name — and attached stills and video clips, all distorted but still her.

"With one tap," he said, voice like a blade, "you're done here. Career, reputation, family... all gone."

Kristen stared ahead, pulse hammering. "I understand."

"No," he said, wagging a finger. "Say it so I believe it."

Her voice shook. "If I don't do what you ask, you'll destroy me. Professionally. Personally."

Steve grinned. "Good. Now... take off your panties."

Her head snapped toward him. "What?"

"You heard me. Right here. Right now." He tapped his phone, the email draft glowing. "Or I hit send."

Her eyes darted around her, no one was looking. The corner was too quiet. She felt the walls closing in.

He shifted, pinning one of her legs with his. The heat of him against her skin made her stomach churn. "Don't make me repeat myself."

Her hands shook as she obeyed, slipping the lace from under her skirt. She folded them once and set them on the table.

Steve's smile widened. "Classy. Now, the skirt stays up. And hands—" he tapped the table—"here. Palms down."

Kristen complied, tears blurring her vision.

Steve slid to the end of the booth, and Kristen felt the slight relief of no longer being caged against the wall. She drew a shallow breath — too soon.

His hand clamped around her right knee, warm and unyielding, and pulled it over his left leg.

"Slide over here," he said.

The tone wasn't loud, but it carried like a taut, unbroken chord.

Kristen moved reluctantly, every inch closing the space between them, feeling like a trap snapping shut.

Then — without warning — his palm pressed firmly against her shoulder, forcing her back against the booth. His other hand moved with deliberate precision, crossing boundaries in a way that made her stomach twist, and her breath catch.

The chatter of the coffee shop faded. All she could hear was her own pulse pounding in her ears and the low, steady rhythm of his breathing as he *kept going*.

Her body locked, every muscle tight. She stared past him at the room beyond, willing someone — anyone — to look up. But no one did.

"Now," Steve murmured, leaning close enough for her to smell the coffee on his breath, "hand or mouth?"

Her stomach turned to ice. "What are you asking me?"

"You know." His thumb hovered over *Send*. "Five seconds."

He counted down, low and steady.

"Five..."

Kristen's breath caught.

"Four..."

No help. No escape.

"Three..."

"Hand," she blurted.

Steve chuckled, reaching for his phone again. The camera app opened. The red record light blinked.

"Good girl. Now lay your right hand on these pretty panties..." He slid them closer. "...and raise your left like you're swearing an oath."

Kristen hesitated, bile in her throat.

"Repeat after me," Steve said. His smile was all teeth.

Kristen's hand trembled as she placed it over the folded lace. Her other hand slowly lifted, stiff at the elbow, as if she were making a grotesque pledge.

Steve angled the phone just right, framing her face, her hand, and the panties in one tight shot.

"Now," he said softly, "repeat after me."

Kristen stared straight ahead, jaw tight.

"I..."

Her voice caught. She swallowed hard. "I..."

"...swear to obey Steve."

She didn't move.

Steve's smile flattened. His thumb hovered over *Send*. "Say it."

Her lips trembled. "I swear to obey Steve."

"...in whatever he asks."

Kristen's nails bit into her palm. "In... whatever he asks."

"...no matter when."

"No matter when."

"...no matter where."

"No matter where."

"...and I will never tell a soul."

Her voice was barely audible. "And I will never tell a soul."

Steve's grin returned, slow and deliberate, like a predator finishing a kill.

"Good girl," he murmured, stopping the recording. He slid the panties into his pocket with exaggerated care, then leaned in so close his words brushed her ear.

"That wasn't so hard, was it?"

Kristen stared at the far wall, every muscle in her body coiled, her breath shallow. She didn't answer. She couldn't.

Steve tapped the phone once, locking the screen. "Now we're... officially bound by contract. Think of it as a... partnership."

"There she is," Steve said, voice low with amusement. "Now that wasn't so hard, was it?"

He tapped at his phone, the faint *click-click* of his thumb on glass loud in Kristen's ears. "Gotta save it to the cloud. Can't lose our little agreement."

Kristen kept her gaze down. Her vision tunneled on the tabletop — a cheap laminate surface, tiny scratches catching the low light — but her shoulders trembled.

"Stop crying," Steve snapped. His fingers clamped around her wrist, the sudden heat of his skin making her flinch. "You know what happens if you make this difficult again."

She stayed silent, but her pulse was pounding in her throat so hard she could feel each beat like a bruise.

Then his tone shifted. Playful. Almost conversational. Too casual.

"You know... I liked your Wildcat better. That girl's got spirit."

Kristen's head jerked up. "What did you just say?"

112

Steve leaned back, scrolling lazily on his phone. "Your little fighter. Feisty. I liked that."

He angled the screen just enough for her to see it — the folder name Wildcat, and a single image. Cartoon leopard print panties. Emily's. "Remember this photo?"

A rush of cold spread through Kristen's chest, like someone had poured ice water straight into her lungs. Her fingers curled tight against her palms.

"I remember those," Steve said. "She had them on when we... crossed paths. Shame you interrupted."

Her voice was a whisper. "What did you do to her?"

He smiled like they were sharing a private joke. "I'll tell you what I almost did. She's got fight — can take a punch like a man, not so great at throwing them. And for the record, she threw the first punch."

Kristen's stomach twisted so hard she thought she might be sick right there, the bitter tang of bile already rising in her throat.

"She stood there with that cute little rump toward me, bent over against the wall all on her own. I wasn't even touching her yet. And I was in a giving mood... had just finished with you and still had plenty to spare. Like mother, like daughter. Spitting image, great ass-sets, well, you've seen."

Kristen's grip on the edge of the table tightened until her knuckles blanched white. The air felt too thick, too hot, pressing against her skin.

"I took them right off her, tan lines lighting up that hallway," Steve continued, savoring every word. "Slid them straight to her ankles — she didn't move, didn't fight it, they were already wet. We were just getting started. You can't rush these things. You break them in first... then you can do whatever you want. Honestly? She was more into it than you were, more of a tease. But you ruined everything. She got away because of you."

Kristen's chest tightened, each breath quick and shallow. She could hear her blood pounding in her ears, a rushing noise that drowned out the low hiss of the espresso machine across the café.

"You drugged me," she said, her voice barely holding.

Steve's grin widened. "Oh, now she remembers. You knocked back two glasses without care. I just... added my own blend while you stepped away. Keeps things fuzzy. Makes everything... smooth, you compliant. You can't buy it in a store."

His voice dropped lower, words curling around her like smoke. "But you? You didn't fight. Not like she did. You were almost eager. Didn't even watch the video, did you? Skipped your homework. Every order I gave you, you followed. Our little teasing Wildcat could vouch for that."

The words hit like a series of punches to the ribs. Kristen's fingers trembled against the cold laminate. Her legs felt rubbery under the table, though she hadn't moved.

Steve's eyes glittered. "And you thought I was done. If you hadn't stepped into that doorway, I never would've circled back to you. I would've fucked the fight out of that Wildcat, and she'd have taken your place. But no... You had to watch, interrupt my ravaging conquest. Nobody watches for free."

He let the moment hang, the muted hum of laptop fans and coffee grinders filling the space between them. Then, almost gently, he dropped the blade:

"So, time to pay up. And remember — this is *your fault*."

Kristen sat frozen. The smell of burnt espresso grounds lingered in her nostrils, mingling with the phantom scent of his cologne from that night. The air felt heavier with each breath. She couldn't look at him. Couldn't move.

Her world had just cracked wide open — and collapsed in on itself.

Kristen sat frozen, barely breathing. Her hands lay flat on the table, exactly where Steve had told her to keep them. The tremble in her fingers had spread up her arms. Her spine ached from holding herself so stiff, but she didn't dare move.

Somewhere in the coffee shop, a barista's laughter echoed over the hiss of steamed milk. The aroma of espresso lingered in the air, warm and welcoming— completely contrasting with the cold knot in her stomach.

Steve leaned back, casual now. Relaxed. In control.

Like he always was.

The booth suddenly felt smaller, the walls tighter. Someone nearby tapped at a laptop keyboard, steady and rhythmic, a sound that made her chest tighten because it was so normal.

Steve adjusted his cuffs, rechecked his phone, and smiled faintly.

"You understand now, don't you?" he said quietly, his tone conversational, pleasant, even. "I give the instructions. You follow them. Simple as that."

Kristen didn't answer.

From the front of the shop, the espresso machine let out a sharp hiss of pressure release. The sound jolted her, like it belonged to a different world she no longer had access to.

Steve tapped the table once with two fingers. Not hard. Not loud. But it cut through her like a gunshot.

"I said," he repeated, "you understand now."

She nodded slowly, her throat constricted.

Steve sighed and leaned closer. "Kristen, Kristen, Kristen... that's not how we do things anymore. You speak when spoken to. Go ahead. Let's hear it. Use your voice."

Her mouth opened, but the words barely formed. Her tongue felt heavy, her lips numb. "I... I understand."

He grinned like a man who'd just won something.

"I knew you would," he said. "Took you long enough. You're not in charge anymore, Counselor. I am. That fancy DA title doesn't mean a damn thing now. You're mine, and the sooner you make peace with that, the easier this will go for everyone."

Kristen blinked rapidly, trying to hold back fresh tears, but they came anyway. Quiet. Constant. She wasn't even wiping them away now.

Behind Steve, a ceramic mug clinked against a saucer. The sound seemed to echo inside her skull, a reminder that life was still moving around her. People sipping coffee, eating muffins. Unaware. Uncaring.

Her mind was spiraling, searching for some thread of power, some argument, some reason, but it was all gone. Steve had dismantled it piece by piece. He held every card.

Evidence.

Video.

Photos.

And now, Emily.

That was the part that broke her. That's what made her feel like the air had been stolen from the room.

Steve leaned in again, his voice a quiet threat. "You make the wrong move... you breathe the wrong name... and I send everything. To your colleagues. To the press. To your daughters' friends. You'll lose your job, your license, your family."

His smile faded.

And if you really step out of line, he leaned even closer, his voice now barely a whisper, "I go back for Wildcat. Or maybe I go back now to make a point. Maybe, or if you bore me, I finish the game with her."

Kristen's body tensed so violently that her legs locked under the table. Her breath caught in her throat, and for one awful second, she thought she might pass out.

Somewhere near the counter, a spoon clinked against glass, stirring sugar into coffee. The ordinary sound felt impossibly far away.

Steve tilted his head slightly, watching her.

"Yeah," he murmured. "You do get it."

She was unraveling.

Her heartbeat felt out of sync with the world around her. Every instinct screamed at her to run, scream, claw her way out, but she was paralyzed. A prisoner in plain sight.

She wasn't Kristen Anderson, District Attorney, anymore. That version of her had been shredded.

She was something else now.

His.

A puppet, strings pulled by a monster with a smile.

And she knew, without question, that any refusal, any resistance, would come at a cost. And it wouldn't just be her who paid.

Kristen obeyed, nerves fraying with every second. Steve angled his phone at her.

"Here's how this works," he said. "I ask. You repeat. Cheerful, no hesitation. Like you mean it." He gave a mocking example: *"Do you like skinny dipping?"* becomes *"Yes! I love skinny dipping!"*

She forced a nod. "Yes. I understand."

The camera rolled.

"Is your name Kristen Anderson?"

"Yes."

"Are you the District Attorney for Ravenwood County?"

"Yes."

"Do you have children?"

"Yes."

Then his tone shifted.

"Have you ever altered a court case?"

She hesitated.

"It's not about truth," he said flatly. "It's about control. Say it."

Her voice trembled. "Yes, I've altered a court case."

Her stomach turned.

Steve's next blade: "Do you enjoy getting paid to let men use you?"

Kristen's lips barely moved. "Yes, I enjoy getting paid to let men use me."

"And," he leaned in, "are you excited to be the prize at the auction?"

Her voice was flat, mechanical. "Yes, I'm excited to be the prize at the auction."

Question after question chipped away at her until he finally stopped.

"Good enough for now." He studied the screen, then smiled. "See that checkmark? That means it's saved. Backed up. Permanent."

He leaned close, voice steady. "Three days. You'll get a location. You'll show up—no excuses. Do exactly what you're told, to the letter, or we go to Plan B."

Kristen sat rigid, sweat soaking through her clothes, pulse hammering.

Steve stepped out of the booth and then blocked her way. He held up his phone—a still of Emily, bare-chested in underwear, brushing her hair in her room. "See? Wildcat looks juicy, doesn't she?"

Her breath hitched.

"Three nights. Nine p.m. Exxon on Sunlicked Lane. Wait for my text with the meeting location. If you don't show... Plan B. And trust me, you won't like Plan B."

"I can't—"

"You can." He swiped to another image: once again, the cartoon leopard panties. "It's either you... or her. Or maybe both twins. I could go for a three-way. Your choice."

Her legs trembled.

"Oh—and speaking of Plan B, maybe you should stock up on some," he added. "Can't have you getting pregnant. Get a Brazilian tomorrow. Proof photo, all sides. I want to see that tattoo."

Kristen didn't move. The phone. The recording. The threats, the words he made her say—it all swirled in her head.

Three days.

She finally stood, adjusted her skirt, purse in hand, knees stiff. As she crossed the shop, the barista leaned over the counter. "Hey, lady, come over here," Kristen walked to the counter. "I don't know what you're doing but you can't come in here slinging your ass like that. Booth's trashed, and we have to close it so we can clean it up. Don't come back, or I'm calling the cops." He snapped her picture. "Keeping this for the police. Get out, whore."

She stepped into the night, heart pounding. The real danger wasn't what just happened.

It was what came next.

His voice echoed from down the street.

Plan B and Brazil.

Trapped in an Invisible Cage

Kristen made it home to the sound of Will cooking dinner and chatting with the girls over video call.

"Hey, your mom's home!" Will said, smiling.

From the screen came two cheerful voices, "Hi, Mom, miss you!" and "Hi, Mom, love you!"

Kristen set her briefcase and keys on the counter without stopping, heading straight for the bedroom. *Three days. You'll get a location.* Will glanced after her, noting the way she avoided eye contact.

"Guess traffic was rough, must've needed the bathroom," he said lightly to the girls. They giggled, and he promised to call back later.

When Will entered the bedroom, Kristen was standing in front of the mirror, her expression distant. *Stock up on Plan B. Get a Brazilian. I better see that damn tattoo.*

"Long day?" he asked.

"Yes," she replied, voice flat.

"Want me to get you anything?"

"Shower," she said quietly. *Or I go back for Wildcat.*

Will turned on the water for her. "Dinner's ready whenever you are," he told her, then added, "Glass of wine?" She gave a small nod. Will pulled out a fresh towel and laid it on the handle of the shower door.

As he started to leave, Kristen slowly unzipped her skirt, letting it fall to the floor, not as a gesture, but as if it simply no longer belonged on her.

Will noticed she wasn't wearing any panties, and something in the way she moved—stiff, mechanical—made him pause. She began unbuttoning her blouse, her fingers almost hesitant.

Trying to lighten the mood, he said, "You know, *Commando*'s one of my favorite movies."

"Yeah," she replied flatly. *Hands on the table, palms down. Don't move them.*

"You okay, hon?" he asked, more cautiously this time.

"Yes," she answered curtly, then added, "Stop staring at me and get me that wine."

Realizing she wasn't in the mood for banter, Will quietly stepped into the kitchen, pulling the cork from a bottle of high-octane Moscato—seventeen percent—because whatever had happened, she needed something strong.

Kristen came out of the shower a few minutes later, naked, hair still wet, skin damp, moving as if on autopilot through the house. Without saying a word, she grabbed the glass from the counter, drank it in one long gulp, and let it drop into the sink, where it shattered.

You'll be the prize at the auction.

Startled by the crash, Will spun around just as Kristen picked up the bottle itself. She met his eyes, her expression unreadable.

"Get another one ready," she said. "And bring it out to me."

Will watched as Kristen crossed the living room, slid open the glass door, and stepped out into the night. She left the door wide, the cool air drifting in. Setting the wine bottle at the pool's edge, she raised her arms and let herself tip backward into the water.

By the time Will followed her out with the second bottle, she was floating on her back, arms and legs spread like a snow angel, eyes closed, only her face above the surface.

"I've got the second bottle," he called, but she didn't react.

Kristen suddenly pushed herself upright, treading water. "What?"

"I brought the second bottle," Will repeated.

Will, seeing a prime opportunity, began unbuttoning his shirt, a faint smile on his face. "Want some company?" he asked.

"No!" Kristen's answer came quickly, though her tone softened after. "Just... leave the bottle. I don't want company. I'm not hungry either. I want to be alone."

Will paused, studying her for a moment before nodding. "Okay," he said quietly. "I'm here when you're ready."

Three days, Kristen. Precisely to the letter. Or Plan B.

The Unlocked Door

Casey had asked Will to swing by her apartment before they headed to Tiffany's.

When she didn't answer his call or texts, Will parked out front and walked up, his unease growing with every step. The hallway was quiet—too quiet—and when he reached her door, his pulse ticked up.

It was ajar.

Just an inch. Maybe two.

"Casey?" he called, nudging it open with his knuckles. "It's me. Here to pick you up."

The apartment was warm, humid. Steam drifted faintly from down the hall, carrying the clean, sharp scent of her body wash—something citrusy layered with eucalyptus—and the softer floral note of shampoo. The steady hiss of running water echoed from the bathroom.

She was in the shower.

Will hesitated, then stepped inside and shut the door behind him, locking it out of reflex. Everything looked normal. No signs of a struggle. No broken glass. No overturned furniture.

He exhaled and sat on the couch to wait, eyes scanning the room anyway. Old habits didn't turn off just because the threat was personal.

A moment later, Casey emerged from the hallway, towel draped loosely around her neck, hair still dark and dripping against her shoulders. Her skin glistened faintly in the apartment light, steam clinging to her like a second skin.

She froze.

For half a heartbeat, neither of them moved.

Then instinct took over.

Casey spun into a defensive stance, hairbrush clutched in her fist like a weapon, eyes wide and lethal all at once. "What the—!"

Her heel caught the edge of the rug.

The world tilted.

With a startled yelp, she went down hard—straight onto the couch and directly into Will's lap.

There was a thud, a scramble, and then an awkward, full-body collision as she tried to recover. Wet skin met leather. Leather met panic. Panic met gravity.

She slipped again.

This time she slid sideways, half sprawled across him, water soaking through his shirt as she flailed for balance. Will instinctively caught her shoulders to keep them both from going down, the scent of soap and steam suddenly everywhere.

For a split second, they were a tangled, ridiculous mess.

Casey shoved herself upright, mortified, and shot him a glare that could strip paint. "You will never speak of this," she snapped, jabbing a finger in his direction, "or my grooming habits... unless you want to be tossed into the Sarlacc Pit and die a slow, painful death."

Will bit back a grin. "Noted."

She stalked off to the bedroom, muttering under her breath, leaving a damp trail behind her.

When she returned dressed and composed, the humor drained from the room just as quickly as it had arrived.

They both stood near the door now, staring at it.

"I locked that," Casey said quietly. "Deadbolt. Chain. I checked it. Twice."

Will studied the latch, the frame, the hallway beyond. Nothing forced. Nothing obvious.

"How sure?" he asked.

"About one hundred and ten percent."

The joke was gone. The steam had dissipated. The apartment felt colder somehow.

"Come stay at my place," Will said. "Just until we catch him."

She shook her head without hesitation. "Not happening."

Will looked at her, then back at the door that shouldn't have been open.

And neither of them said what they were both thinking:

Someone had been there.

The Sober Witness

Tiffany sat forward, elbows on the café table, her expression tense as she pieced the memory together.

"There was a guy on the sidewalk. The day Julia disappeared," she said, eyes narrowing. "He wasn't walking like everyone else; he was just there, still, like he was waiting. Watching."

Will and Casey leaned in slightly, listening without interrupting.

"He passed right by me," Tiffany continued. "Didn't say anything, but I noticed his necklace. Crimson red. Shaped like a snake eating its tail. It was strange, stood out, you know? Like something you'd see in a movie or one of those old secret society books."

Casey's brow furrowed. "An ouroboros?"

Tiffany nodded slowly. "Yeah. That's what it's called. I only know because of The X-Files. Season four, 'Never Again.' Scully gets one tattooed after a rough breakup. That episode lived rent-free in my head for years. She was my hero. I even wanted to get a back tattoo just like hers when I was in high school..."

She smiled faintly. "But my mom would've killed me. She hated Mulder, said he was arrogant and too full of himself."

Casey barked out a laugh. "That's fair."

Will raised an eyebrow, but didn't say a word.

Without missing a beat, Casey turned toward him, adopting her best Alec Guinness tone.

"This," she said, nodding solemnly at Tiffany, "is the girl we've been looking for."

Will rolled his eyes.

Tiffany laughed, but then her smile faded as her thoughts circled back.

"There was another guy too. The one he was talking to. I didn't get a good look, but the car he was leaning on, it was sleek, silver black, low to the ground. Loud. Definitely expensive. The kind of thing guys buy when they can't impress women the normal way, you know?"

"Got a type in mind?" Will asked.

"I don't know cars, but it wasn't from around campus. This thing looked like it belonged in a music video, not parked on a college street."

She paused again, her brow creasing.

"I've seen the guy with the necklace before... I know I have. But I can't remember where."

Will and Casey exchanged a look.

"That's okay," Casey said gently. "That necklace might be just the clue we needed. You did well, Tiff."

Will tapped a few notes into his phone, already thinking ahead, parking camera databases, facial recognition pulls, and dealerships specializing in high-performance imports.

One of them had to give.

Because someone had been watching Julia.
And Tiffany had just remembered what their first clear lead might be.

The Truth Shall Set You Free

Emily stopped by the house to grab clean clothes before school.

In the kitchen, she grabbed a glass, bumped it, and water spilled across the counter, with the glass following.

The sound—sharp, sudden—froze her.

A flashback slammed into her.

The words scraped out of my throat like broken glass.

I told Dad.

Everything.

The assault.

What I saw.

How my own body had betrayed me—reacting in ways I didn't understand and didn't want.

I showed him the bruises on my stomach and told him about the weight of Steve's hands, the smell of his breath, and the way his voice crawled under my skin.

The wine.

I knew I shouldn't have, and now think it was drugged.

How I'd kept drinking it anyway—trying to drown out the shame—until the bottle was gone.

I told him how, after my shower, the change hit like a switch being flipped.

The air thickened.

The room softened at the edges.

My thoughts blurred, smeared like wet ink.

And I told him the part I hated most—

That the numbness had almost felt good.

That even with the terrible thing that nearly happened... and the worse things that did...

Some small part of me had floated, light and euphoric at the danger.

A betrayal inside a betrayal, like my own body was mocking me.

Then—

I told him I knew Steve had done the same to Mom.

Only worse.

Filthier.

Because she hadn't gotten away.

The worst part—worse than the drugs, worse than the touch—was the chest-mounted camera.

I'd seen the red light flashing.

I knew he'd recorded me.

I knew he had video of what he did to mom... and to me.

The words cracked apart as I sobbed, choking them out, telling Dad I was sorry.

Sorry, he had to hear it.

Sorry, I hadn't wanted him to know.

And buried under that—

the part that made me sickest—

I was ashamed because, deep down, I thought maybe I'd wanted him to hurt me.

Knowing what that meant.

Knowing what he is.

Knowing what he did to Mom.

And the memory stabbed me:

Leaving Mom there.

Vulnerable.

Walking away, not knowing what he would do next.

Dad's jaw tightened, his eyes locked on me.

Holding himself perfectly still, like any sudden movement might break me completely.

I could feel the war inside him—

Part of him wanted to call someone, make it official.

The other part wants to find Steve right now and end it. End him.

Will's gut twisted into a knot that wouldn't loosen.

Every instinct urged him to believe her without hesitation—but her trembling voice, the inconsistencies in the story, the missing evidence... it kept him staring at a wall he couldn't break.

He knew trauma could twist memories, make reality blur.

But the thought of Steve laying a hand on her lit a cold, focused fury in his chest.

Will reached out, resting a steady hand on Emily's trembling shoulder.

Her eyes were glassy, distant, filled with pain and shame she should never have carried.

"Emily," he said quietly but firmly. "That feeling—the light, euphoric one—it wasn't you. That was the wine. He

133

drugged it. You said it hit right after your shower? That's when it kicked in. That's why it came on so fast."

Her gaze flicked to his, uncertain.

"Our bodies can react in ways we don't control," he went on. "Even when we're scared. Even when we don't want what's happening, it's just biology. It doesn't mean you wanted it. It doesn't mean you asked for it."

Emily blinked hard. Jaw tight.

"Women who've been through this—unconscious, trapped, assaulted—they've said the same thing: their bodies betrayed them. That they felt guilty or ashamed because of it."

His hand tightened slightly on her shoulder. Steady. Warm.

"But none of this is your fault. Not your mind. Not your body. Not one bit of you."

A tear slid down her cheek.

"We'll get you help," Will said, gentler now. "The best there is."

Then his voice hardened.

"And I promise you—

That monster will never touch you,

or anyone else,

ever again.

If it is the last thing I do on this earth."

Murphy's Law Strikes Again

Will had already called Kristen twice. They needed to talk. No answer. He was pacing, trying to make sense of her erratic behavior over the past week, when his phone lit up: **Detective Murphy.**

"Casey?" he answered. Her voice was low, strained, breathless.

"I think someone's following me," she whispered. "I went out for a run... I'm trying to make it back to my apartment."

"Are you armed?"

"No," she said. "Kinda hard to hide anything in Lululemon shorts and a sports bra... and my force powers are running low."

"Not the time for jokes," Will snapped, already grabbing his keys. "Where are you?"

"Columbia Street... just crossed Reed Avenue."

"I'm on the way. Stay on the phone. Talk to me until you're safe inside."

Will tore through traffic, lights and sirens blaring.

Heart pounding, Casey reached her door, her key already pinched between her fingers, she had just dug out of her shorts pocket. She fumbled with the lock, glancing over her shoulder. As she turned the knob, the door jerked open from the inside. She stumbled forward, her hands gripping the handle and pulling her off balance.

Wham!

A fist slammed into her face. Casey crumpled sideways, dazed, down to all fours. The door slammed behind her. A boot connected with her ribs as she tried to crawl away, knocking the wind from her lungs.

Another strike. Another jolt of pain.

She tried to push up, but all she could focus on were the black tactical boots. Her body tensed as strong arms wrapped around her waist and lifted her. Then, in a brutal display of strength, she was slammed to the floor.

The pain bloomed through her hip and back, and the part of her face used as a punching bag.

Her ponytail yanked her head back. A thick arm coiled around her throat in a tight rear naked choke; she'd been in this hold before. Training told her to tuck her chin, to fight. But she was already lightheaded from the blows.

Her feet kicked uselessly. Her fingers scratched at the forearm pressing into her carotids. She was lifted off the ground by her neck.

A shadow loomed in front of her,

Then darkness.

Casey came to in fragments.

Dark first. Then pressure.

Her wrists burned—pulled tight behind her back—and the realization snapped into place with brutal clarity: zip ties. The cheap kind. Too tight. Cutting circulation.

Her mouth moved instinctively—and she sucked in air. No tape.

What was left of it hung uselessly at her jawline, slick with sweat. *Must've peeled off,* she thought dimly. *I'm sweating like Luke Skywalker in a Tauntaun sleeping bag.* The thought came unbidden, absurd, and grounding in its own way.

Her lungs stuttered, dragging in air that felt too thin. Her body was still catching up, still on autopilot, muscles trembling as if she'd just sprinted uphill. Seconds, maybe a few minutes since she'd gone out. Not long enough for things to feel distant. Too long for comfort.

Cold pressed against her back.

Metal.

Her spine stiffened just as a sound reached her ears— *snip... crunch*—fabric resisting, then giving way.

Scissors.

She sucked in a sharp breath as the metal bit into the skin between her shoulder blades. Not deep. Not yet. A dull, stinging line that made her flinch anyway. The sports bra tugged hard as it was yanked free from under her, the elastic snapping away with an ugly twang.

Another *snip*.

Then another.

She felt the blades work their way down the sides of her shorts, the unmistakable rasp of fabric being destroyed. The sensation of them being pulled free followed up and away, sliding off her legs—ending in a soft, humiliating thud on the floor.

Her breath came ragged now, anger cutting through the fear like a blade of its own.

"Seriously?" Casey growled, forcing the words past clenched teeth. Her voice was hoarse, but it carried. "Fuck you."

She swallowed, pain and fury tightening her throat.

"Those were seventy-dollar shorts, you jackass."

Silence.

She laughed—short, sharp, humorless.

"Scissors? Real cute," she went on, venom threading every word. "Ever hear of clothes first, *then* restraints? What is this—" she sucked in a breath and spat the rest, "—this fucking amateur hour?"

Her heart was pounding. Her back stung. Her hands throbbed.

But she was awake.

And she wasn't going quietly.

She barely had time to twist her shoulders before the steel vise of a forearm clamped around her neck again. The world tilted. Darkness surged.

And then, nothing.

Casey awoke disoriented, her body aching and her senses scrambling to make sense of where she was.

Sound hit first.

A loud *bang* cracked through the space, sharp and sudden, followed by the hollow crash of something slamming into metal. The noise reverberated, echoing long enough to rattle in her skull. It snapped her further awake, adrenaline surging before her thoughts could catch up.

The floor was cold against her cheek.

Memory flooded back in pieces—too fast, too loud.

She was on the ground.

Her hands were wrenched behind her back, wrists bound tight, circulation burning where whatever held them bit into skin. Her ankles were tied too, pulled close enough to make any movement awkward and useless. The realization landed like a punch to the chest.

Panic surged.

She sucked in air—and choked.

Tape covered her mouth, sealing it tight. Every breath felt thin, inadequate, the sound of her own frantic inhaling roaring in her ears. Her chest hitched as her body fought for oxygen, instincts screaming at her to move, to run, to do *something.*

She tried to twist, muscles protesting, pain flaring as the bindings held fast.

Focus.

The word surfaced through the haze, a reflex drilled into her bones. Panic would kill her faster than anything else in this room.

Her heart hammered. Her pulse thundered. The metallic taste of fear coated her tongue beneath the tape as she forced herself to breathe through her nose, short and shallow at first, then slower—just enough to keep from spiraling.

She wasn't unconscious anymore.

She was awake.

And whatever had made that noise was still close.

A muffled but primal scream tore through the duct tape across Casey's mouth—raw, guttural, desperate. Her body trembled from the effort, neck straining, face flushed and streaked with tears. The sound wasn't words, but it was full of meaning. It was fear. Rage. Survival.

Every nerve in her body was firing. Her mind fought through static and chaos. No. This isn't happening. Please, God, no.

Then a BOOM, BOOM, BOOM, followed by flying wood and glass rushing past her from behind. Hands grabbing her, her heart pounding in her ears, drowning out the world.

The thundering footsteps. Her entire body tensed as someone reached for her, hands touching her, rolling her over. NOOOOOOO!!! Casey screamed through the tape, bucking and kicking and thrashing until the fog cleared just enough to recognize the voice.

Casey! Stop! Casey! Casey! Casey! Stop it's me!

Will.

Relief crashed into her like a wave.

Her strength gave out all at once, her body folding into Will as he hauled her upright. She barely registered the pain in her legs or the dizziness clawing at her skull—only the solid reality of him there, arms locked around her, anchoring her before she could crumple.

"I've got you," he said, low and steady, even as his hands moved fast.

The sound of the pocketknife snapping open cut through the chaos, sharp and precise. To Casey, it was the most beautiful sound she'd ever heard.

The blade flashed.

Snap.

The zip ties around her ankles gave way, recoiling as she sagged, breath shuddering out of her. Will guided her down carefully as she rolled onto her side, presenting her wrists without being told.

Snap.

Then another.

The tension vanished in an instant as the restraints fell away, her arms dropping free, heavy and tingling, blood rushing back in a painful flood. She sucked in a breath that felt like the first real one she'd taken in minutes.

With shaking fingers, she tore the tape from her mouth, ripping it away in one furious motion. The adhesive burned, tugging strands of hair loose as part of it caught and tangled near her ear, but she didn't care.

Air rushed in.

She coughed once, then again, chest heaving as she dragged in breath after breath—ragged, uncontrolled, *alive*. Her hands flew up to her face, then to Will's jacket, gripping him like he might disappear if she let go.

She was free.

And for the first time since waking up on that floor, the fear finally cracked.

She couldn't stop the tears. "There were two of them," she gasped, voice raw and broken. "There were two." Will held her close, his expression caught between fury and heartbreak. "I've got you," he whispered. "You're safe now."

That's when she broke.

The sobs tore from her like a storm finally rose from the clouds, shaking her frame as if her body had been holding them back for hours, maybe days. Tears spilled in waves, hot and relentless, soaking into Will's shirt. Her fists gripped his sleeves like a lifeline, as if letting go might pull her under again.

He didn't say anything else. He didn't need to. He just stayed there, anchoring her, steadying her, while his own heart pounded with rage and helplessness. His jaw clenched as he stared over her shoulder, already cataloging everything: the busted lock, the scattered items on the floor, the bruises starting to bloom on her skin.

When her voice finally cracked through the sobs, it was barely audible.

"There were two of them... They were waiting for me, Will."

He pulled back just enough to meet her eyes, his burning with a quiet promise. "Then they just made the biggest mistake of their lives."

Will hadn't seen anyone when he arrived, but the back door was ajar. The pounding wail of his siren must have scared them off. Whoever had done this was long gone.

Casey sat on the floor, trembling, zip ties scattered around her like shrapnel. Blood traced thin lines down her back where the fabric had been cut away, and fresh bruises already began to bloom on her hip. A thin cut appeared hidden in her eyebrow.

"I don't want this in a report," she whispered, eyes locked on the floor. "Please, Will... I can't face them, not like this. I don't want them to know what almost happened. I won't survive that kind of attention."

Will hesitated, his jaw tight. Every instinct screamed to call it in, to start the hunt. But when he looked at her, really looked at her, he saw what she was trying to protect: her dignity, her pride, the control that had been ripped away. And for now, he chose her.

"Alright," he said quietly. "We don't report this. Not yet."

He helped her to the bathroom, one careful step at a time, keeping an arm locked around her waist when her knees threatened to fold. The harsh light made everything sharper—the bruises, the shaking, the thin lines of red where the scissors had kissed skin.

Will set her on the closed toilet lid and turned away only long enough to grab his go-bag. He'd retrieved it without thinking, muscle memory taking over, the same way it always did when things went bad. Gauze. Antiseptic.

Closure strips. Gloves snapped on, hands steady even though something in his chest ached with every breath.

"Tell me if it hurts," he said quietly.

"It already does," Casey muttered, but there was no heat in it. Just exhaustion.

He worked methodically, cleaning the shallow cuts first, jaw tightening as he went. When he reached her left hip, he stopped.

The gash there was longer. Meaner.

A deliberate slice.

It sat just inches from the marks still healing along her side—the ones from the alley ambush weeks earlier. Same angle. Same depth. Same unmistakable intent.

Will's hands stilled for half a second.

"Son of a bitch," he breathed.

Whoever had done this hadn't been improvising. This wasn't panic or opportunity. It was practiced. Familiar. The cruelty wasn't random—it was precise.

Same style. Same signature.

He cleaned the wound gently, sealing it with practiced care, but his eyes had gone distant, dark with the realization settling in.

This wasn't just an attack.

It was a message.

And this time, it had been written on Casey.

Casey winced as he wiped away dried blood but said nothing.

"You're not alone in this," Will said, his voice low and firm. "Not for one second. I'm going to find them. And they're going to pay."

Will gently draped a blanket over Casey's bare shoulders as she trembled, still trying to steady her breath. Her hands clutched the fabric tightly, knuckles white, as if letting go would mean losing what little control she had left.

"I don't know why I feel safe with you," she whispered, her voice raw and shaky. "I haven't felt that way... not in a long time. Not since..."

She trailed off, then looked away. Will didn't push. He waited.

"There was someone before," she said quietly. "A boyfriend. He wasn't... kind. If I didn't do exactly what he wanted, he'd make me pay for it." Her voice cracked. "Sometimes I'd black out from him choking. And when I came to, he'd... well... have whatever he wanted... finish and act like nothing happened. Like it was normal."

The silence between them was thick but not empty.

Will reached out, resting a steady hand over hers. "You didn't deserve that. None of it. And you're not alone anymore."

Casey nodded slowly, her eyes glistening. "That's why I joined the force," she said, managing a bitter chuckle. "I thought if I was strong enough, fast enough, smart enough... maybe it wouldn't happen again."

She wiped her eyes and gave a half-smile through the tears. "Sorry for the ugly crying. That's twice now you've seen it."

Casey stood slowly from the couch, the blanket draped around her shoulders slipping as she leaned in and kissed Will gently on the cheek, a simple, grateful gesture that lingered longer than expected.

"Thanks," she said softly.

She let the blanket fall away, revealing nothing but the fading bruises and healing scrapes from earlier, her only armor now. She didn't flinch, didn't cover up. The moment was hers.

"I'll be back in a few," she said over her shoulder, walking confidently toward the back room. "Don't go anywhere."

Will watched her go, lips pressed in a smirk he didn't quite mean to show. After a beat, he followed.

"I'm headed your way," he called, pausing outside the doorway.

"I'm decent," she replied casually.

He stepped in and paused.

Casey was sitting on the edge of the bed in nothing but a bra and panties, drying her hair with a towel. She glanced up and caught the look on his face, and his involuntary *pfft* of disbelief.

"What?" she said with a grin. "I'm clothed, old man. Besides, you've already seen the birthday suit—*twice*, if we're keeping score."

Will opened his mouth, but she cut him off with a playful wink.

"Starting to think you're making a habit of walking in on me naked. You perv."

Will just shook his head, trying—and failing—not to laugh.

"Yeah, well... third time's on you," he muttered.

Will stepped out of the room with a quiet, "Give me a second."

Casey nodded, watching him disappear down the hallway, phone already pressed to his ear.

A few minutes later, he returned, his face calmer, more resolved.

"I made the call," he said. "Kristen's on board. The offer still stands—stay with us until this whole mess is behind us."

Casey hesitated, but only for a moment this time. The fight was losing strength, and the thought of not being alone was starting to feel less like a weakness and more like a lifeline.

"Okay," she said. "I'll take you up on it."

Will gave a slight nod, almost like a thank-you. "Good. We'll lay low, work the case from our end, but off the grid. No distractions. No outside noise."

As they headed toward the door, Will's eyes swept across the shelves packed with Star Wars LEGO sets, framed posters, and collectible figurines. A smirk tugged at his lips.

"You know what they say," he said, nodding toward a tiny Darth Vader helmet. "Always two there are. No more, no less. A master and an apprentice. We are dealing with the dark side."

Casey laughed, shaking her head. "Okay, Yoda."

Will shot her a look. "Yoda? Please. I'm way more Han Solo."

Casey glanced around at her meticulously arranged lineup of Lego Star Wars figures and half-built ships, then pointed a stormtrooper at him.

"Don't judge me, Anderson. Some people do yoga—I build tiny plastic empires. Keeps me distracted. And it's way healthier than rage-quitting and verbally annihilating random preteens in Call of Duty."

They secured her front door as best they could for now and headed to the Anderson house.

Anderson and Murphy: First Case

The night was quiet except for the steady hum of the tires on asphalt. Casey sat in the passenger seat, going over the day's notes, her pen tapping idly against the edge of her notebook, still thinking of what had just happened, trying to remember any detail.

They rolled past the dark stretch of Oakhaven Park. Even in the dim wash of the streetlights, Will knew precisely where the crime scene had been. His hands tightened slightly on the wheel.

Kelly Vance.

The name hit him like a chord still vibrating after all this time. Twenty-three, Criminal Justice major at the university. Dog walker on weekends. Bright-eyed, the kind of kid who sent half a dozen Christmas cards to professors and neighbors. Too young. Taken too soon.

He remembered that day with perfect clarity—the first time he'd worked with Casey Murphy, back when she was still "Officer Murph."

* * * * * *

The flashing blue and red lights of Officer Casey Murphy's patrol unit cut through the predawn haze in Oakhaven Park. Her boots crunched over frost-bitten grass as she approached the cordoned-off section near the pond, the air already heavy with the stillness that always followed violence.

A tall man in a worn leather jacket stood beyond the tape, whispering to a crime scene tech. Detective Will Anderson. She'd seen him around—heard the stories about his work ethic, his stubborn streak, and his uncanny knack for pulling threads nobody else saw.

Casey ducked under the tape. "Detective Anderson?"

He gave a nod, taking her in—uniform, utility belt, no-nonsense stance. "Murphy, right? Thought you'd still be on patrol."

"I am," she said, pulling on nitrile gloves. "Promotion to Homicide went through last week, but payroll says the transfer doesn't 'officially' hit until the start of the next cycle." She shrugged. "Still have to finish out the shift in uniform."

"Lucky me," Will said dryly. He stepped aside, revealing the body. "Female, early twenties. Brown hair. Found an hour ago by a jogger."

The victim lay nude, limbs positioned to form a deliberate K. Her skin was coated in white paint, the effect stark against the blood-red "O" smeared on her stomach—clearly painted with a fingertip. Nipple clips clung to each breast, gleaming faintly under the scene lights.

Casey crouched beside the body, scanning the ground before leaning in. "Clips were put on before she was painted," she noted. "You can see where the paint line stops."

Will gave a small grunt of approval. "Good eye."

She straightened, surveying the park. "No cameras within four blocks. Checked the city registry and the business permits before I got here. Whoever did this knew the blind spots."

Will studied her a moment, then said, "We've had missing college-aged women in the county lately. Four in the last six months. The city's had even more. You think she's one of them?"

Casey's gaze drifted back to the victim. "Doesn't matter if she is or isn't. Everybody counts, Detective. Every single one."

Will nodded once, the corner of his mouth tightening in shared agreement. "I like that. Most rookies in Homicide forget it."

She smirked faintly. "And here I thought you'd say, 'Impressive. Most impressive.'"

He blinked, then shook his head with a faint laugh. "Did you just drop a Vader line at a crime scene?"

"Lightens the mood," she said with a shrug. "And you looked like you could use it."

He glanced at her again, this time with the ghost of a smile. "I look forward to working with you, Murphy."

Secretly, Casey felt a flicker of pride—and something warmer. She'd always admired his reputation for grinding cases into the ground until they gave up their answers.

"So," she said, tilting her head, "why do they call you the Fox Mulder of Oakhaven PD?"

Will chuckled under his breath. "Because I keep an open mind... and I don't believe in coincidences."

Her eyes lingered on the painted "O" on the victim's stomach. "Neither do I."

Oakhaven PD — 11:42 p.m.
The bullpen was quiet, lit only by desk lamps and the dim hum of the vending machine in the corner. Most of the department had cleared out hours ago. Casey sat at her temporary desk, surrounded by open files and half-drained coffee cups, her hair pulled into a loose knot that had started falling apart.

Across the aisle, Will was in his usual late-night posture—elbows on the desk, pen tapping against a legal pad, eyes locked on the open case folder like it was about to confess.

Casey glanced over, a sly grin tugging at her lips. "Tell me, Mulder... you looking for UFOs in there or are we still on the serial?"

Without looking up, Will replied, "If the aliens abducted her, I'd have found the ship by now."

Casey chuckled. "That's comforting."

Will finally leaned back, rubbing his eyes. "I'm cross-referencing missing students from the city with our cold cases. Trying to find overlap."

She tilted her head, genuinely curious. "And?"

He slid a file across to her. Inside were two photos—different women, different years—but the same detail

152

jumped out immediately: both had a faint crescent-shaped scar just above the left knee.

Casey's brows lifted. "That's... not nothing."

"Exactly." He gave her a faint, tired smile. "People see a scar, they think coincidence. I don't believe in coincidences."

Casey held his gaze for a beat, then smiled. "Guess I'm starting to see why they call you Mulder."

He smirked. "Careful, Murphy. Stay here long enough and you'll start chasing crop circles too."

She sipped her coffee, shaking her head. "Nah. Just chasing killers. And like I said—everybody counts."

Something in his expression softened at that, and for a moment the silence between them wasn't the heavy kind— it was the steady, companionable kind that comes from knowing the other person gets it.

Then Will leaned forward again, pen in hand. "Come on, Murphy. Let's see how deep this rabbit hole goes."

Later That Night — Casey's POV

The streets of Oakhaven were mainly empty, the glow from her patrol unit's dashboard casting soft light across the inside of the car. Casey drove with one hand on the wheel, the other curled loosely around a cooling paper cup of coffee she hadn't finished.

She'd told herself she was just helping Will because she couldn't stand leaving a lead unfinished. But as the quiet hum of the engine filled the car, she knew that wasn't the whole truth.

Will Anderson was... different.

Not just the "Fox Mulder" jokes, or the way he seemed to live inside his case files, but the fact that he meant it when he said every victim mattered. No dismissive shortcuts, no prioritizing based on who would make the evening news. He'd looked at that crescent-shaped scar in the photo like it was a breadcrumb left just for him—and she realized she believed he'd follow it all the way to the end.

Casey smirked faintly at the thought. Mulder. Yeah, maybe the nickname fit. But unlike the TV agent, Will didn't seem to be chasing shadows—he was dragging them into the light.

And if she was honest with herself, she admired that.

The stoplight ahead turned green, and she eased forward, the city sliding by in streaks of sodium yellow.

She'd be in Homicide officially by next week. And as much as she'd never say it out loud, part of her was looking forward to working alongside him again.

The Next Morning — Oakhaven PD Motor Pool

Casey was halfway through a drive-by coffee when a shadow fell across her window. She glanced up to see Will leaning against the patrol car's frame, a file in hand, and that unreadable expression he wore when his brain was three steps ahead of the conversation.

"Morning, Murphy," he said. "Got a minute?"

She popped the door open. "If this is about the scar thing, you've been up all night, haven't you?"

Will shrugged. "Maybe. Pulled DMV photos on four other missing women. Two of them have the same scar. Different cities, different years. Could be nothing—"

"But you don't believe in coincidences," she finished, sliding out of the car.

He gave her the faintest smirk. "Exactly."

She glanced at the file in his hand. "So why tell me first? You could've gone straight to the captain."

Will paused. "Because you get it. You said something the other night—'Everybody counts.'"

He exhaled through his nose, almost a laugh. "I've carried that belief a long time. Just never gave it a name."

His eyes flicked away. "Read it once. In a Bosch novel. Same words."

He met her gaze again. "Hearing it out loud—from you—made it real."

He gave a faint grin. "Want to hear something interesting about the show they made from the books? One of my cousins directed an episode in Season Two and another in Season Three."

Casey's lips curved into a small smile. "Guess it's not just fiction then."

"Nope," Will said, tucking the file under his arm. "And if you're going to work Homicide, you need to know—if that's your mindset, we're on the same side of the board."

She raised an eyebrow. "You always talk like you're playing chess?"

"Only when I think I've found someone worth playing with," he replied.

Casey chuckled, shaking her head. "Careful, Mulder. Keep this up, and I might start liking you."

He grinned. "I'm counting on it."

Casey's POV

She was mid-sentence in her notes when she realized Will hadn't said a word in several minutes. His usual quiet was different now—more weighted, like something was pulling him inward.

Casey glanced up from the page. The streetlights slid over his face in fractured flashes, his eyes forward, jaw set. They were passing Oakhaven Park.

She didn't need to ask what he was thinking. That park held too much history for both of them now.

For a second, she considered breaking the silence with something light—maybe a dig about his "Fox Mulder" nickname or his habit of overthinking—but she let it go. Whatever he was turning over in his head, it was his to carry right now.

Instead, she closed her notebook, rested it on her lap, and kept her eyes on the road ahead.

Some conversations didn't need to be forced.

Later — Oakhaven PD Garage

The garage was mostly dark, just a few fluorescent strips buzzing overhead. Will was leaning against his car, flipping through a thin stack of case notes, when Casey walked in with her jacket slung over one shoulder.

"Hey," she said, stopping a few feet away.

He glanced up. "Hey yourself. Burning the midnight oil?"

"Guess so." She hesitated, then tilted her head. "The other night, when we drove past Oakhaven Park... you went quiet. That was about Kelly Vance, wasn't it?"

Will's eyes held hers for a long moment before he nodded. "Yeah."

Casey stepped closer. "She's been on my mind, too. That day... that was the first time I saw you work. First time I saw someone treat a victim like more than just a case number. I remembered thinking, 'Okay, this guy's different.'"

Will set the file aside, his voice low. "Kelly was smart, kind, and she trusted people. She shouldn't have been out there alone that morning. And whoever took her... they didn't just take a life. They took everything she could've been. That's why I told you what I did—about Harry Bosch. Everybody counts."

Casey gave a small nod. "It stuck with me. Still does."

For a moment, neither of them spoke. The garage was quiet except for the faint hum of the overhead lights.

Will broke the silence with a half-smile. "You know, I remember you calling me Vader that day."

Casey smirked. "I stand by it. You had that whole looming, ominous presence thing going on."

"Guess that makes you Luke?" he asked.

"More like Han Solo," she shot back. "Less idealism, more attitude."

Will chuckled. "I can work with that."

158

On the Road to Will's House

The heater hummed low in Will's SUV, the only sound for the first couple of minutes after they pulled out of the PD garage. Streetlights streaked over the windshield in yellow flashes, their shadows shifting across the dashboard.

Casey glanced over from the passenger seat. "You know... talking about Kelly Vance the other night got me thinking about Nance."

Will's jaw flexed. "Yeah. Both in their twenties. Both posed. Kelly in the K-shape, Nance flat on her back with her arms over her head. Both painted white."

"And both left in open spaces," Casey added. "Nance wasn't in a park, but it was still somewhere she'd be found fast."

Will's fingers tightened slightly on the wheel. "That's deliberate. He's not just hiding his work—he's staging it."

Casey shifted, looking out at the road ahead. "The paint on Nance... it was cleaner. Smoother. Almost like whoever did Kelly was still figuring it out."

He gave a small nod. "Serials evolve. Kelly might've been the first, Nance the latest. Which means—"

"—there could be more in between we don't know about," she finished for him.

They fell quiet for a moment, the weight of that thought pressing down on the small space between them.

Casey broke it with a faint smile. "For what it's worth, Anderson... it means something to me that you remember Kelly in detail. Most guys wouldn't."

Will's eyes stayed on the road. "Like I said... everybody counts." He glanced over, a small grin tugging at the corner of his mouth. "Even smart-mouthed partners who call me Vader at crime scenes."

She smirked. "If the cape fits."

Will chuckled, the tension in the car easing just enough. "I think we're gonna make a good team, Murphy."

Casey looked out at the dark road, hiding the small smile that came with that. "Yeah," she said quietly. "Me too."

Kristen

Will eased the SUV up to the curb in front of his house, headlights washing over the front porch. Through the living room window, he spotted movement—Kristen, pacing with a phone in her hand.

He shifted the gear into park and turned toward Casey. "Stay in the vehicle for a minute. I need to talk to Kristen."

Casey frowned. "I thought you said she agreed for me to stay here."

"She did," Will said, already reaching for the door handle. "I just need to ask her two questions, and then I'll be right back to help you with your things."

Her brows lifted slightly, but she didn't press. "Two questions, huh? You better not leave me out here long, Anderson."

Will gave her a small, distracted smile before stepping out into the cold night air.

Will steps into the bedroom. Kristen sits on the edge of the bed, hands clasped, eyes fixed on the floor.

"Kristen," he says, steady but hard, "we need to talk. You're not going to like it."

She looks up, barely. No words.

"Friday night," Will begins, laying it out piece by piece, "after the party, Steve brought you home. You let him in.

You shared wine. Before he left, you had sex with him. In our bed. Our daughter was upstairs."

Kristen's face pinches. Tears start and keep coming. She rocks, slow, head shaking.

"You were loud enough to wake her," Will says. "She saw you. With him. In our bed. Naked. She remembers details she'll never be able to forget."

Kristen's breath turns ragged.

"The worst part isn't even the betrayal," Will goes on. "He attacked Emily. Right outside this door. Fifteen feet from where you lay—drunk, wrapped up in wine and him. He almost took from her what she could never get back."

Kristen lets out a slight, broken sound.

"She fought him off. She saved herself. Not you—her. And when she finally got free, she saw you and Steve go back into this room. No stopping him. Just casual talk. Then he left, like nothing happened."

Will steps closer. "I have two questions. Why? And what has been going on with you since that night?"

"Will... I'm not going to stand here and pretend it didn't happen," Kristen said, her voice shaky. "Everything you just said, I believe you. I know it happened. I just... I don't remember it the way you do. I don't remember Emily being there, or Steve walking through the house, or even what we talked about. All I know for sure is that when I woke up in that bed, I knew I had been... with someone. Sexually. And deep down, I knew it wasn't you."

Her eyes brimmed with tears, but she held his gaze. "I hate saying that out loud. I hate that I don't remember the details, because that means I can't defend myself, can't explain to you how it got that far. But I swear to you, Will, I didn't invite it. I didn't want it. I would never choose him over you. You know how I feel about Steve. I've always kept my distance for a reason. But I let him in that night, and I drank the wine he gave me. After that... it's like my mind just went black."

"Will... I need you to understand something. I didn't know. I swear to God, I didn't know. I had no idea Emily was out there, no idea that he, " Kristen's voice caught. "That he was touching her. I never saw it. I didn't hear it. I didn't see her in the hallway until later, and even then, I... I didn't understand what was happening."

Her hands twisted together in her lap, knuckles white. "You're telling me she saw me, saw *us*, in bed. And that she walked away from that only to be assaulted by him right outside my door? Will, I didn't know. I would have stopped it. I would have thrown him out, I would have fought him, God, I would have killed him before I let him lay a hand on her. But I didn't know. I was gone. Whatever was happening, it had me so far under that I couldn't see anything." I was there, everything was a blur, but everything felt like it was supposed to be happening. In my mind, everything was good, happy, euphoric even. I know how bad that sounds, but that is the truth of what was going on. It's like it was me, but in a hazy dream."

Her voice dropped to a hoarse whisper. "I know how it looks. She saw me with him. She thinks I let him in, that I let him touch her. I get why she feels betrayed. But Will, you must believe me, I never would have let that happen. I wasn't there for her. Not in the way I should have been. And I will hate myself for that for the rest of my life."

She shook her head slowly, almost to herself. "I'm not asking you to pretend it didn't happen. I can't. But I am asking you to believe that I wasn't in control. I didn't know what I was doing or that I wasn't myself. Because whatever happened in this house that night, it wasn't me making those choices."

Will's jaw tightened, his voice low. "Kristen... you let him into the house."

Her lips parted, but no words came.

You told me you were tired and just wanted to be home. Then you drank the wine he poured for you. You don't even remember opening it, do you? His eyes stayed on hers, searching for something to make sense of all this.

She shook her head, trembling.

"I think he drugged it," Will said. "I think that's why everything's foggy. Why you believed it was me. But, Kristen..." He took a step closer, his tone heavy with hurt. "You must understand how it looks. You let him in. You were alone with him. And now Emily..." His voice cracked before he could finish.

Kristen's breath caught, but Will pressed on, steel in his voice now. "If he planned this, he's not going to stop. Not with you. Not with Emily. Not with anyone. So, I'm going to find him. And when I do," He cut himself off, his eyes cold. "There won't be a second chance."

Will walked out of the bedroom to see Casey standing just inside the doorway at the bottom of the stairs, crying with rage on her face. Casey hadn't meant to linger, but the moment she caught Kristen's voice breaking in the next room, she froze. The words seeped through the doorway like smoke: Emily, assault, Steve. The more Kristen said, the tighter Casey's jaw clenched.

She could still smell the sweat from the two men who had forced their way into her apartment hours earlier, still feel how her pulse roared in her ears as she fought them off. She had kept her fight inside until they took it from her, but the echo of their hands reaching for her still hadn't left her skin.

And now here was Kristen, saying she hadn't known, saying she hadn't seen. Maybe she hadn't. But to Casey, every moment of that confession felt like a knife twisting. A teenage girl had been left alone with a predator fifteen feet from her mother. Casey's throat burned.

Will turned from Casey's tear-streaked face toward the hallway to see that Kristen appeared in the doorway, her face streaked and swollen from crying. The moment she saw Casey standing there, she seemed to crumble. Her back pressed against the bedroom doorframe, and then she slid down it until she was sitting on the floor.

Reaching out a trembling hand toward Casey, she broke down completely, wailing, sobs tearing out of her in raw, uneven bursts. The sound filled the hallway, jagged and desperate, as if she was reaching not just for Casey's hand, but for something she knew she might never get back.

She didn't say anything. Didn't trust herself to. But in that moment, Will could see it; she wasn't just hearing a case anymore. She was hearing *herself* in the story. Hearing the breath she'd almost lost. And seeing the nightmare, Emily hadn't been spared.

Kristen's hands were trembling so hard she had to lace her fingers together to keep talking. Her gaze flicked between Will and Casey, her voice raw.

When you told me, 'If Steve planned this, he won't stop.' Not with you. Not with Emily. Not with anyone, you didn't know how right you were." She swallowed hard, fighting the urge to look away. "Because he's not stopping, Will. He's still doing it."

Will's jaw tightened. Casey's expression went cold.

Kristen's voice dropped. "I found out... he recorded it. Everything. The night with me. The attack on Emily. All of it. And he has... Emily's underwear from that night. The cartoon leopard ones." She closed her eyes briefly, as if saying it out loud burned her from the inside.

She forced herself to continue. "He's been using it. The video. The threats. Telling me if I don't... if I don't do what he says, on camera, he's going to send an edited version to the entire Ravenwood County employee email list. A version where it looks like I'm willing, where it looks like I participated in all of it."

Will took a step toward her, his voice low and dangerous. "Kristen..."

But Kristen's tears broke free again. "I thought I could handle him, keep him from coming after Emily again. But every day he pushes harder. And every day I feel like I'm running out of ways to keep him from pressing 'send.'"

Kristen's voice shook so badly that Will could barely hear her at first.

"I thought... if I met him somewhere public, I could end it. Stop it before it gets worse. So, I told him to meet me at Jack'd Up, the coffeehouse. I thought maybe, in a crowd, he wouldn't try anything." She shook her head, almost laughing bitterly. "I was wrong."

Her eyes darted between Will and Casey, searching their faces, bracing for disbelief.

"He sat beside me," she said, voice tight. "Pressed in close. Pushed me up against the wall of the booth." She swallowed. "People were everywhere. They could see us. Hear us. Or they chose not to. For the first few minutes, it was just... talk. Normal enough that no one would've looked twice."

Her hands twisted together in her lap.

"Then the threats started."

She looked down, breath hitching. "He leaned in and told me exactly what he'd do to Emily if I didn't cooperate. Told me how easy it would be. How fast." Her voice trembled, but she kept going. "He had his phone out. An email already open. Photos of me attached. All he had to do was tap the screen."

A pause. Longer this time.

"And then..." Her voice faltered. "Then he made me do things. Right there. In the booth."

Casey went very still.

"He touched me," she said, the words flat with shock. "Violated me. Made me lift my skirt. Made me take off my underwear and put them on the table like they were a joke. Like I was." Her jaw tightened. "He commented on them. Mocked me. Belittled me. Broke me."

Her eyes glistened, but no tears fell.

"He made me say things on camera," she whispered. "Disgusting things. Things I'll never forget hearing come out of my own mouth." She shuddered. "Then he told me to keep my skirt up. Said if anyone walked by, it was my fault if they saw. He made me sit a certain way—hands flat on the table. Don't move. Don't cover myself."

She finally looked up again, shame and fury warring in her expression.

"And the camera... he wanted it personal. Traceable." Her voice cracked. "He made me say my full name. Where I work. Name all my children." A tear finally slipped free. "So there'd be no mistaking who I was. So I'd know I could never pretend it didn't happen."

Silence filled the room—thick, suffocating.

What she'd endured wasn't about sex.

It was about control.

Tears streaked her cheeks as she went on. "I had no choice. I complied because he said if I didn't, he'd send everything to the entire Ravenwood County employee list. And now... he's still threatening me and still threatening Emily. He says if I don't do exactly what he wants, he's going to do it to her. He talks about the dark web, about... auctions. Selling me to the highest bidder to be their 'party girl.'"

She pressed her hands to her face, then dropped them, trembling. "I must meet him in three days. He told me to be at a gas station at 9 p.m., and he'll give me the real location then. Will, what do I do? How do I stop him? I can't refuse. If I do, he'll hurt Emily. But if we take him down... the worst part is, I know he's not alone. There are others. People we don't even know about. "To make it worse, one of the male baristas called me a whore, I guess he saw the whole thing and thought I was a prostitute.

"Will... there's something I haven't told you," Kristen said, her voice trembling. "He told me to go out and buy something, medicine, Plan B, and keep it stocked, like I'd need it again. He said he should have told me about the day after he had sex with me, but he didn't; he did not use protection."

Then he told me to do something else, something humiliating, get a Brazilian wax, and to send him proof I'd done it. He made it clear that if I didn't, there would be consequences.

I realized what it all meant the next morning. He sent me texts with my replies. I'm thinking he sent the texts to himself from my phone when I was passed out, but it seemed so real, and I couldn't bring myself to tell you. I was scared, Will, terrified of what he might do to me if I said anything. And every day I've kept it to myself, it's felt like he's still right here, holding that power over me."

"I don't want you to have anything else to do with him," Will said, his voice low but firm. "You're done meeting him. We'll deal with the fallout when, or if, it comes."

Kristen's eyes flared, her voice trembling with a mix of anger and fear. "You think that's it? You think we can ignore him and he'll go away? Will, if I stop, he will follow through. You don't understand, he's already doing this to other women. And there are others we don't even know about. I've seen enough to know he's serious."

She took a step toward him, her hands clenched. "If I walk away, he'll carry out every threat he's made against me, against Emily. You're asking me to let it happen, to sit back and watch while my life burns down. That's you victimizing me all over again. I can't do it, Will. I *have* to go through with it. I'm trapped, and you don't have the power to stop it."

Casey stepped forward, cutting through the rising tension. "Well... you're both right." She turned to Kristen. "Unfortunately, I think you should tell him you'll be at that meeting. And as humiliating as it may feel, do exactly what he's asking, give him the proof he wants. I know you think that's the worst thing you could do, but hear me out."

Her tone hardened. "Those photos, no matter how much they violate you, are bait—a trap. You play along, make him believe you're one hundred percent compliant, as long as he stays away from Emily. We use that as leverage. We use it to take him down."

She glanced at Will, then back to Kristen.

"I can break him," she said quietly.

Guys like that—predators—they think they're untouchable. That the rules don't apply to them. And when they get comfortable... they brag."

She leaned back slightly, eyes distant now, voice cooling to something hard and precise.

"I once got a confession out of a pedophile just by playing along. Didn't push. Didn't threaten. I told him the girl wanted him. Told him it wasn't his fault she wanted to be with a real man." Her mouth twisted faintly. "His face lit up like Christmas morning."

Kristen's stomach turned.

"And he said," Casey continued evenly, "'Hell yeah. That's right. She did.'"

A beat.

Casey's eyes hardened. "Case closed."

She leaned forward again, all focus now. "That's how we get him. We let him think he's winning. We let him talk. And then we hang him with his own words."

Kristen is the Bait

Casey stepped in, eyes blazing. "Here's how we do it, we follow you to the meeting spot. You go in first, make him think it's business as usual. Once you're inside, we move in and take him down, him and anyone else sick enough to be there. Strike first. Strike hard. No mercy, sensei."

She looked Kristen dead in the eye. "We might not know each other well, but I want to end this Mo-Fo more than anyone on this planet. And I mean it when I say I felt every word of what you told Will about the assault. I'm sorry I overheard it... but now? I'm here for you, girlfriend, two hundred percent."

Will's voice was steady but measured. "We put a wire on you. GPS tracker in your car. And we'll use the Family Tracker One app on your phone."

Casey shook her head. "The wire's risky. If they search you... or make you strip before you get close to Steve, it's over before it starts."

Will's eyes narrowed. "I've got a friend who might have just the thing for that."

Kristen shifted uncomfortably, her arms wrapping around herself. "I don't know about all this planning. I can just... comply. I can compartmentalize it, block it out, whatever happens. I would give my life to save my family."

Casey's voice dropped to a fierce growl. "If I have anything to say about it, no other man is ever going to lay a hand on you, unless it's Will."

Will stepped out of the room, shutting the door behind him. His mind was already moving three steps ahead. He scrolled through his contacts until he landed on a number he'd never thought he'd use.

It took him back years, to the city, when he was working Vice/Narcotics. A missing teen, runaway with a low-life boyfriend who turned out to be a coke dealer. Four days of tearing through the city's underbelly, finding every dead end imaginable, until finally he kicked down the right door.

She was locked in a filthy room, strung out, wearing nothing but a t-shirt. Will remembered the look in her eyes, vacant, glassy, already halfway gone. He'd nearly beaten the boyfriend to death right there. It almost cost him his badge.

Her father, quiet, polished, dangerous in a way Will couldn't place, had thanked him. The man, Orin Mercer, worked for a clandestine agency under the State Department's umbrella. Will never asked for details. He knew better. The father handed him a plain card with an unlisted number. *If you ever need anything, no matter how big or small, call me.*

Now, Will did. The phone didn't even ring once.

"Mr. Anderson..." the voice on the other end said smoothly. "I've had my eye on you for some time. What can the Matrix do for you?"

Will didn't waste a second. "I need something a female can wear without detection, GPS, live audio, live video. Real-time. And it has to be discreet. There's a chance they'll strip her down to check for a wire."

There was a pause, just long enough to let the weight of it sink in.

"I see," the voice said at last. "Tell me when and where. And, Detective... be ready. Once we do this, there's no going back."

Will ended the call and slipped the phone into his pocket. He knew his contact would deliver fast and quietly.

Less than two hours later, a matte-black SUV rolled to a stop at the curb. No plates. Tinted windows so dark they swallowed the streetlights. The rear passenger window slid down just far enough for a black-gloved hand to extend a hard-sided case. Will took it without a word, as Will started to turn the man in the back, his voice echoing a low, guttural sound: "Oblivion sends his best." By the time he reached the porch, the SUV was already gone, swallowed by the night.

Inside, Casey and Kristen waited. Will set the case on the table and cracked the latches. The lid came up slowly, revealing a nest of precision-cut foam, each cavity cradling something that looked almost ordinary, until you looked twice.

"These," Will said, lifting a tiny, stainless-steel stud, "are full-spectrum mics. Disguised as earrings, but they can also be worn as skin studs. They'll transmit crystal-clear audio in real time from anywhere in the room. Range is over half a mile."

He picked up a polished, hollow belly-button ring. "Camera. 4K resolution, wide-angle lens. No RF spikes, no heat signature. You can be fully stripped, and they'll never spot it without a forensic teardown. Same tech works in a toe ring, an ear cuff, even under a thin adhesive on bare skin."

Next came a microchip the size of a sesame seed. "GPS tracker. This is going to tell us exactly where you are, even if they move you."

At the center of the case sat a plain silver charm—the kind you'd see dangling from a bracelet at any mall jewelry counter.

"The brain," Will said. "It syncs every device. Streams everything to a secure node in real time. Nobody but me and my guy will have access."

Kristen stared at the gear, color draining from her face. "If they strip me—"

"They won't find it," Will cut in, his voice flat, hard. "It's built for deep cover. Even if you're standing there with nothing on, they won't see a thing."

A beat.

"Besides," he added, without thinking, "if they do strip you, they wouldn't notice it anyway. You could be holding the Mona Lisa and they'd still miss it. Have you seen yourself lately? Straight fire."

There was a long, dangerous silence.

Kristen turned slowly toward Casey. "Will—"

"—shut the *fuck* up," Kristen finished, eyes never leaving him.

Casey didn't even try to hide her smirk.

Will exhaled. "Yeah. That one's on me."

Casey leaned forward, her eyes locked on Kristen's. "With this, we'll hear him, see him, and track him. The second he slips, the second he brags, he's done. And I swear to you, when we hit him, we'll make sure he never gets back up."

Will closed the case with a sharp click. "Three days," he said. "And we take the fight to him and anyone else in our way."

Pact of Fire and Wine

Kristen was dreading the waxing appointment, but Casey wouldn't let her go alone. "If you're doing this, I'm doing it," Casey said, arms crossed like it was already decided.

The two of them sat side by side in the salon's waiting area, trading nervous jokes to cover their discomfort. By the time it was over, both were laughing at how much they'd hyped it up in their heads.

Afterward, they headed back to Kristen's house. The hot tub was already bubbling when they stepped out onto the deck, the steam curling into the cool night air. Casey popped the first bottle of wine, then another.

Two bottles disappeared in easy conversation, then maybe a third... possibly a fourth. They lost count somewhere between stories about cases gone sideways and confessions neither had told anyone else.

For the first time in a long time, Kristen felt something she hadn't expected: relaxed. And not alone.

"Okay, okay, we have to get this over and done," she grumbled, already half-laughing. "I'm going to send that bastard my inflamed cooch. Honestly, at this point, I don't care." She waved the phone vaguely. "Help me take these,

Casey. I'm way too drunk to hold it steady. And you know what? I'm throwing in a titty pic too. Fuck it."

Before Casey could respond, Kristen flung her bikini bottoms into the air. They arced gracefully—then snagged on the edge of the patio umbrella before sliding back down and plopping into the hot tub.

The two of them stared at it for a beat.

Then completely lost it.

Casey dipped under the water, resurfaced with the soggy bottoms in hand, and tossed them skyward. "Fly away, your free little birdy!"

They both started on their tops at the same time, laughing so hard it hurt. Kristen snatched Casey's top mid-motion and tossed it over her shoulder, nearly missing the deck entirely.

"Traitor," Casey snorted.

Kristen shoved the phone into her hands. "Just—point and shoot."

The photos were a mess—crooked angles, steam fogging the lens, uncontrolled giggling—but they sent them anyway.

"Bait," Casey announced solemnly, hitting send. "Sent."

Kristen grabbed the phone back and, without hesitation, lobbed it straight into the pool.

A splash. Then silence.

Then the two of them collapsed into helpless laughter, the sound echoing under the back patio's canopy as steam curled around them like a shield.

For a few precious moments, there was no fear. No waiting.

Just defiance, new friendship, and the kind of reckless joy that felt like taking something back.

The steam from the hot tub wrapped around them like a blanket, the night air cool on their faces. The wine had loosened the sharp edges of their thoughts, and the conversation drifted from lighthearted jabs to deeper things neither of them usually voiced.

Kristen stared at the rippling water for a long moment before speaking. "Casey... I keep replaying it in my head. Everything. I know I didn't ask for any of it, but... I still feel like I failed. Failed Will. Failed Emily. Failed myself."

Casey turned, resting her arms on the edge of the tub. "You didn't fail. You were targeted. He planned it. That's not on you."

Kristen shook her head. "Doesn't matter. The guilt's there. Like a weight I can't get rid of." Her voice caught, and she took another sip of wine, almost like it might wash the feeling away. "And now I'm supposed to sit here and trust that we can stop him before he hurts someone else."

Casey reached over and set a steady hand on Kristen's arm. "We *will* stop him. I promise you that. I've been where you are, thinking you've lost control, thinking they get to define what happens next. They don't. You do."

Kristen met her eyes. There was no judgment there, just the solid presence of someone who understood in a way few others could.

For the first time since that night, Kristen felt her shoulders loosen, not because the fear was gone, but because someone else was holding part of it for her.

Kristen set her empty glass on the edge of the tub, the steam curling around it. "You really think we can end this? Not just arrest him, but... end it. Him. Whatever he's part of."

Casey didn't hesitate. "I don't think. I know." She leaned in, her voice low, steady, the kind of tone that came from having made this kind of promise before. "We find the tech guy. We tear apart his network. And Steve? He won't have anywhere left to run."

Kristen gave a tired laugh. "That sounds like a declaration of war."

"It is," Casey said flatly. "And I don't lose."

They sat in silence for a beat, the distant hum of crickets and the bubbling of the hot tub filling the night air. Kristen reached over and extended her hand. "Then it's a pact. No matter what it takes."

Casey took it without hesitation, gripping firmly. "No matter what it takes."

The handshake lingered for a moment, both knowing this wasn't just talk over wine, it was a line drawn in the sand.

Casey reached for the cooler by the hot tub steps and popped the cork on yet another bottle. "If we're making a pact, we need to seal it properly," she said, pouring them both another generous glass.

Kristen laughed, the wine and the warmth of the night easing the tension that had gripped her for days. "What's the proper way, according to Detective Murphy?"

Casey grinned. "By forgetting about the world for a little while. And maybe... doing something reckless."

Kristen arched an eyebrow. "Reckless?"

"Yep." Casey took a sip, then set her glass down. "I dare you to streak around the house and jump straight into the pool. Last one in buys a case of wine tomorrow."

Kristen nearly choked on her drink. "You're serious?"

"Dead serious. Game on."

They both stood at the same time, laughing like teenagers as they scrambled out of the hot tub. The cool night air hit their skin, and they took off in opposite directions around the house, feet pounding over the damp grass.

From the other side, Kristen could hear Casey's mock battle cry, and she pushed herself to run faster, both breathless with laughter.

With a simultaneous splash, they hit the pool almost at the same time, sending up arcs of shimmering water under the patio lights.

Kristen surfaced, brushing her hair back. "Okay... that was worth a case of wine."

"Good," Casey said, grinning as she floated beside her. "Because you lost."

They both laughed, letting the night wash over them, the worries of the last few weeks kept at bay for just a little longer.

They drifted to the shallow end, breath still uneven from the run and the shock of the cold water. The patio lights reflected off the surface, casting ripples of gold across their faces.

Kristen leaned against the pool wall, tipping her head back to stare at the stars. "You know," she said quietly, "I can't remember the last time I laughed like that. Or the last time I didn't feel... weighed down."

Casey rested her arms on the edge beside her. "You've been carrying a lot. Too much."

Kristen's voice wavered, though the smile lingered. "I needed this. Just... to feel alive again. To feel like me, even if it's only for a night."

Casey glanced over, her tone gentle but sure. "You are still you, Kristen. He didn't take that. And you're not alone in this. Not anymore."

Kristen gave a small nod, letting the silence stretch between them, broken only by the soft lap of water against the tile.

For the first time in weeks, she felt the tension in her chest loosen, not gone, but lighter, like she could finally take a full breath.

The next morning, Will pulled into the driveway just after dawn, holding a cup of coffee in one hand and a case file in the other. He had stopped by to check on Kristen and debrief with Casey before they got started. But he didn't expect the scene that greeted him as he stepped through the side gate.

Two bare backsides strutted across the yard with the casual confidence of queens returning from war.

Kristen, with her hair a wild mess and holding what looked like the last third of a wine bottle, confidently marched toward the back door. Casey followed behind, equally undressed, clutching a pool float like it was a victory flag.

Will froze mid-step. "Uh... morning?" he said, his voice cracking somewhere between cop and bewildered husband.

Kristen turned and blinked at him, wine bottle still in hand. "Oh, hey, babe," she said, completely unfazed. "You want in on mimosas? Oh wait, we drank the orange juice... and all the wine."

Casey waved the pool float like a salute. "Don't act shocked, Will. We made a pact. It involved justice, vengeance, and nudity. All very official. Had to celebrate it properly."

Will slowly set the case file down on the patio table, eyes wide. "You two... are usually the ones yelling at rookies for showing too much cleavage at a press briefing."

Casey shrugged. "And now we're hairless, empowered, and hydrated. Your move, Anderson."

Kristen tossed her head with a dramatic flair. "Yeah, Will. Don't shame the naked revolution."

Will raised his coffee to his lips, smirking as he turned toward the house. "I'm going inside before HR calls."

As the back door closed behind him, the two women burst into laughter and high-fived, their friendship sealed with late-night wine, streaking, and a promise to take down a monster together. He tried to focus on his coffee, flipping open the case file he brought, but the voices outside were impossible to ignore.

"Whoa, girl, just noticed, those buns are on point!" Casey's voice rang out, full of mischief.

Kristen shot right back, "Yours look like they could stop traffic!"

"Well, actually... they have."

Will shook his head, setting the file down and taking a long, deliberate sip of coffee. "Professionals," he muttered under his breath, half amused, half exasperated.

Through the glass, he caught a glimpse of the two of them still parading around the yard without a care in the world, tan lines catching the late summer rays, laughing like old friends. After the weeks they'd both had, he decided they'd earned it.

Setting the Trap

Three nights later, the clock on the dashboard ticked over to 8:57 p.m. The rain had come in hard, slicking the asphalt and painting the gas station's cracked pavement in streaks of neon from the flickering sign overhead.

Kristen sat in the driver's seat, her hands clamped to the wheel, belly-button ring and studs already live, charm bracelet humming faintly under her sleeve. Will's voice came through the hidden earpiece, low and controlled.

"You're good on signal. We've got eyes and ears. Just remember, play it like you always do. He can't know anything's changed."

Casey's voice cut in, harder. "And if he tries to move you anywhere, we don't know, stall. We'll be right there."

Kristen swallowed. "Copy." She hated how small her voice sounded. I'm scared I'm going to blow it Kristen thought. Be tough, you got this, it will all be over after tonight.

The first set of headlights rolled in at 9:02, a silver sedan she didn't recognize pulling into the far corner of the lot. The driver's silhouette was wrong, too broad, too heavy. Her stomach dropped.

The passenger door swung open, and Steve stepped out. No rush in his stride. Like he owned the ground under him.

He approached the car with a smile that didn't reach his eyes.

Through the hidden mic, Will's voice went low. "Target visual confirmed. Kristen, let him talk first."

Steve leaned on her open window, the stench of cologne mixing with the rain. "Let's go," he said simply, tossing her a folded scrap of paper. Inside was an address, no street name, no town, just coordinates.

"Where is it?" Kristen asked, keeping her voice neutral.

"You'll see." He gave her a look that said Don't ask again.

Back in the surveillance van, Will traced the GPS ping on the secure feed. "He's taking her out of town. Remote area. Casey, you and I go in silent, no lights."

"Copy," Casey said, checking the slide on her sidearm. "Strike first, strike hard."

Kristen put the car in gear. Every turn took her farther from the lights, farther from any help but the two people following in the dark. The bracelet's charm blinked once, signal steady.

She knew the second that blink stopped, she'd be on her own.

The coordinates led Kristen miles out of town, down a cracked two-lane road lined with skeletal trees. No street lamps. No houses. Just the wet hiss of tires on asphalt and the occasional flash of high beams from Will and Casey's unmarked SUV shadowing far back.

The GPS tag blinked steadily on Will's screen. "We're good. She's still in range," he said, mostly to reassure himself.

Kristen's headlights finally swept over a corrugated metal building squatting at the end of a gravel lot. One side bore a rusted-out sign that had once advertised farm equipment. Now it just looked abandoned.

Steve stepped out of his car and waved her forward, motioning for her to pull up near a massive sliding steel door. The rain hammered harder, wind slicing through her coat as she stepped out.

He punched a code into a panel, and the door groaned upward. Kristen hesitated at the threshold, but Steve's hand on her back nudged her inside. The door dropped behind them with a thunderous clang, the kind of sound you felt in your bones. Then came the heavy chunk of locking bolts sliding home.

It was colder inside; the air tinged with metal and machine oil. Bright lights flickered overhead, bathing the space in harsh white.

Kristen's breath locked in her chest. The space wasn't just a warehouse, it was a stage. Every inch of it was arranged with precision and purpose. Cameras on silent gimbals slid along the walls, their glass eyes tracking her every move.

A steel-framed swing hung from a reinforced beam overhead, swaying gently as if it had been waiting for her. To the left, a padded contraption she'd only ever seen in disturbing images, a bondage horse, sat under a halo of harsh light. Along the walls, cuffs, chains, and lengths of rope hung from hooks in neat rows, like tools in a craftsman's shop.

This wasn't chaos. It was a system. And she was now part of it.

Steve walked ahead, gesturing toward the swing suspended under the glare of the studio lights. "Get comfortable. We've got work to do. And Kristen, don't get any ideas about running. This place is Fort Knox. You comply, things go smooth. You back the system..." He gave a cold smile. "...Let's just say you don't want to know. Think of the worst thing you can imagine, and you're still not close."

He stepped closer, voice dropping into something uglier. "Comply, or I'll have that Wildcat and her twin dragged out of your sister's house by their hair, brought here to watch the most depraved things a man can do... done to you. And then I'll make them the next show. While we're at it, maybe that busty blonde sister of yours joins the lineup for dessert, she's got that little orchid tattoo, right? Kind of like your pretty little daisy."

Kristen's gut twisted hard. A deep, cold dread settled in her chest. They had to have heard that. Will and Casey had to have heard every word.

"Kristen?" Steve's voice snapped her back.

"Yes," she said flatly. "I'm going to play nice for you."

His grin widened. He reached to a nearby table and poured amber liquid into a shot glass, sliding it toward her. "It's not what you're thinking, nothing like the wine. This is just to celebrate, take the edge off. Relax you. I need you to be awake and coherent. Down the hatch." Kristen lifted the shot glass, the amber liquid catching the glare of the overhead lights. She braced herself for the burn of whiskey, but instead, it slid over her tongue smooth and sweet, like liquid cotton candy. Too easy to drink.

She could've tossed back another without thinking, but the fact that it came from Steve's hand made every swallow feel like a mistake. Even finishing this one churned her stomach.

As the sweetness lingered, Kristen's eyes stayed on Steve. He was watching her too closely, like a man waiting for a fuse to burn down.

The taste might've been harmless, but she'd learned the hard way that with him, it was never just about the taste. Every move he made came with strings attached.

Her stomach knotted. Too easy to drink... too easy to hide something in.

Steve smiled faintly. "See? Nothing to worry about."

Kristen forced a tight smile back, masking the tension in her jaw. Inside, her mind was already racing, trying to count the seconds since she'd swallowed, wondering if Will and Casey were close enough to get here before whatever was in that glass had time to do its work.

Best Laid Plans

Casey, nervous and wanting to be sure, slid her Sig Sauer P365XL Rose from her thigh rig, racking it just far enough to confirm the chambered 9mm round. "Strike first. Strike hard. No mercy," she muttered, her voice low and deliberate.

The moment the heavy steel door clanged shut behind Kristen, Will's eyes dropped to his tablet. The GPS signal flickered, stuttered, and vanished.

"Signal's gone," Casey said, smacking the side of the receiver as if that might bring it back.

Will's jaw locked. "They've put her in a dead zone. We find that building, or she's on her own."

Inside, Kristen's stomach turned as the blinding lights snapped on overhead. Three men in black hoods fanned out around her, moving in a slow circle like predators. Steve stood back, arms folded, his expression almost casual.

"Check her," Steve ordered.

The first man stepped in close, forcing Kristen to tilt her head back to meet his eyes.

"Arms up." His voice was low, practiced.

Another moved behind her, gripping her waist and shoving her feet apart. "Wider."

The wand swept from the crown of her head to her shoes. Fingers combed through her hair—methodical, deliberate—his gaze locked on hers. She'd seen searches like this in county lockups before. But this wasn't security. This was performance.

"Shoes."

She slipped them off. They were flexed, examined, and placed neatly on a table.

"Empty your pockets."

Each item was taken and lined up with precision.

"Jacket."

The air bit at her arms as she handed it over. Folded. Added to the stack.

"Shirt."

Her pulse jumped, but she obeyed. No comment. Just folded and stacked.

The wand swept again. "Pants."

She hesitated. The pause was noticed. The man behind her unfastened them himself, tugging them down past her knees before stepping back. She took them the rest of the way, handing them over. Folded. Added to the pile.

Now in her base layers, the room felt colder.

"Arms out."

The pat-down resumed—slower, deliberate.

Behind her, metal snapped open. A cold edge grazed her shoulder. Snip. Then the other side. Bra straps slackened.

"Hold still."

The clasp was undone and the garment whisked away.

The man with the blade stepped into view. The light caught an engraving on the handle. Her initials. Will's knife.

He held her gaze before crouching. The blade grazed her hip—slice—then the other—slice—severing her underwear's waistband so they could be taken without her bending. This time, no folding. Just tossed aside.

Kristen fixed her eyes on the far wall. Every movement was slow, deliberate—a reminder she had no control.

Something on wheels scraped closer behind her. She didn't need to see it to know it wasn't for her comfort.

Where are you, Will?

"Sit."

She was pushed back onto the table. The foot end rose, legs angled upward. Padded supports locked her ankles in place. With a hydraulic hiss, the center dropped away, leaving her entirely exposed. Cool air drifted across her skin.

Metal scraped metal. A tool lifted from a tray. Her pulse thundered.

The exam was clinical in method, brutal in detachment. Cold pressure where there should be none. Precision without care. Procedure without consent.

Tears blurred her vision as humiliation crashed over her. She locked her body, every nerve screaming to run, to fight. She couldn't move.

When it ended, the instrument clattered onto the table. She flinched.

The restraints were unfastened with the same slow precision.

"Stand up."

Her legs were unsteady as she rose. Every movement, every command clicked into place—this wasn't security protocol.

It was a ritual.

A ritual meant to strip her dignity, reduce her to an object, and remind her she had no control.

She didn't know how much longer she could hold on. Only that Will and Casey had to be close.

When their search turned up nothing, Steve's mouth curled into a slow, smug grin.

"Rig her," he said.

The three men moved in without hesitation, their coordination almost mechanical. Thick straps were pulled tight around her wrists, chest, and thighs, buckles cinched until they bit into her skin.

Metal hooks clinked into place, connecting the harness to a heavy winch bolted into the ceiling.

With a low, grinding whine, the motor engaged, hauling her upward. Kristen's feet left the ground, her body hanging rigid in the air. Every strap was a reminder; she couldn't move, couldn't run, couldn't stop whatever was coming next.

Steve stepped over to a workstation, adjusting a mounted camera and angling blinding lights toward her. A nearby monitor flared to life, a shadowy live feed already streaming to an audience. Dozens of usernames scrolled up the screen, each followed by climbing dollar figures.

"Let's start the bidding," Steve announced, his voice dripping with salesmanship. He began reeling off personal details about her, her height, her build, her health, like a car salesman pitching to a buyer. "She's rare stock. All-natural. Tame enough to handle, wild enough to break."

Kristen's head felt heavy, her thoughts sluggish. A chemical haze fuzzed the edges of her awareness, but one truth cut through: she was trapped, on display, and she didn't know if Will or Casey would ever find her.

Outside, Casey locked a fresh magazine into her custom-painted MP5, the matte-white Cerakote and black accents giving it the unmistakable look of a stormtrooper's blaster. Even the Galactic Republic logo was stenciled cleanly along the receiver, a touch of rebellion in her otherwise lethal kit.

Will's eyes flicked to it, one brow raised. "That's not department issue. Your obsession knows no end,"

"Nope," Casey said flatly, racking the MP5. "Hokey religions and ancient weapons are no match for a good blaster at your side, kid."

They moved together down the row of warehouses, methodically clearing them one at a time. Each was a dead space, hollow shells of dust, rust, and the hollow echo of their footsteps. No heat, no movement, no life.

Casey checked her watch. "We're losing time, Will."

"I know," he muttered, scanning the next building. His jaw was locked, the tension running down into his shoulders. "If they moved her while we were sweeping, we're screwed. I need to make a call."

Will stepped away from the steel building frame, pulling his phone and hitting a number buried deep in his contacts. The line clicked twice before a low, even voice answered.

"Oblivion."

"It's Anderson," Will said. "I need eyes on a cluster of warehouses, sending coordinates now."

A pause, the faint sound of keys clacking in the background. Then Mercer's voice returned. "Got your location. Pulling a sat feed now... stand by."

Several seconds of silence passed, then a faint hiss of static over the line. "Back two warehouses have thermal signatures. Can't tell which ones are people—something's throwing interference. Could be shielding, could be a jammer. Whatever it is, it's intentional."

Will's jaw tightened. "So they know how to hide."

Mercer hesitated before answering. "I've seen this kind of masking before... only a few groups in the world use it, and none of them are the kind you want to walk in on uninvited."

"Which means?" Will asked.

"Which means," Mercer said quietly, "your clock just started ticking a hell of a lot faster. And Anderson—watch your six. If they've got this setup, they're probably watching me watch you."

Will slipped the phone back into his pocket, his expression darker than before. Casey caught it immediately.

"Oblivion? That's dark, so... What'd Oblivion say?"

"Back two warehouses are hot," Will said, keeping his voice low. "Thermal shows movement, but there's interference—like they're masking the heat signatures. Mercer says it's deliberate. Only pros pull that off."

Casey's brow furrowed. "Pros? Or the kind of pros that don't let witnesses walk away?"

"Both," Will replied flatly. "He also thinks they might already know we're watching."

Casey's eyes flicked toward the rooftops, scanning instinctively. "Which means we're burning daylight just standing here."

"Yeah," Will said. "If we're going in, we pick one, commit, and move fast—because the second we hit that door, they'll know exactly where we are."

Inside the actual location, Kristen's head drooped heavily in the harness, the bright lights blinding her from all directions. The bidding on the feed kept rising, shadowy figures on the monitor silently increasing their offers. Every so often, Steve would lean into the camera to deliver another sales pitch. She could barely process the words through the haze, but she knew time was running out.

Will and Casey moved fast, alone, every step echoing in the cold air. Mercer's voice still rang in Will's head—*two warehouses running hot, interference masking the heat signatures.* No backup. No margin for error.

Will's eyes swept the stretch of buildings ahead, and something made him stop cold. "Hold up."

Casey followed his gaze. One of the two back warehouses stood just far enough apart from the rest to feel wrong. A low, steady hum vibrated through the air.

"HVAC," Will muttered. "It's running."

Casey angled her light, catching thick bundles of cable feeding out from the wall, running up a nearby pole. "Power and data lines. That's no warehouse grid."

Will's voice dropped into something darker. "That's a live feed."

Casey gave a single nod, jaw tightening. "Then we just found Kristen."

Will and Casey circled the building, keeping low, scanning for a way in.

"No side doors," Casey muttered. "No windows, no vents. They've sealed this thing up like a vault."

Will ran a hand along the corrugated steel wall, thick, reinforced, and cold to the touch. "Not just sealed... fortified. Whoever built this didn't want anyone getting in."

When they came back around to the front, Casey stopped and let out a low whistle. The entrance was a solid steel slab set in a reinforced frame, the hinges and locking mechanism sunk deep.

"That," she said, "looks like it could shrug off a Death Star turbo laser... or at least a pissed-off Wookiee with a battering ram."

Will smirked faintly. "Let's just hope it's not guarded by a squad of stormtroopers with better aim than the usual."

Her grin was quick but sharp. "Either way, Solo, we get one shot."

Will's smirk faded, eyes locked on the door. "Which means if we want in, we're going through it—and we'll have to do it right."

Always Wear Clean Underwear

Casey adjusted her grip on the MP5, the matte-white Cerakote catching a faint glint from the security light overhead. "Then let's make it count—and I have an idea. Do you trust me?"

Will frowned. "What kind of idea?"

"A distraction," she said, eyes locked on the fortified door. "If their cameras catch me looking like I don't belong here—vulnerable, unarmed—they might take the bait and open up."

Will's face twisted. "That's insane. We pound on the door, we hit hard, we make them open it."

Casey just stared at him, then tossed her tac vest to the ground. "Seconds count. This'll be faster. Give me a hand."

Grumbling under his breath, Will helped her strip off her tactical belt and thigh rig, shoving the gear behind a stack of pallets. She stood in just her Oakhaven PD polo and 5.11 pants, stripped down and non-threatening.

She thought it wouldn't work unless I sold it.

Without warning, she peeled the polo over her head—neon green bra glowing under the security light like a flare in the dark.

Will's eyes widened. "You're out of your damn mind."

"Exactly," Casey said, smirking. "That's the point."

"Neon green, really?" Will muttered.

"No judgment zone here, pal—we don't have time," she shot back.

She unfastened her belt and let her lightweight pants fall to her knees, the cold night air immediately brushing against her skin. The matching neon green bikini briefs caught the glow of the security light, standing out vividly against the darkness around them.

"Boots first," Will said. "Always boots first, then pants."

Casey leaned into Will for balance as he unzipped her Merrell Moab boots, pulling them free one at a time. She kicked her pants away, the fabric landing in the gravel with a muted thud.

Her hair came loose with a quick pull, falling over her shoulders as she adjusted the MP5 strap.

Will's jaw tightened. "Casey, this could blow up in our faces. If I can't get to that door fast enough, they've got you as a hostage—or worse, they decide you're expendable. No vest, no cover. One wrong move and—"

She cut him off with a half-smile that didn't quite hide the steel in her eyes. "I'm glad you care, Anderson. Really. But right now, I'm your only hope of getting that door open without blasting half the building down. Trust me—we don't have another play."

Will exhaled slowly, pulled his phone from his pocket, and stepped back into the shadows. He hit a contact labeled Rivers – DHS.

The line picked up on the second ring. "Rivers."

"It's Anderson. You know those trafficking rings we've been talking about?" Will said, his voice low but sharp. "I think I just walked into the center of one. Send help—ASAP. GPS pin incoming. No questions, get here."

"You're not in your jurisdiction—" Rivers started.

"Don't care," Will cut in. "They've got people inside, our people. I've got one shot to get them out. You're either part of this or you're explaining to your boss why you didn't answer the call."

There was a pause, then Rivers' voice hardened. "Copy. I'm on it. Hold your position."

"Cavalry's coming. But until then? We're it."

"Then let's make it count," she said, squaring her shoulders toward the fortified door.

Will's phone clicked off after the call to Rivers. He turned back to Casey, replaying her words in his head.

A smirk tugged at the corner of his mouth. "You realize you just went full Princess Leia on me, right? Help me, Obi-Wan Kenobi, you're my only hope."

Casey raised an eyebrow, still holding the MP5 low and ready. "Anderson? You're making Star Wars jokes now?"

"You're the one making them," he shot back, his gaze flicking to her neon green underwear. "Only difference is, Leia didn't do it half-naked, holding an SMG, with the shit about to hit the fan."

Casey gave him a flat look. "Pretty sure if she had, Han wouldn't have left the Death Star."

201

Will chuckled despite the tension. "Just... don't get yourself killed before I can say 'I told you so.'"

"Then stay close enough to save my ass if this goes sideways," she said, turning toward the door.

Now, she slung her MP5 by the strap so it rested across her front. If she angled it just right, it would look like nothing more than a shoulder bag to anyone watching a grainy security feed.

"They see a lone woman pounding on their door, they'll think opportunity, not danger," she explained.

Will gave her one last look. "You sure about this?"

Casey smirked, even as tension coiled in her voice. "Not even a little. But it's the only shot we've got to get that door open."

Casey dug into the go-bag, pulled out a spare mag for the MP5, and slid it into the back waistband of her neon-green undies.

"Don't let that fall out," Will said, half-serious. "We need every bullet we can spare."

She shot him a quick smirk. "Relax. If it moves, I'll know."

"Just make sure you get in if they try to shut the door," Casey said, eyes fixed on the steel slab ahead.

"I'll damn well try my best," Will replied.

Casey shot him a hard look. "Do or do not, Will, there is no try. That's your wife in there."

Casey jogged up to the heavy steel door, bare feet splashing in the puddles on the cracked pavement. The cold bit into her skin, but she ignored it. She gripped the MP5 by its sling, letting it hang against her side so, on camera, it looked more like a bag than a weapon.

She slammed her open palm against the door. Bang. Bang. Bang.

"Hey!" she shouted, her voice sharp enough to cut through the rain. "Open up! You hear me?!"

Will crouched in the shadows, just out of the camera's range, watching her every move. The earpiece crackled with his voice. "You've got their attention, hold position."

From the podium, Steve's voice rolled smooth and confident through the mic, playing to the masked faces and dark silhouettes watching on the feed. Bidding numbers blinked and climbed in the corner of the monitor, each chime a reminder of just how well tonight was going.

Then—BANG BANG BANG.

The noise rattled faintly through the steel door on the far side of the warehouse. Steve paused mid-sentence, one eyebrow twitching. He looked toward the security feed and saw the camera over the entrance flicker to life.

"Hold on, gentlemen," he said to the bidders, giving them a smile that was all teeth. "Looks like we might have a little... interruption."

One of the guards leaned closer to his own monitor, squinting. "Uh... boss? It's a lady. Either she's lost, or she's a stripper who missed her cue. Or maybe one of those social media DIY singing telegrams."

Steve gave a dry laugh. "Wonderful. Either they go away, or..." His gaze slid to Kristen, still hanging in the harness under the harsh lights. "...they stay. And become the next item up for bid."

The guards chuckled darkly. Steve leaned into his mic again, addressing the bidders. "Stand by, gentlemen. Might be about to add a little bonus to the lot."

Casey banged harder, throwing in a shiver for effect, letting her hair hang forward to mask her face from the high-mounted lens. "I'm freezing out here! Let me in!"

From somewhere inside, the metallic click of a lock disengaging echoed faintly through the steel. Will's grip tightened on his sidearm.

Casey took one slow step back, just enough to give herself space to move if the door opened. Her heart hammered in her chest, not from the cold, but from the knowledge that in seconds, it could swing open, and she'd be face-to-face with the men holding Kristen.

The locks disengaged with a heavy clunk and the massive steel door began to swing open. Casey shot a glance up at the overhead camera and murmured into her mic, "You'll know when to charge."

It creaked wide enough to reveal two hooded men. One stepped forward, voice sharp. "What are you doing here?"

The other guard's gaze slid over her bare arms and neon underwear, lingering low, his smirk dripping with filth. "Well, damn... didn't know the buffet came with dessert in a to-go box. You on the specials board, sweetheart?"

Casey let her shoulders sag, playing the harmless act—then snapped upright and bellowed at the top of her lungs: "IT'S A TRAP!"

Will burst from cover like a freight train. Casey drove her elbow into the smirking guard's jaw with a sickening crack, dropping him instantly. His limp body wedged in the doorway, blocking it open.

Will barreled through right behind her, sidearm snapping up. The second door guard raised his pistol from what seemed like nowhere at Will and fired. Will double-tapped him in the center of his chest and was past him before he ever hit the ground.

The interior erupted. Four more hooded men scattered for cover among the lights and camera rigs of the studio space. "Six guards total and Steve!" Will shouted. Muzzle flashes strobed through the room as the first rounds cracked past Will's head.

Casey dove behind a stack of equipment cases, returning fire in tight, three-round bursts from her MP5. One of the shooters spun and went down. Will flanked left, catching another in the shoulder and sending him sprawling into a light stand.

A ricochet sparked off the concrete near Casey's bare foot. "Two left!" she called. Will leaned out, fired twice, and one more assailant dropped his weapon with a shout. The last man bolted toward the far end of the warehouse.

But Steve was already moving, slipping between the chaos and the live-feed lights. Kristen's suspended form swayed under the glare as he snatched a duffel bag and disappeared through a side passage.

"Steve's running!" Will shouted.

They gave chase, weaving through dim corridors stacked high with crates. The air reeked of machine oil and damp concrete. Steve glanced back once, then pushed harder toward a set of emergency-lit stairs leading down to a storage bay. The slap of Casey's bare feet echoed behind him, the sound sharp enough to make him look twice.

Will was a step behind her when a figure lunged from the shadows, one of Steve's goons, and hit him hard from the side. The impact slammed them both into a stack of crates, rattling the metal frames.

"Go!" Will barked, shoving the man off and grappling with him as Casey surged past, never breaking stride. She was already halfway down the stairs, MP5 in hand, neon green flashing against the gloom as she closed in on Steve.

He hit the bottom of the stairs at full speed and stopped dead. A solid steel bulkhead door loomed in front of him, bolted shut from the other side. No exit. No escape.

Casey slowed her approach, MP5 steady, sights locked on his center mass. "Nowhere left to go, Steve."

He turned, chest heaving, sweat tracking down his temple. His eyes darted to the walls, the corners, the ceiling, anywhere there might be an opening. There wasn't one.

"On your knees," she ordered.

Steve smirked, trying to mask the panic edging into his voice. "Not your color, Detective."

Casey didn't blink. "On your knees, asshole."

He hesitated, shifting his weight like he might lunge or run, but there was nowhere to go. Casey stepped in closer, her weapon unwavering, her voice dropping to a low, dangerous calm. "Don't make me say it twice."

This time, the fight left him. He sank to his knees, muttering something under his breath. Casey moved fast, holstering her weapon just long enough to slap cuffs on his wrists, wrenching them tight enough to make him flinch.

With a sharp tug, she hauled him to his feet. "Walk," she ordered, shoving him forward.

She dragged him back toward the main floor, where Will was just finishing with the last of the other men, Will's eyes met hers, a flicker of relief passing between them before he looked at Steve.

"Nice catch," Will said.

"Nice fight upstairs," she replied, giving the cuffs another tug to keep Steve moving.

"Got him," Casey said, giving the cuffs a final tug. "Auction's closed."

Cleaning up and Getting Dressed

Kristen hung limp in the harness, the straps biting into her arms and waist. Her eyes were half-open, unfocused, her head rolling slightly with each sway. Will moved in first, cutting the primary lines while Casey steadied her.

"Easy... I've got you," Will murmured, lowering her to the cold concrete. He wrapped a heavy blanket around her shoulders, shielding her from the harsh glare of the studio lights. She leaned into him instinctively, still dazed from whatever Steve had pumped into her system.

Across the floor, the toll of the fight was plain: three of Steve's men lay still in dark pools, two more groaning on the ground, wrists cinched with zip ties, and another was the door stop. The air stank of cordite and ozone.

Casey took one last glance at the scene, then jogged toward the front door. "I'll be right back," she called over her shoulder.

"Where are you going?" Will asked.

"Before the cavalry rolls in, I need to not look like the kind of woman who was banging on a door half-naked with an MP5," she shot back, disappearing into the rain.

A few minutes later she strode back in, tactical vest and Oakhaven PD shirt back in place, hair tied up again, zip tied the guy by the door and came back in.

Will smirked at her. "By the way... where exactly did you hide your handcuffs?"

Casey didn't miss a beat. "Wouldn't you like to know, partner?" she said with a sly grin, stepping past him to check the other zip-tied survivors.

Will shook his head but couldn't help the corner of his mouth twitching upward.

Red and blue light began strobing through the high warehouse windows, slicing across the steel beams and casting jagged shadows across the floor. A heartbeat later, the rising wail of sirens bled into the space, growing louder until the low hum of approaching engines joined it.

The sound swelled into the grinding stop of cruisers and tactical vans on the gravel lot outside. Doors slammed. Boots hit the ground in unison.

Casey glanced toward the entrance with a quick, satisfied smirk. "Cavalry's here. Right on time."

Will shifted his grip on Steve's arm, wrenching the cuffs tighter. "Good," he said, voice low and cold. "Let's hand them a gift."

He shoved Steve toward a pair of uniformed officers moving in to take custody, then crossed the floor to where Kristen sat, still wrapped in the heavy blanket. Her eyes were glassy, her movements sluggish.

Will knelt beside her, steadying her as he helped her to her feet. He guided her toward two arriving paramedics, making sure the blanket stayed tight around her shoulders.

"Keep her warm," he told them firmly. "Keep her on oxygen, she's been dosed with something."

One of the medics nodded, already pulling an oxygen mask from a kit. Will lingered for a moment, his gaze fixed on her face, before finally stepping back to let them work.

Then he went straight to the camera rig still pointed at the empty harness. The auction feed was still live, though the viewer count had dropped sharply the second the shooting started. Will's fingers moved fast, yanking the main storage drive from the back of the encoder, then pulling the backup from a hidden slot beneath the monitor.

"Got 'em," he muttered, stuffing both into an evidence pouch. He followed the thick data cable back to a secondary box mounted on the wall, ripped that free too.

Casey strode over, MP5 now slung casually over her back. "You think that's everything?"

"No," Will said. "But it's enough to prove the auction was live. And with any luck, the network logs Will give us IPs, maybe even payment trails." His gaze dropped to the evidence pouch, eyes hard. "We can trace the buyers."

Casey held out her hand. "Then give them to me. I've got the tools for that, and the software's already set up at my place. We can start digging tonight."

Ravenwood Sheriff's Department SWAT came filing in over the downed guard, weapons low but ready.

"Sheriff's Department—coming in!" one of them barked.

A sergeant swept the scene with a quick, practiced eye—the three dead, two more zip-tied and groaning, another still out cold in the doorway. Steve was cuffed against the wall, glaring like he thought it might still matter.

The sergeant gave Will a nod. "Looks like you two were busy."

"Yeah," Casey said, still keyed up, "and we're not done yet."

Will stepped closer to the sergeant. "We'll talk later. Agent Evan Rivers with DHS is on his way with his people. I need to get to the hospital—check on my wife."

The sergeant just nodded again, reading the urgency in Will's face. "Go. We've got it from here."

Checking the Hard Drives

Casey didn't wait for clearance. The moment she left the warehouse, she drove straight to her apartment, the evidence bag in the passenger seat like a silent dare—two storage drives pried from Steve's so-called "studio vault."

Inside, she swept the coffee table clean, sat, and slid on a pair of nitrile gloves. The drives were cold in her hand, heavier than they looked. She plugged in the first one.

The file explorer popped open instantly. Too fast.

Her brows drew together. Nearly empty. No partitions, no buried folders—just a single file.

She opened it.

The screen lit up with a still image: a middle finger, dead center in frame, lit by the same stark lights from Steve's studio.

At the bottom, in bold white block letters:

SUCK IT, PIGS.

Casey's jaw tightened. She yanked the drive and plugged in the second. Same result—same image, same insult.

Then, as she started to eject it, her laptop's fan roared to life. A warning box flashed across the screen: FILE WIPING IN PROGRESS – 3%.

Her pulse jumped. She slammed the power button and ripped the cable free. The screen went black.

Booby trap. Steve hadn't just taunted them—he'd built in a kill command to erase whatever was really on those drives the moment they were accessed.

Casey sat back, breathing hard. "Alright, Steve," she muttered. "You want to play dirty? Let's play dirty."

The door opened behind her. Will stepped in, spotting the dead laptop and the evidence bag. "Please tell me that's not as bad as it looks."

Casey gave him a grim smile. "Worse. But he's not getting the last laugh."

Digital Resurrection

Will's frown deepened as Casey powered her laptop back on, the drives now resting on the table like unexploded grenades.

"He set a self-wipe," she said, fingers flying over the keyboard as the system crawled through a forced reboot. "As soon as you open that one file, it triggers a script. Whole drive gets nuked."

"Anything left?"

"Maybe. But not if we poke it the wrong way again." She reached for her phone and scrolled to a contact buried deep in her list. Kessler.

Will arched a brow. "Thought you and Eli Kessler weren't on speaking terms after the... 'Vegas incident.'"

"We're not," she said, hitting dial. "But he owes me. And if anyone can pull data off a rigged drive without killing it, it's him."

The line clicked. A lazy voice answered, "Casey Quinn. Well, hell. Did the sun freeze over?"

"No time for jokes," she said. "I've got two SSDs booby-trapped with a zero-fill wipe script. Trigger's in the only visible file. I need the data under it—intact."

Kessler whistled low. "Old-school insult over a hidden payload? Cute. Send me the hardware. Courier only. And

Casey—" His tone sharpened. "If these drives are tied to the name I think they are, you might not like what you find."

"I'll take my chances."

She hung up and looked at Will.

"You trust him?" he asked.

Casey shrugged. "I don't trust anyone. But I trust his work."

Will glanced at the drives, then back at her. "Fine. But if this blows up in our faces..."

"It won't," she said, sealing the drives into a padded evidence pouch. "Steve wanted to erase these for a reason. That reason's going to nail him."

"So, Casey what was with the "Casey Quinn comment?" Will inquired.

"Well since it's you I'll tell you; I was never going to speak of it again to embarrassing, considering were basically family now guess you should know in case I run for President one Day." Casey joked. "So here is the dirt!"

Casey leaned back on the couch, nursing her glass of Eagle Rare, already regretting starting this story.

"Okay, so... McSorley's. Halloween night. Costume contest. I decided I was gonna do Harley Quinn, but not, like, lazy Harley Quinn. Homemade Harley Quinn. I'm talking—cut-up tee, hand-painted hot pants, fishnets, the works. Spent days on it. Honestly? I looked damn good."

Will smirked. "So where's the part where this turns into a disaster?"

Casey shot him a glare. "Patience, Anderson. Anyway, I get there, feeling like a queen, and the MC announces a Harley Quinn dance-off. Of course, I join. First thirty seconds? I'm killing it—bat over the shoulder, spin moves, crowd is screaming. Then—" She made a ripping motion with her hands. "RRRIP. Back seam on the shorts just... detonates. Like a paper bag in a hurricane."

Will covered his mouth, trying not to laugh. "No..."

"Oh yes. And here's the thing—I can't stop, because if I stop, it's obvious. So I keep dancing, trying to face the crowd, but then this Deadpool dude decides we're doing a butt-bump thing. I dodge too slow, and—guess what?—rip gets bigger. Now I'm basically one wrong move away from becoming a cautionary tale."

Will snorted. "This is already a cautionary tale."

"I'm not done," she said, pointing at him with her glass. "The bat slips out of my hand mid-spin, clatters across the stage, crowd thinks it's part of the act. People are throwing Joker cards at me. By the time the song ends, my fishnets are doing 90% of the modesty work. I bolt offstage, tie my flannel around my waist, and vanish. Thank God I wore those fishnets and they were a size too big, so they bunched up in the front."

Will was laughing openly now. "You didn't win, I assume?"

"Oh, I didn't win the contest. But apparently, I won something called 'Best Crowd Reaction." She rolled her eyes. "And here's the cherry on top, Anderson, someone filmed it. Whole thing. It's on Instagram, TikTok, probably a subreddit I don't want to know about. There's even a slow-motion replay of the rip, set to that dramatic Inception BWAAAH sound. And my Sergeant saw it."

Will nearly choked on his drink. "Oh my God—"

"Yeah," Casey said flatly. "So now, whenever Harley Quinn shows up in a movie, half the department just looks at me and says, 'Hope those seams hold up this time, puddin'.'"

Will grinned like Christmas came early. "Casey, you realize you just gave me blackmail material for the rest of your life, right?"

"You do, and I'll spill, and I'll tell my version of your Halloween pumpkin suit incident. Kristen didn't spare any embarrassing details." Casey retorted. "Fair..." Will Said. "Puddin' for Prez!" Casey punched him in the shoulder.

As she slid the pouch into her messenger bag, she couldn't shake the thought: whatever was hidden under that little crude message, Steve hadn't wanted it seen. Which meant it was precisely what they needed.

Will Gets an Earful

Will had barely made it to his truck when his phone lit up—

Captain Dan Rogers flashing across the screen. He almost didn't answer. Almost.

"Yeah?"

"What the hell was that at the warehouse, Anderson?" Rogers' voice hit like a shotgun blast in Will's ear. "I heard the radio traffic, rolled up to see what was going on—and guess who met me at the tape? Ravenwood Sheriff's Department. And guess what kind of welcome I got?"

Will stayed silent.

"They iced me out," Rogers snapped. "Told me it was handled. *Handled.* Like I'm some damn tourist at my own crime scene."

"This wasn't—" Will started.

"Don't you start," Rogers barked. "I'm done, you hear me? Done. Your badge is worth exactly *nothing* right now. You and Murphy think you're Dirty Harry out there? You're not. You're just a couple of loose cannons who've been playing cowboy without filing a single piece of paper. I've seen *zero* reports on this 'Steve' or whatever case you think you're working. Zero."

Will clenched his jaw. "We've been—"

"Save it. You and Murphy get your asses back to the PD. Now. Sheriff's bringing Steve in for questioning—on *your* case, the one you never bothered to tell me existed. And I'm gonna be sitting in on that interview. So you can either show up and try to explain yourselves, or you can clean out your desks."

Rogers hung up without waiting for an answer.

Will stayed there for a long time, staring at the phone.

Casey came around from the far side of the lot, MP5 still slung over her shoulder. "What was that about?"

"Rogers," Will said. "He's ordering us back to the PD. Sheriff's bringing Steve in."

Casey's brow furrowed. "And you believe that?"

"No," Will said flatly. "Not for a second. But we've got no proof—yet. Every time we've started pulling threads on him, Steve's crap blows up in our faces and we're chasing fires instead of following the money."

"So we're walking right into whatever Rogers wants?" Casey asked.

"Yeah," Will said, sliding behind the wheel. "And this time, we watch every move he makes. Because if he's dirty, this might be the only chance we get to prove it."

Steve's Interrogation

The interrogation room smelled faintly of stale coffee and disinfectant. Fluorescent lights buzzed overhead, washing everything in a harsh, unforgiving glare.

Steve sat slouched at the table, ankle shackles clinking when he shifted. His hands were cuffed in front of him, fingers laced loosely like he was on a lunch break instead of under arrest. The smirk etched across his face seemed less like an expression and more like something he'd been born with.

Through the one-way glass, Will stood with his arms crossed, his jaw tight. Beside him, Captain Dan Rogers muttered under his breath, every syllable laced with irritation.

Inside the room, Casey paced once behind her chair, then stopped. Her hands gripped the backrest, knuckles pale, the urge to lunge across the table at Steve written all over her face.

The door opened with a quiet click. A tall man in a dark suit stepped inside, his DHS credentials clipped to his belt. Without a word, he took the empty seat beside Casey, laying a slim case folder on the table between them.

Steve's smirk deepened, his eyes flicking from Casey to the new arrival. "Oh," he drawled, "guess I rate the big leagues now."

Casey leaned forward, arms braced against the cold metal, the DHS agent quietly listening standing just behind her.

"You want to talk?" she asked flatly. "Then talk."

Steve's grin widened.

"Kristen's wine? Yeah, that was me. She left to check on Emily, came back clueless. That stuff makes you compliant as a puppet—go here, do this, suck that, take it wherever I tell you. No complaints. No hesitation. And the best part? She double-dosed herself. Real thirsty, that one. Gave me double the time for repeat performances, extra takes for the camera. Made for a real show—more money for us."

Casey's jaw tightened, but she didn't bite.

"Haven't seen the video yet, have you?" Steve went on. "You should. Might learn something. Hell, you could make a killing yourself—bounce those tits up and down on some stud, or a chick with a strap-on. You look like the strap-on type, being a cop and all."

The muscles in Casey's neck went rigid, but her eyes stayed locked on his.

"Oh, and those ripped panties of hers?" Steve's tone was almost cheerful. "Sold 'em. Put the clip of me tearing them off on the dark web first. Thirty bids. Sold for five hundred. Can you believe it? I fuck her, and *I get paid for her underwear*."

Casey's voice was ice. "And Kristen's future?"

"That was the big score," Steve said, leaning back in his chair like he was recounting a business deal. "Auction her to the highest bidder. Keep the video handy. She'd do whatever I said if she knew the alternative—Plan B."

His smirk deepened. "Had my chest rig on the whole time. Got it all. Every second. Every angle."

From the other side of the observation glass, Will stood frozen, every muscle coiled. His hands flexed at his sides like he was already imagining them around Steve's throat.

Steve leaned forward, lowering his voice like he was sharing a secret. "And Emily? Yeah, I tried. Would've gone further if Kristen hadn't wandered out. Doesn't matter—the message was sent. She *felt* it. Long, hard, like a punch to the gut."

He chuckled. "Could've tamed that kitty and mounted her like a trophy."

Casey heard the faint creak of movement from the observation room. Will.

Still listening.

Still waiting.

Still deciding if he could resist breaking through that door.

Steve let the words hang before smirking.

"Speaking of messages... I sent a few messages from Kristen's phone while she was out snoring like a pig. Made it look like she was *all in.*" He chuckled. "The tattoo pic? That was the moneymaker. Easy enough. Got the money shot on her face, and the moneymaker on her phone—that sealed the deal."

He tilted his head, savoring the memory.

"Even left her a little... token of our time together. Did she tell you about the buried treasure I left in her box? I do that a lot. My married ladies love a keepsake."

Casey's knuckles tightened against the table. "You're admitting to multiple victims, then?"

"Oh, more than you think," Steve said, his grin widening. "Right now? Three other women. All married. They're the best. The money's better from the web, and they fold faster. Threaten to blow up their perfect little lives, they'll do whatever you tell 'em—or whoever you tell 'em to."

Casey's voice stayed flat. "So why didn't we find your video or gear when we hit your house and your so-called vault?"

Steve's laugh was low and smug.

"Because you were looking for the wrong thing. The vault's just the showpiece. The real stash—videos, rig, buyer lists—that's not in any place you have jurisdiction over."

"Then where?" she pressed.

He just leaned back, cuffs rattling. "Earn it, Detective."

Steve's tone dropped into a conspiratorial whisper.

"You think I'm the big fish? I'm just the middleman—Pimp Daddy Steve. I set up the meets, keep the girls in line. The wizard? He's the one with the dedicated server. Edits the videos. Packages them for clients. Makes it all look like art."

He grinned wider, leaning in like he was selling her a vacation package.

"There's dozens of us. Full-time production. All the girls you could want. Walk onto Ravenwood campus, pick one out, give her a free drink, hook up the cameras. Little fucky-fucky, little sucky-sucky, and they'll do *anything* to keep mommy and daddy from finding out. Most of 'em are more afraid of their friends knowing than their parents. Social media made me a king."

Casey could feel her blood boiling, but she forced her face to stay neutral. She knew Will was in the next room, hearing every word.

And she knew exactly how close he was to coming through that door.

Steve smirked. "Tell your partner to get comfortable, because I'm about to make your night."

He rattled off a passcode. "My phone's in your evidence lockup. Punch that in, kill the lock, then open the folder labeled *Wildcat*... if you dare."

Casey stepped out, came back with the phone. She keyed in the code, disabled the lock, and found the folder.

Her expression hardened with each swipe—still frames of Emily, different days, different states of undress. Each image stamped with a date and time.

Then—stills from the night of the assault. Frozen moments she would have given anything to unsee.

The last photo stopped her cold: a close-up of Emily's cartoon leopard panties. Same date as the attack.

Casey's grip tightened. Her chest rose sharply, a burn building behind her ribs. Without warning, she stepped forward and slammed her forearm into Steve's throat, driving him back in his chair and spilling him to the floor.

"*Fucking bastard!*" she shouted.

The other detective caught her arm before she could follow through. "Easy!"

Steve rolled to an elbow, rubbing his throat, then started laughing—low, ugly, deliberate.

"That all you got?" he rasped. "You haven't even seen the best part. Check the folder marked *Trophy Trash*."

Casey's thumb hovered, then tapped.

Dozens of faces stared back from the screen—Kristen among them—each frozen in a moment they hadn't chosen. Between them were video files, every one marked with a timestamp.

She didn't open them. She didn't have to.

Her voice went cold. "Every one of these is going into evidence."

Steve just smirked. "Better hurry. My partner's probably adding new ones as we speak."

Casey's thumb hovered over the screen, but she couldn't bring herself to open a single file. She didn't want to see Kristen like that—

not now, not ever.

Steve leaned back, eyes locked on her, his grin pure malice.

"*Trophy Trash,*" he said, savoring every syllable. "Get it? Only trash would do those things. Worst one I ever had. She went from trophy to trash just like that. Got the video to prove it."

The chair legs screeched as Casey moved toward him, but the other detective caught her arm. "Don't," he warned.

Steve's laugh rose, ugly and triumphant. "That's not the best part. *That's not the best part!*" His eyes glinted. "Open *Irish Crème.* Go on. Do it."

Casey's jaw clenched. She scrolled until she found the folder. The first file was a video.

When she tapped play, her blood went cold. Her bedroom filled the screen. *Her* bed. *Her.*

The phone trembled in her grip. A low hum came through the speaker, followed by a sound she recognized instantly—her own voice. She stabbed the stop button.

"Irish Crème Murphy," Steve grinned. "Get it? No, you don't get it—nobody gives it to you like you give it to you."

Casey snapped. She hauled him out of the chair and drove her knee into his groin. Steve folded with a grunt, but she followed him down, hammering her fists into his back.

The door slammed open. Will stepped in, grabbing her shoulders and dragging her back. "Enough!"

Steve staggered upright, smirking through the pain. "Guess I should've labeled that one *Scorched and Spread Red.*"

Will's fist moved before his brain caught up, cracking Steve across the jaw. Blood trickled from the corner of Steve's mouth, and he licked it like a prize.

Casey ignored him, scrolling through the rest of *Irish Crème*. Her breath hitched when she hit a still image: her own apartment floor, her body bound and gagged, shot from above, from a phone, not one of the spy cameras. Resting on her lower back between tied hands was a small, round object.

She zoomed in.

An *Ouroboros*.

Her gut twisted hard. The room fell away under the pounding in her ears.

Steve was watching her reaction, savoring it. "Want to know who set those cameras in your house? Or your apartment?"

"Talk," Casey said. "Who took this picture!"

"That wasn't me. That was my tech guy," Steve said, smug. "At the request of a client. Goes by *GodBodyCount* and *ErosGoneWrong* on the dark web. Never met him. Likes to act like God's gift to women. My guy streamed him *everything*—your place, your safe space, all of it neat and tidy on his server."

The phone buzzed in Casey's hand, the brief vibration mimicking the start of an incoming call.

Then nothing.

The screen flickered, showing a small green robot for half a second—something she barely registered before it went black. A heartbeat later, the display lit up again, flashing a familiar splash screen: SouthernLink Wireless in bold white letters against a navy background, the unmistakable golden palmetto tree centered beneath it, arcs radiating from its limbs.

Her stomach dropped.

The screen refreshed once more.

Hi. Welcome. Please set up your phone.

Factory reset.

Wiped clean.

Casey's fingers tightened around the device as a lead weight seemed to form in her gut, dragging everything else down with it. He hadn't just been watching. He hadn't just gotten inside.

He could reach out and erase her—whenever he wanted.

Slowly, she lifted her eyes toward Will, dread crawling up her spine.

He was still talking, still focused on the case file in his hands.

He hadn't seen her face yet.

And for one terrible second, she didn't know how to tell him what that blank screen meant.

Will's voice was flat. "His name."

Steve smiled wider. "Not so fast. One, You want him? Two, you want that server? Then, Kristen gives me *full immunity*. No charges, no trafficking, no assault—nothing from those videos or whatever you find. That's my price." Casey instinctively handed the phone to Will and leaned over the table.

"You think you can bargain your way out of this?" Casey's voice was pure ice.

Steve leaned back in the chair, cuffed hands laced behind his head, eyes glittering with the thrill of still having power. "Now I want a lawyer, I want DA Kristen Anderson, well, I had her already, but immunity, Check and mate, you bitch."

That's when Casey pivoted on the table and drop-kicked him straight in the chest, slamming him back into the wall and dumping him—and the chair—onto the floor.

Steve's lungs seized the moment his back slammed into the wall. Air wouldn't come. For a few seconds, the world narrowed to white pain radiating from his chest, each heartbeat like a nail driven into his ribs.

He coughed hard, tasting iron, and rolled to his side. Every instinct screamed to get up slow, keep the swagger, don't let them see the hit land. He'd played this game too long to give them the satisfaction.

But in the dark edges of his vision, a thought slid in—unwelcome, sharp. Murphy isn't like the others. She's not scared enough to fold. And Anderson's watching her back.

Steve forced a chuckle through the ache, dragging himself upright and dropping into the chair like it was all part of the plan. His lip split wider when he grinned, but he kept it, because the smirk was armor.

He'd been in tighter spots. He had backups, caches, people in the shadows who owed him favors. They could tear him down here, but they couldn't touch the rest. Not yet.

Still... he couldn't shake the look in her eyes before she hit him. That wasn't cop-anger. That was personal. And personal, I had a way of getting messy.

Another Page in His Book

Oakhaven Park glowed under the strobe of cruiser lights, the alternating red and blue bleeding over damp grass, twisting the pavilion's shadows into long, shifting fingers. The wind carried the earthy tang of wet leaves, layered with something sharper—an acrid bite that cut through the night air.

Fresh paint.

A yellow crime scene barrier flapped lazily in the breeze, its motion at odds with the heavy stillness inside the perimeter. Beyond it, white-suited techs moved like ghosts, their gloved hands steady, their voices hushed—no one wanted to break the suffocating weight that hung over the scene.

Page Kettering, 22, was reported missing three days ago. Third-year business major. Former honors student. She lay dead in the center of a weathered picnic table, transformed into something cold and deliberate. Her skin was completely coated in a smooth, chalky layer of white paint, not a streak out of place.

A deep red "O" had been finger-painted across her stomach, the uneven ridges of the mark catching in the portable floodlights. It glistened wet, the pigment so fresh it looked like it might smear if touched.

Her arms were stretched high above her head, fingers spread wide, palms turned skyward. Her legs were splayed at exact, measured angles, perfectly aligned with the table's corners. From above, the body formed an unmistakable X—precise, intentional, ritualized.

Casey's voice cut through the static hum of the lights. Low. Certain. "She's posed... exactly like Julia Wells."

Will's gaze stayed locked on the display. He didn't need to be reminded of Julia—two days missing, then found the same way. Her image had been splashed across the front page, immortalized in the killer's mocking editorial. Every line of that piece had been a dare, baiting them to try and stop him.

"This isn't a copycat," Will said, his voice tight. "Same guy. Same ritual."

A forensics tech glanced up from where he knelt beside the table. "Paint's still wet. Whoever did this... was here minutes before patrol rolled up."

Will's jaw clenched hard enough to ache. His eyes swept the dark tree line beyond the perimeter lights, the shadows thick, unbroken. "Then he's watching us. Just like before."

Casey didn't blink, her gaze still fixed on Page's lifeless face. "Or worse... he's counting on us to watch him."

Will's voice dropped into something colder. "Watch him fall. It's time to nail this bastard."

A Call Back to the Office

Rogers caught them halfway down the hall, his face already flushed, voice low but cutting. "You two think you can just beat the hell out of a suspect in cuffs and walk away clean? I'm filing a formal IA complaint. And don't be surprised if assault charges follow."

Will stopped, squared to him, his tone calm but hard-edged. "Do whatever you have to do, Captain. That piece of garbage threatened my family. I'll gladly take a misdemeanor for putting him on the floor."

Rogers' jaw worked, but Will didn't give him a chance to interrupt.
"And let's be honest—this would never see the light of day. The DA has had Steve on her radar for the last week or so, or were you not listening to a damn word that came out of that snake's mouth? She'd be just as happy if I—or Casey—put two in his chest and one in his forehead. So go ahead. Make your complaints."

Rogers' eyes narrowed. "You think you're untouchable?"

Casey stepped in, voice sharp enough to cut. "No, Captain. I think you're a dirty cop. Because if you'd listened to a single word Steve just spewed in there, you wouldn't be standing here talking to us like this. You'd be kicking down doors to find the rest of the girls he mentioned."

Something flickered in Rogers' expression—just for a heartbeat—before the mask slid back in place. It wasn't a shock. It was recognition.

"Watch yourselves," he muttered, turning on his heel.

Casey's eyes followed him until he was out of earshot. "That look he gave us... he knows more than he's saying."

Will's jaw tightened. "Yeah. Either he's protecting Steve, or he's protecting whoever Steve's working for. Either way, one day, we'll prove it."

234

Casey Needs a Drink

Casey stared out the passenger window, arms crossed like she was holding herself together by force. The silence wasn't awkward—it was loaded.

"I wanted to kill him," she said finally, voice low and hard.

Will didn't answer right away. He knew better.

"In that interrogation room... Steve sat there like he was untouchable. Every confession was a flex. He talked about Kristen as if she were for sale. Emily like she was disposable. Me like I was next."

Her jaw tightened. "And then someone just so happens to nuke his phone remotely? He just sat there smirking as he'd planned it. Like the system was working for him."

Will's fingers whitened around the wheel. "Because it is," he muttered. "Guys like him... they don't get punished. They get plea deals."

"I don't trust him, Will. He knows more—a hell of a lot more—and he's playing us."

"You think he's tied to the killer."

"I think he's part of it. He knew details of the scene we never released. Talks like it's a production—and he's not just some low-level creep. He's connected, he knows."

Will's voice was flat. "And you think they'll cut him loose for a name."

235

"I know they will. Immunity, then he twists it and walks. Meanwhile, all we've got is Kristen's word. She walked into that warehouse and did everything they told her—no 'kidnapping' on paper. And Emily? You want to put a traumatized minor on the stand and let a defense attorney shred her? The Sixth Amendment will kill us before the trial starts. And with immunity, he will get to do his dirty deeds and be a rat on the outside."

She looked at him, eyes cold. "We need his videos. Cloud, server farm, whatever. The truth's out there."

He gave her a sideways look. "Okay, Scully. Welcome to the dark side. But you're right—either we find something to bury him, or I put him in the ground myself."

Her mouth twitched into something between a smirk and a warning. "Careful, Anderson. You're starting to sound like me."

They pulled into the parking lot of Jack'd Up, the local coffee shop. A rare moment of normalcy in the middle of chaos.

"Coffee first, conspiracy later?" Will offered, trying to lighten the mood.

Casey smirked faintly. "Only if they have the good muffins today."

Inside the shop, the bell chimed above the door. Jack, the owner, gave a wave from behind the counter. "Detectives," he greeted. "Busy week?"

"Something like that," Will muttered as a hooded figure brushed past them and out the door.

As Casey scanned the room, something near the back caught her attention. Her brow furrowed.

"Will," she whispered, nudging him. "Look. That guy sliding into the booth... the one on his laptop."

Will turned subtly.

"He's wearing it," Casey said. "The necklace was just leaning out from under the neck of his shirt. Crimson-red. A serpent devouring its own tail."

Will's pulse kicked up a notch. "The ouroboros. How'd you see that?"

"And that's not all," Casey added, lowering her voice. "I'm sure he's using a VPN, bouncing his IP. And... he's uploading something."

They watched as the man tapped a few keys, closed the laptop, and stood, slipping out the side door before either could react. I think that was Julien Cain, he works here.

Will looked at Casey. "Coffee break's over."

Casey nodded, reaching for her badge. "Let's go hunting."

Will was already moving. He shoved open the side door just in time to see the suspect, Julien Cain, round the corner of the building, hoodie drawn up, laptop bag slung tight over one shoulder.

"Cain! Police!" Will shouted.

Julien didn't look back. He bolted into the alley behind Jack'd Up, his feet slamming the pavement, echoing off brick walls slick with old rain and shadow.

Casey was right behind Will, ignoring the fresh sting in her healing shoulder as they gave chase.

"Split him?" she barked.

Will nodded. "You go left, cut through the lot! I'll stay on him!"

Casey veered off, ducking between two parked cars and hopping a curb as Julien tore through the narrow alley and burst out the other side, straight into the edge of Oakhaven's old warehouse district.

He was fast, but sloppy. He glanced back too often, and his panic made him reckless.

Will stayed on him, closing ground slowly but steadily. "Come on, come on..." he muttered, dodging trash bins and vaulting a low chain barrier.

Julien disappeared around a corner.

Will followed and nearly collided with a stack of pallets, which had been knocked over to block the path. He skidded, stumbled, but kept going.

Ahead, Julien reached a narrow loading dock, scrambling up the concrete lip. But as he pulled himself up,

Casey appeared from the opposite end.

"Don't move!" she yelled, gun drawn, feet planted.

Julien froze, torn between choices, and made the wrong one. He turned, ducked low, and ran toward the warehouse door.

Will took the shot, clean and precise—a warning. The bullet cracked into the wall inches from Julien's path.

Julien stumbled, crashed through the door, and vanished inside.

Will reached the entrance seconds later. He and Casey exchanged a glance.

"Warehouse is condemned," she said, breathing hard. "No power. No cameras."

Will took out his flashlight.

"So we go in the dark," he said.

Casey nodded grimly. "Let's find out what he's hiding."

They entered the shadows, the door swinging closed behind them with a heavy, echoing clang.

Inside, the silence was unnerving, thick, close.

A soft hum vibrated through the floor, and a single red light blinked in the distance.

Casey swept her light across rusted machinery, old crates, and peeling signs. Then, movement.

A shadow darted between pillars.

"He's not alone," Will said, raising his weapon.

The hunt had truly begun.

Will moved first, sweeping his light in tight arcs, the beam slicing through the darkness. Casey followed close behind, her weapon drawn, her breathing steady but shallow.

The warehouse smelled of rust and mildew, with the faintest trace of something acrid beneath it, burned plastic? Bleach?

They stepped over rotted pallets and torn insulation scattered across the floor. Cracked skylights overhead leaked dull moonlight, offering ghostly outlines of long-abandoned machinery and forgotten crates.

"There," Casey whispered, gesturing toward a faint red glow pulsing from behind a rusted-out office door at the far end of the floor.

Will nodded, signaling for her to circle wide while he approached straight on. As he neared, the door creaked open slightly, ajar.

He pushed it in with the muzzle of his gun.

Inside, the tiny office had been repurposed. Power cables snaked from a portable generator humming low near the corner. On a metal folding table sat a rigged-up workstation, three monitors, a satellite router, and what looked like a series of external drives labeled in Sharpie: ARC-1, SKEIN, SESSION_O.

Casey stepped in behind him, lowering her weapon as her eyes widened.

"Will... this isn't just some kid with a laptop. This is organized."

A photo collage was taped to the wall above the screens, dozens of printed images, notes scribbled in red ink, maps of Oakhaven with plotted routes, pins, and dates.

Some of the photos were crime scene images.

Others were surveillance shots.

One showed Julia Weeks walking across the Ravenwood quad two days before she was found.

Another, a still frame, showed Will and Casey at a diner. The timestamp was from three nights ago.

Will stepped closer, scanning the chaos of information. At the center of the board was a single phrase, written in block red letters:

"WILDCAST NETWORK – DO NOT INTERRUPT"

His stomach turned.

"Jesus Christ..." he muttered. "They've been watching us."

Casey moved to the drives and picked one up. "This network... we've seen that name before, on the darknet drop linked to the victim files. Someone's uploading this. Organizing it. Monetizing it."

"Not just murders," Will said, jaw tight. "This is performance. Exhibition."

He turned to the monitors. One still blinked. The last file transfer hadn't completed.

UPLOADING: SESSION_04 - 97%

Casey reached for the keyboard, trying to stop it, only to find the input locked behind encryption.

The moment snapped together in Will's mind. "That guy at Jack'd Up. He wasn't just running, he was delivering. This is a node. One of many."

A clatter echoed from somewhere deeper in the warehouse.

They both froze.

Casey raised her gun again, voice low. "We're not alone."

The clatter echoed again, sharper this time, like metal striking concrete.

Will swept his flashlight toward the sound, catching only empty space between the old machinery. The red glow of the monitors behind them flickered once, then steadied.

Casey turned toward the door. "We need to pull the drives and get out of here. Now."

She reached for the closest external drive, detaching it from the console just as the overhead lights, long dead, sputtered to life.

All at once, the warehouse was bathed in a harsh, flickering yellow glow.

Will tensed. "That generator didn't power the whole building."

Casey froze, eyes scanning the rafters. "Which means someone else just flipped a switch."

A click echoed from the far end of the warehouse, the unmistakable sound of a door locking.

Will turned to the main entry. The large roll-up door they'd come through was now sealed.

He rushed to the side exit. Also locked.

"We're boxed in," he muttered.

Casey was already moving, tucking the drive into her jacket and scanning the floor for cover.

Then a hiss, high-pitched and mechanical, filled the air.

Small nozzles embedded in the ceiling vents began releasing a faint mist, almost invisible except where it caught the light.

Will's instincts screamed. "Masks, now!"

They both scrambled, snapping on their tactical respirators that were left on a shelf just feet away, just as the vapor began to thicken. The chemical scent stung the eyes, even through the filters.

"Gas," Casey said. "It's not lethal... not yet."

A voice crackled through one of the old speakers mounted near the rafters. Grainy. Distorted.

"Detectives. Always so curious. So sure of your own moral compass."

Will turned slowly, tracking the sound. It was coming from the back wall where the speaker wires vanished into a control box.

"You came here for truth. For justice. But you're standing in something much bigger. You're not investigators anymore. You're part of the story."

Casey drew her weapon. "Come out and say that to my face, you coward."

The voice chuckled.

"Oh, I Will. But first... lights out."

A sudden pop, then total darkness.

The warehouse lights cut out in an instant, plunging them into black silence.

Only the faint hum of electronics and the soft hiss of the gas remained.

Then a sound behind them, quiet footsteps, circling. More than one.

Will clicked on his tactical flashlight. The beam cut a narrow cone through the mist, just in time to catch a figure moving behind a support pillar. Hooded. Masked.

"We've got company," he growled.

Casey checked the mag in her weapon. "Let's give them a story they won't forget."

Will's flashlight darted across the misty warehouse interior, catching glimpses of movement, shadows slipping between steel beams, boots scraping against concrete.

"They're flanking," he muttered. "Left and right."

"Then we punch straight through," Casey said. She swapped her near-empty mag with a fresh one, the click loud in the silence. "Pick a door and make a hole."

Will turned toward the nearest side exit, one they'd found locked earlier. But if they could get close enough...

Another figure darted between crates ahead, too fast to shoot.

Will grabbed some flashbang from a random chest rig lying on a pallet, pulled the pin, and tossed it low and long.

Thunk-thunk-thunk,

BOOM.

The blast lit the fog like lightning. A concussive pop followed by shouting, stumbling, and chaos.

Will and Casey broke into a sprint.

Two masked men reeled near the exit, disoriented. Will dropped one with a swift elbow to the jaw and fired a round into the other's leg, dropping him.

Casey hit the door hard, but it was still locked.

"Stand clear!" Will shouted. He stepped forward, raised his sidearm, and fired twice into the locking mechanism.

The steel groaned, then popped.

They burst through into the cool night air, lungs burning even through their masks.

The side lot behind the warehouse was a mess of weeds and old loading ramps. A van was parked near the fence, a nondescript utility vehicle, engine still idling.

Casey's eyes narrowed. "Too convenient."

Will checked his corners. "Or too late to ask questions."

They sprinted for it, boots hammering the gravel.

As they reached the van, a figure emerged from the shadows beside it, another masked man, rifle raised.

Casey didn't hesitate. Two quick shots, center mass. The man dropped.

Will yanked open the driver's side door and slid behind the wheel. Casey jumped into the passenger seat, already pulling the drive from her jacket.

"Hang on," Will said.

He slammed the accelerator, and the van tore out of the lot, tires spitting gravel.

Behind them, more figures spilled out of the warehouse, but it was too late.

Will hit the road and didn't let up, eyes fixed on the mirror, hands locked on the wheel.

Inside the van, the hard drive pulsed faintly in Casey's hand. She stared down at it, then at Will.

"That wasn't just a network," she said. "That was a war room."

Will nodded grimly. "And we just stole the battle plans."

The van rumbled down a forgotten county road, headlights cutting through the rising fog as dawn threatened the horizon. Neither of them had spoken since leaving the warehouse.

Will finally pulled into an overgrown turnout, concealed by a row of thick pine trees. They'd used it before, decades ago, back when the department ran undercover training in the area. No one uses it now. No cameras. No questions.

Will killed the engine.

Silence.

Casey sat still, fingers clenched around the external hard drive she'd nearly been shot retrieving. It was warm from the heat of her hand.

She passed it to Will. "Time to see what hell we just stole."

He nodded, pulling his laptop from the back of the van. They'd learned not to rely on the department's tech, not since things started leaking. He connected the drive and waited.

The laptop whirred. The screen lit. The drive blinked once.

Then... nothing.

"Come on," Will muttered, refreshing the input. He unplugged it, reconnected it.

Still nothing.

Casey leaned over. "Try a data recovery tool. Maybe it's just the boot sectors."

Will tried. Scanned. Waited.

A pop-up appeared:

DRIVE CORRUPTED. FILE SYSTEM UNREADABLE. CRITICAL SECTORS DAMAGED.

Will stared at the screen, jaw tightening.

Casey leaned back slowly, her voice low, bitter. "All that... and it's toast?"

He didn't answer right away. He unplugged the drive and turned it over in his hand. A jagged gouge ran along the casing, probably from the moment she took fire. Or maybe when the flashbang hit the floor. It didn't matter now.

"We lost it," he said flatly. "They either damaged it on purpose... or we just got unlucky."

Casey let out a shaky breath. "No backup. No copy. No trail."

Will glanced out the windshield at the tree line, expression hardening.

"They'll think we're off the board now," he said. "Empty-handed. Blinded."

Casey looked at him. "You want to use that?"

He nodded. "Damn right I do. They think we've got nothing. That's our edge now."

She stared at the broken drive in his hands. Then gave a tired half-smile. "Fine. But next time? You're carrying the tech."

To Catch a Demon

Two Hours Later – Oakhaven PD, Off-Grid Room, Sublevel Archives

The flickering fluorescent lights overhead made the room feel more like a bunker than a records room. That was the point. Only a few trusted people even remembered this sublevel existed.

Will set the damaged hard drive down on the dusty table and leaned over the whiteboard he'd wheeled in from the hallway. On it, a web of names, images, and red lines spiraled outward from one center photo: JULIEN CAIN.

"Tech-savvy. Low-profile. No priors," Casey said, pacing. "But he knew how to encrypt, bounce his signal, upload to a dark site in under two minutes while sipping espresso. He's not just a barista with a shady side gig."

Will circled Cain's name. "He's a gatekeeper. A handler. Not the top, but close enough to know who is."

Casey looked up. "So we bait him?"

Will nodded. "We make him think we recovered the drive, decrypted it, and pulled something game-changing, something worth killing over. Then we wait to see who comes for it."

Casey crossed her arms, thinking. "We stage a leak. Something public enough to rattle the network, but quiet enough to make Julien feel like it's still containable... if he acts fast."

Will smirked. "We make it look like we posted a fragment from the drive. Just one frame. One breadcrumb. Something they'd recognize."

Casey tapped her fingers on the desk. "What about that photo of the ouroboros pendant? The one he was wearing? It wasn't in evidence; it was in our direct line of sight."

Will pulled out his phone, found the image from the coffee shop's security cam, and zoomed in. "Perfect. We release it anonymously through a forum they monitor. Add a cryptic message: 'Recovered and mirrored. Insurance files live.'"

Casey raised a brow. "You're really enjoying this cloak-and-dagger thing, aren't you?"

He shrugged. "Been a while since I felt like we had the upper hand."

She turned serious again. "You think he'll take the bait himself?"

Will leaned forward. "If he doesn't... someone above him Will. Either way, they'll send someone to verify the leak, or silence us."

Casey smiled. "So we leak the photo. Wait for Cain to panic. And catch him trying to clean up the mess."

Will grabbed a marker and drew a big red X over Cain's photo. "Exactly. We don't need the drive. We just need him to think we do."

Later That Night – Jack'd Up Coffee

They sat in a borrowed surveillance van across from the café, watching through long-range lenses and a hacked security feed. Julien returned around midnight, nervous, checking over his shoulder, moving faster than usual.

Casey's voice was low over comms. "He's not acting. He's scared."

Julien entered through the back door, glancing around before disappearing into the back office.

Will checked his watch. "Right on time. Let's see who he calls... or who shows up to silence him."

Jack'd Up Coffee – Rear Alley, 12:17 a.m.

Inside the van, the feed from the hacked security cam flickered as Julien Cain paced in the back office, fingers trembling as he typed furiously on his laptop. He paused now and then to check his phone, glancing toward the back door like he was waiting for someone, or something.

Casey's voice crackled in Will's earpiece. "No call yet. But he's sweating bullets. He took the bait."

Will leaned forward. "He's stalling. Waiting for backup. I don't think he's here to delete files. He's here to survive."

Then movement.

A black SUV pulled into the alley behind the shop, its headlights dark. Two men stepped out, bald, dressed in tactical black, moving in perfect sync.

They weren't here for coffee.

Casey's eyes narrowed. "That's not his legal counsel."

Will popped the van's side door and grabbed his weapon. "Time to move."

But before they could exit, a third man stepped out of the SUV.

Will paused. "Wait... is that?"

The third figure wasn't dressed like the others. Hoodie. Jeans. Civilian. Unarmed.

But familiar.

The face came into focus beneath the alley light.

Detective Mason Dyer.

Presumed dead. Reported missing eight months ago after disappearing mid-investigation on a sex trafficking ring in Charleston. One of their own. One of the best.

Casey blinked. "That's not possible."

Will swore under his breath. "No. That's Dyer."

But Dyer wasn't with the team.

He was moving toward them.

Not toward Cain. Not toward the hit squad.

Toward the van.

And then, gunfire.

One of the black-clad men raised his suppressed weapon and fired toward the café door. The front glass shattered, and Julien's scream echoed through the alley.

Will and Casey spilled out of the van, returning fire as Dyer dove behind a dumpster.

"Will!" Dyer shouted. "I'm on your side!"

Casey ducked behind the open van door, eyes wide. "You'd better be telling the truth, Mason!"

Dyer popped out just long enough to shoot the man on the left in the leg, dropping him clean. The other assailant turned toward Dyer, then dropped from Will's shot a heartbeat later.

Silence.

Only the sound of Julien hyperventilating behind the shattered café door remained.

Will and Casey approached Dyer cautiously, weapons still half-raised.

"Talk fast," Will said, eyes hard. "You died. You disappeared."

Dyer lifted his hands slowly, blood on his knuckles but no wounds. "I was deep cover. Embedded. The Ouroboros Network's deeper than you know. I've been tracking it since Charleston. You just kicked a hornet's nest."

Casey's jaw clenched. "And you let us walk into it?"

"I came to pull you out of it," Dyer said. "You weren't supposed to be part of this. But now that you are... we need to finish it."

Will lowered his weapon, mind racing. "Then start talking. Fast."

Behind them, Julien Cain whimpered, still alive, but now with no one left to protect him.

Casey stepped toward the shattered doorway. "You want to end this network?"

She looked at Dyer.

"Then he's our key."

Julien, looking all out of sorts, twitched like a cornered rat as Will loomed over him. Then, out of nowhere, his face twisted into a crooked laugh—loud, defiant. He lifted his wrists toward Will as if offering them up.

Will didn't take them. Instead, he grabbed Julien by the shirt, yanked him forward, and slammed him down onto his stomach. Julien hit the floor hard with a grunt, and Will drove his knee into the small of his back, grinding it in as he locked the cuffs tight around his wrists.

From his pocket, Will pulled a worn metal Miranda card and dropped it on the floor inches from Julien's face.

"Read along," Will said, his voice flat, ice-cold. Then he began, each word slow, precise, and heavy:

"You have the right to remain silent.

Anything you say can and will be used against you in a court of law.

You have the right to an attorney.

If you cannot afford one, one will be appointed for you."

His tone was void of mercy—more sentence than formality. When he finished, Will leaned in just enough for Julien to feel his breath.

"Do you understand these rights as I've read them to you?"

Julien gave a snort, his lip curling. "Yeah, yeah... I understand. I understand you're a pissed-off cop trying to play Dirty Harry."

Will's fist knotted in the back of Julien's collar, jerking his head up just enough for his neck to strain. His voice dropped to a lethal whisper.

"No. You understand you're done. And if I were you, I'd pray the justice system gets to you before I do."

Art Speaks

Oakhaven PD – Off-Grid Room, 4:09 AM

Julien Cain sat alone at the metal table, hands resting flat, fingers twitching slightly. The overhead light flickered above him, casting shadows that stretched across the walls like grasping hands.

He no longer looked scared.

Just tired.

Casey stood behind the glass, watching from the adjacent observation room with Will and Dyer. Her arms were crossed, her expression guarded.

"He hasn't said a word in ten minutes," she muttered.

Will's jaw clenched. "Then let's see if silence is his way of taking control."

They entered the room together.

Will sat across from him. Casey leaned against the wall, her presence sharp, silent.

Dyer remained by the door, arms folded, watching like a wolf.

Julien didn't lift his head.

"You want to talk now?" Will asked.

Julien tilted his chin up just enough for the light to catch his eyes, no longer wide with fear, but glassy and distant.

"I've thought about this moment," he said softly. "For years."

Casey narrowed her eyes. "Which moment?"

Julien's gaze moved to her, then to Will. His voice was almost serene.

"The moment someone asked the right question."

Will leaned forward slowly. "What question is that?"

Julien smiled faintly.

"Why I chose the 'O.'"

Casey went still. Will didn't blink.

Julien nodded slowly, his hands twitching again.

"They thought it was symbolic. Some message. Some coded threat. But it's just... complete. It's the beginning and the end. The return. The perfect cycle. And it's been beautiful."

The temperature in the room seemed to drop.

Will stared at him. "You're saying, "

"I'm not a cog," Julien interrupted. "I'm the engine. The mastermind. The artist. Every scene? Every pose? I designed them. I filmed them. I uploaded them."

Casey took a step forward, fists clenched. "You murdered those women."

Julien didn't flinch. "No. I preserved them. Gave them purpose. They became symbols. Witnesses to a system that devours the forgotten."

What is with the letters, the paint, the positioning?" Casey asked.

"The letters? Oh, that was *art*, Detective—an *art grade*. You hand me the alphabet, I'll paint you a masterpiece. One—she was just 'OK,' average brushstroke in the collection. Two—she liked it at the Y, all nice and symmetrical. Three—ha—X marks the spot, Detective Anderson knows about that spot. Four? Couldn't make up her mind if she liked the football team or the baseball team—might've been *both*. You should see her pay-to-view page... now *that's* performance art. And the last one? That was me leaving you clowns a love note—a reminder. You still don't get it. You never will. You don't *understand* art. Or the artist."

He laughed under his breath, shaking his head like they were the idiots here.

"The paint? That was their baptism. After their cleansing. Wiped them clean of all the filth they'd done—or the filth they wouldn't admit to. They were a fresh canvas when I was done. Pure. Perfect. A vision of my making. Their beginning... their end... a new beginning for them, all in one stroke." "I had two more works of art I had already laid out the canvas for, one got away, and the other was taken from me.

Dyer's voice came low, dangerous. "You're not an artist. You're a butcher with a Wi-Fi connection."

Julien looked at him, calm. "You didn't catch me. I chose to stop. And now... I want the world to know."

Will leaned in, voice like ice. "Then why run tonight?"

Julien's smile faded.

"Because they didn't know. The network. The investors. The sick little voyeurs on the other end of the stream, they thought I was just the guy behind the screen. Not the one behind the knife."

He looked down at his hands, stretching his fingers.

"I was so good at being invisible... I forgot what it felt like to be seen. They needed a face to see, to go with the artist, not just my work."

Silence hung in the room like smoke.

Casey's voice came cold and steady. "We'll see how invisible you are when you're in a 6x8 cell for the rest of your life."

Julien tilted his head again, eyes distant.

"We'll see."

Oakhaven PD – Off-Grid Room, 4:43 a.m.

The room was silent, thick with the buzz of fluorescent lights and the low hum of recording equipment. Julien sat at the table, his hands folded neatly, that same unnerving calm plastered across his face.

Casey stood across from him, rigid. She didn't sit. Didn't blink.

"I want to know why," she said.

Julien raised his eyes to hers.

She stepped forward. "You marked me. You choked me out. You placed that pendant on my back. You staged it, took a photo like I was one of them. Why didn't you finish it?"

A slow smile tugged at the corner of Julien's mouth.

"Because Will was coming," he said simply. "Sirens on. Lights flashing. Right on cue."

He gave a slight tilt of the head toward Will, who stood silently near the door. "Funny. He saved your life and doesn't even know how close it was."

Casey's jaw clenched. "So that's the only reason I'm still breathing?"

Julien's expression flattened, something more sinister flickering behind his eyes.

"I had plans," he said quietly. "You were going to be... special. Precise. I'd already prepped everything. Clean razors. Studio lighting. I was going to shave you, pile up those little red short and curly hairs inside the O, leave them for Will, like I did with Julia and the photo,"

"Don't," Will snapped, stepping forward, voice sharp with restrained fury.

Julien chuckled softly. "Touchy subject."

Casey didn't flinch. "You were trying to humiliate me. Strip me down and make me part of your narrative. But I didn't break. That's what eats at you, isn't it?"

Julien's eyes flicked up. For the first time, his confidence wavered.

"You were supposed to be a message," he said. "To him. To all of them. But you ruined it by surviving."

Casey leaned in, voice cold. "No. I ruined it by fighting. And now? You're not the storyteller anymore, Julien. You're just the ending."

Julien leaned back in the chair, eyes distant, voice smooth, almost academic in its detachment.

"I wasn't born evil," he began. "I was born observant."

He tapped two fingers lightly on the steel table, a slow rhythm that matched the tempo of his thoughts.

"The Cain estate was built to impress, but it was a mausoleum in disguise, cold marble, colder people. My father thought feelings were weaknesses. My mother only touched me when there were cameras around."

He looked up at Will, then Casey.

"Do you know what that does to a child?" he asked, not really expecting an answer. "It teaches them that love is a performance. That people only matter when they serve a purpose. Or a story."

Julien's lips curled into a shadow of a smile.

But I adapted. I watched. Learned what people needed. How to mirror it. Charm was easy once I realized it was a transaction. Smile, compliment, listen, just enough. And they give you everything.

He shifted in his seat.

"The coffee shop?" he said with a scoff. "That wasn't some humbling job. It was brilliant. Constant traffic. Girls with headphones, homework, and just enough loneliness, and just enough to catch my eye, signaling that they needed to join the club. All I had to do was pay attention. Make them feel seen. People open up when they think they're safe."

His voice lowered, but his tone never wavered.

"I didn't pick victims. I selected performances. Each one... a vignette. A living echo. And when they were perfect, when the vulnerability was honest, I preserved them. Captured them. Elevated them."

Casey's knuckles tightened on the edge of the chair.

Julien turned to her, calm and unapologetic.

"Don't pretend you don't understand. You walk into every room calculating who's a threat, who's weak, who will break under pressure. The difference is, I act on it. I make the invisible visible. That's art."

Will's voice was gravelly. "As it has been said, you're not an artist. You're a predator with delusions of poetry."

Julien just smiled.

"Funny thing about predators... they always know how to wait. And they always return."

Oakhaven PD – Interrogation Room
5:27 a.m.

Casey sat across from Julien Cain, hands clasped, eyes fixed on him. The quiet hum of the camera recording above them was the only sound for a long moment.

Then she asked, flatly, "Julia Weeks. She wasn't lonely. She wasn't vulnerable. So why her?"

Julien's expression didn't change, but his fingers twitched once.

He leaned back slightly, almost casually.

262

"She wasn't like the others, I'll give you that," he said, voice cool. "But perfection doesn't always come from weakness. Sometimes... it walks right through your door, wearing crimson lace."

Casey stiffened.

Julien smiled faintly, the memory clearly alive behind his eyes.

"It was a Tuesday. Mid-afternoon. She came in with her boyfriend and your friend, Will. Sat in the booth near the window." He gestured with a slight tilt of his head. "She dropped her phone. Bent down to grab it. Half-lay across the bench... and that skirt of hers?" He gave a low whistle. "Got caught up on the seatback."

Casey's stomach turned.

"Crimson lace panties, sheer," he said. "Thin tan lines against sun-kissed skin. A perfectly accidental moment. But not to me. Or to Will."

Casey's brow furrowed. "What are you talking about?"

Julien's grin widened, cruel now.

"He looked. Your golden boy detective. I watched it happen. He didn't linger, but he saw. He even blushed. His face said everything: surprise, guilt, interest."

He leaned forward now, eyes glinting.

"That's when it clicked. She wasn't just stunning. She was connected. To Billy. To Will. That made her a thread. And every good web needs a central thread."

Casey's voice dropped. "You followed her from that?"

263

Julien shook his head. "I didn't have to. Steve already had eyes on her."

The temperature in the room seemed to drop.

"Steve abducted her?" Casey asked quietly.

Julien nodded. "He doesn't kill. That's not his role. Steve's logistics. Middle-management. He finds. He moves. He prepares. But he doesn't paint."

"So he delivered her," Casey said, bitterness rising in her throat.

"Yes," Julien said. "Tied with a bow. Like a gift."

Casey stared at him, fury roiling just beneath the surface.

"She died because you saw a flash of red lace?"

Julien's smile faded. He looked at her, and for a split second, there was something close to sincerity.

"No. She died because she was beautiful, unafraid, and part of the story, special."

Will's Point of View
Oakhaven PD – 5:30 a.m.

Will stood behind the one-way glass, arms crossed, watching Julien's face as he spoke to Casey. He couldn't hear every word from this distance, but he didn't need to. He saw it in Casey's posture, rigid, controlled, but radiating anger. He saw it in Julien's expression, smug, sick with pleasure, like a man telling bedtime stories drenched in blood.

And then Casey's voice came through the monitor.

"So why Julia?"

Will held his breath. That name still hit like a bullet.

Julien's answer came too easily. Too quickly.

"She dropped her phone... crimson lace... He didn't linger, but he saw. He even blushed." He let out a laugh.

Will's stomach turned.

Then the words that hollowed him out:

"No. She died because she was beautiful, unafraid, and part of the story, special."

Will's jaw clenched so hard it hurt. The memory snapped into place with terrifying clarity.

Julia laughed and reached under the booth. That brief flash of color, skin. The involuntary glance. And yes, he had looked. Not lecherously. Not with intent. It had been a moment. A reflex. And then he'd immediately looked away, guilt chewing at him, and saw more than he should.

But Julien had seen it.

And in that single heartbeat, he had marked her.

Will's breath caught. His vision tunneled.

She had died because of him. Because of a glance. Because of something as meaningless as a muscle twitch and a second of surprise. A girl he loved like a daughter, Billy's girlfriend, gone, because of his presence... his existence in that booth.

He backed away from the glass, slowly, carefully, like the room might collapse if he moved too fast.

Casey turned her head, locking eyes with him through the mirrored wall. She saw it on his face. The guilt. The realization.

Will forced his jaw to unlock. Swallowed hard.

He wanted to rip Julien apart with his bare hands. But more than that, he wanted to go back in time, to sit in a different booth. To turn his head one second sooner. To stop it all before it started.

But he couldn't.

So instead, he whispered, too low for anyone to hear:

"I'm gonna bury you, Julien. You and the bastard who brought her to you."

He turned and left the room, fists clenched, a storm brewing in his chest.

All these questions, everything Julien says brings memories back to meeting Steve, Julia still fresh on his mind.

Julien Cain is sitting in the interrogation room, dreaming, blocking out the room. He's back on the dark web.

Alliance

Julien first crossed paths with Steve in the shadows of the internet. On *GodBodyCount*, Steve was a trusted facilitator, a broker for those Willing to pay for more than just videos. Julien, operating as *ErosGoneWrong*, had been watching from the sidelines for months, bidding here and there and testing the limits of what the network could offer.

Beneath the polished exterior, Julien was a manipulator with a deviant streak. On the dark web, he was one of Steve's clients, hiding under the handle *GodBodyCount*. Online, he operated as *ErosGoneWrong*, or the more cryptic OBRX (short for Ouroboros X), on his public social media accounts.

Their first direct exchange came after Julien messaged Steve about a specific "type," intelligent, athletic, unattainable on the surface. Steve, always hungry for business and leverage, delivered a sample. The transaction went smoothly, and both men recognized in the other a kindred predator.

When they finally met in person, it was in the back of the Jack'd Up Coffee House after hours, the place reeking of espresso and secrecy. Steve found Julien's polished, almost aristocratic manner amusing; Julien appreciated Steve's unfiltered ruthlessness.

Julien offered connections, private spaces, and a network of influential names who could keep trouble buried. Steve offered supply, real people, broken down into commodities. It was a match that felt inevitable.

From then on, Steve funneled content and "opportunities" Julien's way. In return, Julien acted as both client and recruiter, whispering in the ears of those he knew would never speak publicly but would pay handsomely for the right kind of depravity.

It was an alliance born not out of friendship, but out of shared appetite, and the understanding that each man could destroy the other if they ever stopped playing along.

The Other Julia

Earlier, the bell over the coffee shop door gave a lazy jingle as Julia Wells stepped inside with Billy Anderson. The pair laughed about something as they made their way to a booth in the far corner, her skirt swaying just above the knee.

Julien Cain was behind the counter, all easy charm and polite smiles, steaming milk for a latte like he hadn't already clocked her the moment she crossed the threshold. Her voice carried in short bursts of laughter, and even from across the shop, her presence seemed to draw the eye.

A minute later, the door opened again. Will Anderson, Billy's father, stepped inside, scanning the room before making his way over to their table. From behind the counter, Julien watched the three greet each other, their conversation relaxed, comfortable. *Detective Anderson.*

Julia reached for her phone and realized it wasn't on the table. "Hold on," she laughed, dipping down to check under the booth. The phone had slid deep against the wall, forcing her to lean almost flat to reach it.

Julien's gaze sharpened. When Julia slid into the booth, her skirt had caught on the back edge of the seat, bunching up against her lower back. Later, as she leaned over to retrieve her phone, it stayed hooked there, riding higher than it usually would. She didn't notice, but he did.

The position gave him longer to look than should have been possible, a lingering view of crimson red fabric framed by the tan lines along her thighs. In the low light, it glowed like a beacon in the dark, impossible to ignore.

She straightened, laughing with Billy and Will as if nothing had happened. But for Julien, the image was already seared into his mind. The signal had been delivered, and he'd received it loud and clear.

It wasn't just the color. To Julien, it was *that* color, the deep blood-red of his Ouroboros tattoo, the eternal serpent eating its tail. In his mind, the connection wasn't a coincidence; it was a sign.

The flash of her skin beneath revealed faint tan lines, pale against the rest of her. To Julien, they weren't just marks from the sun; they were borders, frames, something to be trespassed. The imperfections made her real. Real made her attainable.

Julia straightened, laughing again as she held up the recovered phone. Will and Billy carried on the conversation as if nothing had happened. But from behind the counter, Julien's focus never wavered.

That glimpse, that color, those lines, they all fed the thought forming in his mind. Julia wasn't just another customer anymore.

She was the next target, and a bonus that she knows Detective Will Anderson. *She will be a nice prize.*

And now that she'd caught his attention, she wouldn't slip out of it.

Julien locked the coffee shop behind him, stepping into the night. The drive home to the Cain estate felt shorter than usual, his thoughts consumed by a single image: crimson fabric framed by tan skin, burning like an ember in his memory. The more he replayed the moment, the clearer the sign became. The color matched the deep red of the Ouroboros perfectly, he'd tattooed on his chest, the serpent endlessly consuming itself, a cycle he felt destined to complete.

Inside his private study, Julien logged onto his secure network, the glow of monitors reflecting off his face. He navigated swiftly to the encrypted site *GodBodyCount*, feeling an immediate rush as the familiar dark interface loaded.

A blinking message awaited him from *MatchMakerKing*.

MatchMakerKing: *"Inventory just updated. Let me know if something catches your eye."*

Julien's mouth curled into a slow, unsettling smile as his fingers hovered over the keyboard. He quickly typed his reply, pulse quickening with each keystroke.

ErosGoneWrong: *"No need tonight. Found one of my own. She's perfect, exactly my type."*

Dots danced as Steve typed back.

MatchMakerKing: *"Perfect is a strong word. You sure about this one?"*

Julien leaned closer, the memory vivid, intoxicating.

ErosGoneWrong: *"Never been more certain. Athletic, confident, unattainable, and she wears our favorite shade of red. She's exactly what I'm looking for."*

Steve responded swiftly, businesslike but intrigued.

MatchMakerKing: *"Then consider it done. Send details. I'll make sure your perfect one gets exactly what she deserves."*

Julien leaned back, breathing deep, his smile widening. Julia Wells had no idea yet, but the wheel had started turning, and she'd soon be drawn into its relentless spin.

Julien leaned forward again, fingers poised above the keyboard, the dim glow of the monitor highlighting the twisted excitement on his face.

ErosGoneWrong: *"There's an added bonus with this one. She's close with Billy Anderson, and his father is Will Anderson, the detective who's sniffing around our artwork."*

Dots flickered again as Steve quickly responded.

MatchMakerKing: *"Well, now that's intriguing. You're saying she's connected directly to our favorite detective?"*

Julien's smile turned predatory as he typed back.

ErosGoneWrong: *"Exactly. Imagine the possibilities. We get the girl, we send a message, and we rattle Detective Anderson all at once. Poetry, wouldn't you say?"*

A pause, longer this time, before Steve's reply appeared on the screen.

MatchMakerKing: *"You've got a beautiful mind. Send me everything you have on her. Let's make this masterpiece unforgettable."*

Julien attached the information he'd gathered: Julia's schedule, her address, her patterns from the coffee shop visits, each detail carefully collected and now weaponized.

He clicked SEND, feeling an electric surge. Julia Wells wasn't just a target now; she was a statement. A work of dark art designed specifically for Detective Will Anderson.

Steve closed Julien's message and leaned back, eyes narrowing thoughtfully. He studied the attached files, Julia's home address, daily schedule, and a few discreet photos snapped from Julien's vantage at the coffee shop.

He zoomed in on one image: Julia Wells, mid-laugh, carefree. The crimson fabric Julien had mentioned was still fresh in Steve's imagination. But it wasn't the color that excited him; it was the possibilities. Julien had been right; this girl represented something more than just another target. She was leverage.

Within the hour, Steve parked his nondescript sedan a half-block down from Julia's townhouse. The quiet street sat bathed in shadows, broken only by pools of yellow streetlight. He checked his watch and noted the time, exactly on schedule, according to Julien's notes.

Julia's front door opened, and she stepped out onto the porch, unaware of Steve's eyes tracking her every move. She adjusted her purse over her shoulder, phone in hand, as she moved toward her car. Steve noted every detail, the confident stride, the casual glance she gave her surroundings, oblivious to any threat.

"Perfect," Steve whispered under his breath. He snapped a quick photo and uploaded it to the secure server for Julien to see. The message attached was direct and straightforward:

MatchMakerKing: *"Your intel was good. Surveillance underway. She's exactly where you said she'd be."*

Julien's reply came instantly.

ErosGoneWrong: *"Excellent. Keep me updated. Let's make sure Detective Anderson knows exactly what he's up against."*

Steve watched Julia drive away, feeling that familiar rush, this wasn't just business anymore; it was personal. He had Detective Will Anderson in his sights, and Julia Wells was about to become the centerpiece of a very dark game.

Two nights later, Steve was back outside Julia's townhouse. The street was silent, every window dark except for the soft glow from Julia's bedroom upstairs. He glanced at his watch again, just past midnight, exactly as expected. Julia was home, alone, unaware of him waiting patiently in the shadows.

With practiced efficiency, Steve left the sedan parked down the block and approached quietly, taking a path through neighboring yards until he reached Julia's back fence. He vaulted it smoothly, landing quietly in her small garden. A motion-sensor porch light flicked on, bathing him briefly in pale illumination. Steve froze, counting silently. The seconds ticked by, his pulse steady, before the yard returned to darkness.

He moved toward her back door, pulling a small set of lock-picks from his pocket. The lock yielded quickly under his skilled fingers. He eased the door open slowly, stepping into the kitchen. Julia's home was neat, comfortable, the air still faintly scented with lavender candles she'd burned earlier.

Steve paused, taking in the details: family photos on the fridge, books scattered on the countertop, a half-full coffee cup. Quiet footsteps overhead told him exactly where Julia was. He didn't ascend, not tonight; intrusion was enough. He pulled his phone from his pocket and took photos of the inside, just enough for Julien to see he'd been here, so that he could reach her at any moment.

He opened a kitchen drawer and found a small, handwritten notebook. Steve flipped through quickly, names, addresses, simple notes. He photographed a few pages and put them carefully back where he'd found them. Julia would never notice he'd been here, but Julien, and eventually Detective Anderson, would know precisely how close he'd gotten.

Satisfied, Steve quietly exited, relocking the door behind him. Back in the safety of his car, he sent Julien the new batch of photos along with a message:

MatchMakerKing: *"She's vulnerable. Access confirmed. Ready to proceed when you are."*

Julien's reply was swift, concise, filled with barely restrained anticipation.

ErosGoneWrong: *"Excellent. The game begins now."*

Steve smiled in the dark, engine idling. Julia Wells had no idea she was about to become the pawn in a much larger, far darker game.

Julien leaned back in his chair, sipping from a glass of bourbon as he scrolled through the images Steve had just sent. Each photograph of Julia's home, her private space, her belongings, felt like a quiet triumph. He smiled slowly, savoring the control he now wielded.

The message was clear: Julia was within reach. And through her, so was Detective Will Anderson.

He closed the messages from Steve and opened a private folder labeled "OBRX – Special Projects." Inside were detailed plans, schedules, names, and notes, each file meticulously organized. At the top was Julia Wells, her photo now prominently placed alongside his notes from the coffee shop. Her movements, friends, and daily routines were outlined with chilling precision.

Julien took another slow sip of bourbon, letting the warmth spread through him as he mentally reviewed his next steps. Julia had no idea she'd become the centerpiece of a masterpiece he'd envisioned long before their paths had crossed. He would orchestrate every detail, control every move, right down to the moment he revealed his hand to Detective Anderson.

He opened the secure chat again and typed a new message to Steve:

ErosGoneWrong: *"Proceed with the next phase. Let's ensure Detective Anderson can't miss the message. I want Julia perfectly intact, emotionally destroyed, but physically unharmed. She must be the messenger who delivers our art to him."*

Steve's reply flashed on-screen:

MatchMakerKing: *"Understood. The detective won't miss this."*

Julien set down his glass, eyes glittering with anticipation. Everything was falling precisely into place. Soon, Julia Wells and, by extension, Detective Will Anderson, would discover exactly how deep the serpent's bite could go.

Swallowed by the Day

Steve had been watching Julia for days, mapping out her habits with the kind of precision that made his work almost effortless. He knew she took late-night walks when she couldn't sleep, often circling her quiet block with headphones in, lost in her own little world.

The night he struck, the street was empty, only the faint glow of porch lights dotting the sidewalk. Steve parked his van a block away, dressed in unremarkable clothes and a ball cap pulled low. He waited, engine off, in the darkness until he saw Julia step out of her front door and head down the sidewalk, just as she had the night before.

He timed it perfectly. As she neared a small alley between two houses, he stepped out, walking casually until their paths crossed. Julia barely glanced up, headphones still in, before he moved fast, pressing a chloroform-soaked cloth over her mouth and nose. She gasped, struggling, but his grip was firm and practiced. Within seconds, her resistance faded, and she slumped into his arms.

Moving quickly, Steve carried her to the van, gently but efficiently laying her on a padded blanket in the back. He checked her breathing, steady, just as planned, then injected a measured dose of sedative to keep her calm and compliant. He closed the doors, slid behind the wheel, and pulled away without a sound.

By the time anyone noticed Julia was missing, Steve was already miles away, her phone powered down, all digital traces erased. She never saw his face, never heard his voice.

Just after midnight, Steve's van pulled quietly onto the gravel driveway of the Cain estate, headlights off, engine idling. He glanced into the back; Julia Wells lay sprawled across the cushioned floor, eyes half-open, breathing steady but shallow. The sedative he'd used was strong enough to keep her pliant but conscious enough to follow simple commands exactly as Julien requested.

Julien stepped from the shadows of the porch, calm, poised, utterly in control. He approached the passenger-side door and opened it casually.

Steve spoke quietly, "Just as requested. She's awake, cooperative, no harm done."

Julien smiled faintly. "Excellent. Let's keep it that way."

He opened the van's side door, gently touching Julia's arm. Her eyes fluttered, trying to focus, her pupils wide and glazed. Julien leaned in, voice smooth and reassuring.

"Julia, listen carefully. Stand up. We're going inside."

She nodded slowly, sluggishly pushing herself upright with Julien's guidance, her movements dreamlike and loose. Julien carefully wrapped a thin jacket around her shoulders, more for appearance than comfort. To an outside observer, they might seem like a couple returning from a late evening out, nothing unusual, nothing alarming.

Steve watched silently, admiration blending with unease. Julien's precision always unsettled him.

Julien led Julia slowly toward the house, one hand gently placed on her back. She moved obediently, trusting his voice, her steps unsteady but manageable. Once at the door, Julien paused, glancing back at Steve.

"You've done well," Julien said quietly. "You'll hear from me soon."

Steve nodded, closing the van door quietly. "Enjoy your masterpiece."

Julien's smile widened slightly, dark satisfaction flickering in his eyes as he guided Julia into the dimly lit interior of the Cain estate. The door closed quietly behind them, leaving Steve alone in the dark, feeling both accomplished and suddenly insignificant.

Inside, Julien gently led Julia forward, whispering soothing reassurances, his voice soft yet cold. Julia moved without resistance, unaware she was walking deeper into a carefully laid trap, unaware she was about to become the living message he'd meticulously crafted for Detective Anderson.

Two days later, Julien sat in the quiet gloom of his private study, eyes fixed thoughtfully on his laptop screen. Julia was safely contained, sedated just enough to keep her compliant and unaware. Still, he knew the Cain estate wouldn't be suitable for what came next, especially if he wanted Detective Anderson to truly understand the message.

He opened a secure channel, sending a direct message to Steve's MatchMakerKing account:

ErosGoneWrong: *"I have a special request. Your warehouse studio, the one you used for Kristen. Is it secure and equipped for recording?"*

The reply arrived quickly, precisely, and businesslike.

MatchMakerKing: *"Completely secure. Audio, video, and streaming capabilities. Privacy guaranteed. Why?"*

Julien typed slowly, thoughtfully choosing each word.

ErosGoneWrong: *"Julia deserves the proper setting for her performance. I want it recorded, professionally, discreetly. No interruptions, no interference. It's the perfect stage."*

Steve's response was immediate, clearly intrigued by Julien's approach:

MatchMakerKing: *"Studio's yours whenever you need it. Consider it booked. When?"*

Julien leaned back, tapping his finger against his lips as he weighed his timing carefully. After a pause, he typed:

ErosGoneWrong: *"Tonight. The sooner the better. I'll bring her myself. Make sure everything's ready, lights, camera, and the restraints."*

The dots danced momentarily on the screen as Steve typed:

MatchMakerKing: *"Understood. I'll meet you there. This will be unforgettable."*

Julien smiled coldly, closing the laptop. Steve was right, it would be unforgettable. Detective Anderson would never look at the world in the same way again.

Change of Scenery

Julien stood before the antique mirror in his bedroom, buttoning up his tailored black shirt with practiced ease. Around his neck hung a crimson-red Ouroboros pendant, perfectly matching the serpent tattoo etched into his chest, a constant reminder of his purpose, his cycle of control and power.

He adjusted the pendant, feeling its familiar weight against his skin. Tonight, it required precision, careful attention to detail, down to the last symbolic touch.

Satisfied, Julien crept down the hall to the guest room, where Julia lay motionless but awake, eyes unfocused on the ceiling. The sedative he'd carefully measured kept her compliant but conscious enough to move and follow basic commands. Exactly as planned.

"Julia," he said softly, his voice low and reassuring, "it's time for us to go."

She turned her head slowly toward his voice, eyes heavy-lidded, pupils wide. "Where?" she mumbled faintly.

He smiled gently, taking her hand and guiding her upright. "You'll see. Just follow me. Everything's going to be fine."

She stood slowly, swaying slightly. Julien steadied her with one hand, draping a coat loosely around her shoulders to obscure her condition from prying eyes. Carefully, he

283

guided her down the grand staircase, her feet moving slowly but steadily with his support.

Outside, the night air felt crisp, cold, and charged with anticipation. Julien helped Julia into his black SUV, carefully positioning her in the passenger seat and buckling her seatbelt with deliberate gentleness. Her head fell back against the seat, eyes half-open, lost somewhere between dreams and waking.

He circled the vehicle, climbing behind the wheel, feeling the Ouroboros pendant press lightly against his chest, a silent reminder of the role he played in this eternal loop. Tonight, Julia was more than a victim; she was art, carefully designed to deliver the strongest possible message to Detective Will Anderson.

Julien started the engine and drove off slowly, headlights cutting the darkness, heading toward the warehouse studio where Steve was waiting to bring their shared masterpiece to life.

Julien's SUV rolled quietly to a stop just outside the warehouse, its shadowy bulk stark against the dim industrial lights. Steve was already waiting by the steel door, a subtle smirk playing at the corners of his mouth. Julien gave him a curt nod as he stepped out.

"You're right on schedule," Steve said calmly, unlocking the heavy door. It groaned open, revealing the meticulously prepared warehouse studio within, with lights dim but ready, cameras already positioned, waiting silently.

Julien helped Julia out of the passenger seat, guiding her carefully. Her feet shuffled slowly, uncertain, drugged eyes wide but unseeing. Steve watched approvingly, noting the Ouroboros pendant gleaming at Julien's throat.

"Nice touch," Steve remarked dryly. Julien said nothing, focusing instead on gently moving Julia toward the prepared set.

Inside, the studio lights hummed quietly to life, bathing the dark, meticulously arranged space in a subtle, cold glow. Julien's gaze moved deliberately around the room, chains, cuffs, the reinforced frame of the harness suspended overhead, every detail perfectly arranged to reflect the message he intended to deliver.

He eased Julia toward the waiting restraints, speaking softly and calmly, guiding her gently until she stood exactly where he wanted her beneath the rigging.

"Hold still," he whispered quietly, his voice soothing yet cold. She nodded slowly, oblivious to her surroundings, compliant from the sedation. Julien motioned for Steve to approach.

"Secure her," Julien ordered, stepping back to observe. Steve moved with practiced efficiency, fastening thick leather restraints around Julia's wrists and ankles, locking them into the harness overhead. Julien watched silently, the Ouroboros pendant heavy against his chest, its symbolism not lost on him. Tonight represented a completion of the circle, a rebirth of his own twisted power.

Once Julia was safely restrained and positioned precisely beneath the lights, Julien moved to the control table, activating the cameras, and the screens flickered to life around the studio. He leaned toward a microphone, adjusting it carefully.

"Julia," he said softly, voice calm but commanding. "Tonight, you have a very important role to play. You are the messenger. You're going to help me speak directly to Detective Will Anderson. Do you understand?"

Julia's head lifted slightly, her eyes clouded but responding to his voice. She nodded slowly.

Julien turned toward Steve, a dark, satisfied smile spreading across his face.

"Let's begin."

With the cameras positioned and the warehouse cloaked in darkness, Julien turned to Steve. "Let's prepare her."

Steve moved methodically, producing a pair of surgical scissors from a tray. He and Julien worked in quiet coordination, first removing Julia's sweater, then carefully slicing through the seams of her jeans, peeling away the fabric piece by piece. The soft scrape of the blades against denim was loud in the otherwise silent warehouse. Her shoes were tugged off and set aside.

Julien watched her face for any sign of recognition, but the sedative had her drifting, eyes glazed, head rolling loosely as she hung by her wrists. With practiced efficiency, Steve cut away her fitted tank top, and Julien cut away her

286

low-rise bikini briefs; they were the perfect cut for those hip-hugger jeans she chose to wear. Julia hung suspended in the harness, wrists and ankles pulled tight by the restraints, her body angled slightly forward in the glaring spotlight. The harsh beam lit every contour, casting deep shadows behind her and swallowing the rest of the warehouse in blackness. All that existed in the frame was Julia, vulnerable, silent, alone.

Around her neck, a delicate silver necklace caught the light, the charm at its center dangling heavily toward the floor. Gravity had pulled it off-center, the thin chain cutting a faint line across her collarbone. The charm itself, a small, ornate crescent, twisted in the air, sending shards of reflected light flickering across her chest.

Julia's eyes moved slowly, her head tilting as she scanned the empty space. The sedative left her in a fog, mute and adrift, but a flicker of awareness lingered behind her gaze. She didn't speak. She only watched the void, waiting.

Julien stood just beyond the edge of the spotlight, his own crimson Ouroboros pendant resting heavily against his chest. His gaze was locked, not on Julia's face, but on the silver necklace she wore. The charm, unique, personal, held his full attention, as if it were the final, perfect detail in the tableau he'd created.

He studied it with a predatory intensity, the reflected light from Julia's charm dancing in his eyes. To him, it wasn't just an accessory; it was a symbol, a silent message. The line between victim and art had never been clearer.

They adjusted the harness, tightening the restraints at her wrists and ankles. Steve tested the rig, ensuring Julia hung straight and motionless. Satisfied, Julien walked to the bank of lights and slowly dialed the background into total darkness, allowing only a single spotlight to illuminate Julia's body from head to toe. On the monitors, she was the only thing visible: a lone, vulnerable figure suspended against a void, framed by shadows.

Julien checked the cameras one last time, ensuring every angle captured the display exactly as he intended. To the viewer, Julia was all that existed: her body, her silence, the stark light of the lens.

He leaned in, voice cold and soft. "Perfect. No one watching will see anything else."

Steve nodded, glancing at Julia, then at Julien's Ouroboros pendant glinting in the pale light. The preparations were done. Everything was in place.

The Message

"Hold up, I need one more thing before I begin," Julien announced.

Julien stepped forward, eyes never leaving Julia as she hung in the spotlight. "Lower her," he instructed softly.

Steve moved to the winch and slowly let out the tension, bringing Julia down until her knees touched the cold concrete floor. She remained upright primarily, wrists still secured but now within easy reach. Her body swayed gently, head drooping, the silver necklace charm resting against her chest.

Julien approached, his movements precise. From a nearby table, he picked up a pair of red hinged handcuffs, the metal gleaming in the harsh light. He ran a suspended steel cable through the cuffs, the click of the mechanism echoing in the cavernous space. With practiced care, Julien unfastened the leather restraints from Julia's wrists, holding her steady as her arms dropped limply to her sides.

Then he guided her hands together in front of her, methodical, almost gentle, before locking the red handcuffs snugly around her wrists. The cable threaded through the cuffs ran upward and out of frame, pulling her arms into position and leaving Julia kneeling, bound and exposed. The crimson metal stood out starkly against her skin.

A message, unmistakable and deliberate.

Julien stepped back, his eyes never leaving her as the camera continued its cold, unblinking stare. Every detail had been chosen. The red cuffs weren't just restraint—they were symbolism. A taunt aimed straight at Will Anderson. Julia, marked and displayed, had crossed the line between victim and warning, her body repurposed as part of the threat.

He moved behind her, disrobing as he went, careful to position himself so his face and torso remained outside the frame. Still, his presence filled the space. He knelt close enough that she could feel him, close enough that the camera could not ignore him.

Julien draped one arm around her, crossing it deliberately in front of her chest—not to claim her, but to shield her. To control what was seen. To decide what remained hers.

The gesture was precise. Calculated.

His dark crimson Ouroboros pendant slipped forward, dangling low and nearly brushing her right shoulder. It caught the light as it swayed, the serpent devouring its own tail, gleaming clearly in the camera's view.

Nothing here was accidental.

Everything was meant to be seen.

"Steve," Julien said, voice low and businesslike, "get her attention. I want her eyes open. I want Will to see her, not just the image, but the look in her eyes. This is about the message, not the spectacle."

Steve stepped into the light, kneeling to Julia's level, and spoke her name sharply. "Julia. Look up. Look at the camera." His tone was just stern enough to break through the sedative haze.

Julia blinked, her eyes lifting to the lens. For a heartbeat, she was fully present, frightened, vulnerable, aware. The necklace glinted sharply in the light, the only flash of silver in the stark scene.

Julien squeezed and cupped her breast to show his control, steady and firm, his face hidden above and behind hers, the Ouroboros charm dangling in the shot as he'd intended.

"Take it," Julien said.

Steve pressed the shutter, the camera's click echoing in the emptiness. The image would show Julia on her knees, the necklace and charm gleaming, Julien's arms around her, protective, possessive, cold. No faces. No nudity. Just a message, carefully staged for maximum impact.

Julien stood, glancing at Steve. "I need to work. If you would please take your leave."

Steve gave a slightly mocking bow. "As you wish, maestro." He started toward the exit, then paused, tossing one last joke over his shoulder: "Don't forget to turn out her lights, I mean, the lights, when you're done."

Julien didn't respond, already focused on Julia and the stage he'd set.

Steve stepped into the night, shutting the heavy door behind him. In the parking lot, he pulled out his phone and dialed a number from memory. The call rang once before a gravelly voice answered.

"Captain Rogers."

"Hey, Dan, it's Steve. Your nephew wants to see you at the warehouse in about two hours. Don't come early."

A pause. "Understood. I'll be there."

Steve hung up, glancing back at the warehouse. Inside, Julien's masterpiece was only beginning. He smirked to himself, both disturbed and impressed, then climbed into his car and drove off into the dark.

Oakhaven PD – Interrogation Room
5:47 a.m.

Casey was exhausted. Her shirt itched around the bandage on her shoulder, and her stomach growled, needing to eat. But her gaze was steady, locked on Julien Cain, who sat with his usual smug smirk, fingers laced in front of him like he was awaiting a chess opponent instead of being interrogated for murder.

She waved off the others in the observation room.

"Get me something hot," she told one of the officers. "Breakfast sandwich, maybe. I need caffeine and calories if I'm going to listen to this bastard gloat."

The door clicked shut behind them. Just her and Julien now. Remembering an old phrase from her Irish grandmother, quoting some guy she doesn't remember, "Now listen, love — if you're after a rich man, tell him he's the cleverest lad in the room. And if it's a smart one you're courting, tell him he's the finest lookin' you've ever seen. Works every time, so it does." She also added. "It also helps if you are pretty."

She leaned forward, resting her elbows on the table with faux admiration.

"I have to admit, Julien... I've been studying your work. The precision. The messaging. It's all so... calculated like a true artist. You're not just smarter than we gave you credit for. You might be the smartest man I've ever met."

He tilted his head, surprised, intrigued.

"That's quite the compliment from you, Detective Murphy."

"No lie," she said, brushing her fingers against her jaw. "I mean, your timing, your planning, the psychology of it all. That kind of brilliance, " she smiled, ", gets my attention."

Julien leaned in, confidence swelling like a balloon.

"You should've let me finish," he murmured. "That night... You were on the floor. Completely still. It was art. And I was going to, shave..."

"What?" Casey said sharply, the smile gone. "Finish, what?"

Julien's eyes gleamed. "You know what—a little trimming of the hedges. You'd have appreciated it. I wanted you awake for it. We brought my razor just for you."

Casey stared at him, letting the rage simmer just below the surface.

Then she threw her real blade.

"Too bad you couldn't get it up."

Julien blinked. His mask slipped.

"All this, this elaborate violence, this control, it's not about power. It's compensation. For rejection. For the fact that you'll never get a woman without terror. Because you know, deep down, if you didn't force them, " she leaned in, eyes hard, "they'd laugh, laugh because Julien can't get pussy!"

Julien's face flushed. His mouth twisted.

"Those girls... they pretended like I was beneath them. Like, I didn't matter. But look at me, I'm the embodiment of a god! My family built this town!" He slammed the table. "My bloodline owns this town! You think a little badge gives you control? My uncle runs your damn department!"

Casey's eyes narrowed. "What uncle?"

But Julien was still raging.

"Rodgers, he knew everything! He helped me cover it up! Hell, he was next in line for you! I was going to have you then him, but your little party pooper boyfriends' warning told us to run, blaring those sirens. You were out next example, then the DA was next, not like I didn't tell you!"

In the adjacent observation room, Captain Rodgers had been watching with arms folded, unmoving.

Until now.

The second his name was spoken, he turned.

Then bolted.

The door to the observation room slammed open. A half-second later, they heard the commotion in the hall.

"Hey!" someone shouted.

THUD.

Rodgers crashed into the officer delivering breakfast, sending the coffee and sandwich flying across the corridor. Will, coming in from the stairwell, caught part of the spill and shoved Rodgers hard against the wall.

"Rodgers?" Will barked. "What the hell are you doing?"

Casey burst through the interrogation room door, breath shallow.

"Will!" Casey yelled as she burst into the hallway. "Julien just said Rodgers is his uncle! He lost it the second Julien dropped the name."

From inside the interrogation room, Julien's voice slithered through the doorway, smug and self-satisfied.

"Yeah, he's my uncle. My mom's his sister. Guess that little detail didn't make it into your background check?"

Will's jaw clenched. He turned to Rodgers, who stood rigid just outside the observation room door, face pale, sweat forming fast.

"Rodgers, " Will started, but then,

CLINK! CLINK! CLINK! BANG!

A flashbang canister clattered to the floor, hissing, too late.

The concussive blast filled the hallway with a blinding light and deafening thunder.

Casey hit the ground, ears ringing. Will stumbled back into the wall, vision seared.

"HE'S RUNNING!" someone shouted, voices chaotic in the haze.

By the time the smoke cleared and officers swarmed, Captain Rodgers was gone.

Gone.

Out the side door. Out of the lot. Tires squealing.

Will swore under his breath, scanning the exit.

"He's headed home," he said. "You don't run unless there's something worth hiding."

Casey steadied herself, wiping at her watering eyes as adrenaline surged.

"We have to do this right," she said, breathless. "No missteps. No technicalities."

Will nodded sharply.

"Search warrant. Now. Call the judge."

He turned to the nearest officer, voice slicing through the confusion like a blade.

"Secure his office. Lock down the network. And get me a warrant application team, ten minutes ago."

Casey narrowed her eyes, fire lit behind them.

"If Rodgers has anything buried, we're about to dig it up."

Casey stood behind him, breathing hard. Her rage had turned cold and sharp.

"Looks like we've been hunting in the wrong direction."

The Payload

Two hours later, Casey's phone buzzed with an encrypted message.

From: Eli Kessler

Subject: You're going to want to sit down.

She opened it. Inside was a single secure download link that expired in 1 hour. Beneath it, Eli's note:

Got your data. He hid it under a triple-layer shell—dummy partition, looping checksum, and a zero-fill tripwire. Cute. But he made one mistake: he used recycled encryption keys. Your boy Steve isn't as smart as he thinks.

Also—Casey—this isn't just evidence. It's a damn confession.

Casey plugged in her secure drive, downloaded the package, and opened the folder.

Dozens of video thumbnails filled the screen, each timestamped over the past three years. The first few looked like standard "studio" work—sick, predatory, but expected. Then her gaze froze on one file name in particular: *DanR_0418.mov.*

She double-clicked.

The video opened to a dim room. Steve sat behind the camera, his voice low and coaxing. In front of him, Captain Dan Rogers leaned into the frame, speaking directly to a woman tied to a chair.

The woman was crying.

"Listen to him," Rogers said calmly, almost kindly. "Or you don't go home."

Casey's hand curled into a fist. She scrubbed forward through the video. Rogers and Steve both appeared multiple times—sometimes together, sometimes alone—with different women, all of them scared, all of them trapped.

And in the corner of each frame, barely visible unless you knew where to look, was the same symbol burned into the wall: a crude "O" with a slash through it.

Will stepped into the room mid-playback, his eyes immediately narrowing. "Is that—"

"Yeah," Casey said, voice tight. "It's him. With Steve. And at least three of these young women match our missing persons list from the surrounding area."

Will stared at the screen, jaw set. "Search warrants typed up, let's go see Judge Matthew. This is it. Time to get the hammer and put the nail in Steve and Rogers' coffin."

Casey smirked, sealing the evidence bag. "Please. No need for a hammer when you've got a thermal detonator."

Will's eyes stayed cold on the screen. "Just remember— Vader didn't need a detonator. He just closed his fist and crushed the life out of anything in his way."

Casey's grin thinned, but her eyes stayed locked on his. "Good thing I'm not here to crush them, Anderson. I'm here to make them watch the walls close in."

Dan Rodgers

Will and Casey sat in the dim light of the judge's chambers, watching as Judge Joe Masters skimmed their probable cause statement. He didn't ask a single question, just signed the search warrant with a heavy flourish and slid it back across the desk. No one said a word; there was nothing to say. They had what they needed.

Dan Rogers' property sprawled across thirty tangled acres at the edge of the county. The house itself was unremarkable—a low, brick ranch set back from the road—but at the rear of the property stood two hulking metal workshops, like silent sentinels.

The teams split up fast. Uniformed officers went through the house, weapons drawn, voices clipped and careful. The dynamic entry turned up nothing but emptiness—no Rogers, no one else. Will and Casey exchanged a glance that said not surprised.

They left the house behind and trudged down a rutted gravel path toward the workshops. The first shop was all business: a battered farm tractor, a couple of earthmovers, shelves stacked with oil cans and rusting tools. Nothing out of place, nothing out of the ordinary.

The second shop was a different world entirely—a grown man's fortress of solitude and ego. A massive TV dominated one wall, surrounded by oversized speakers and a weathered leather couch. The bar sparkled with good bourbon and cheap vodka, bottles lined up in military rows. Police memorabilia—old badges, commendations, shadowboxes—covered another wall, alongside posters of pinup girls in bikinis, tanned and grinning, forever frozen in mid-laugh.

Casey's eyes landed on an especially tasteless drawing pinned above the bar: two topless girls in bikini bottoms, handcuffed and being frisked by a cartoonish version of Rogers himself. He had one hand on a girl's breast, the other tugging at the string of the other girl's bikini, a speech bubble floating above him: I'll find that contraband. Casey felt a wave of nausea rise in her throat. She swallowed hard, pushing it down.

There were baseballs and signed jerseys, all perfectly preserved in glass-fronted cases, trophies from another, cleaner life.

But then, tucked into the corner of a cluttered bookshelf, something caught Casey's eye—a framed photograph. She leaned in, squinting.

It was Rogers, grinning in the sunlight, an arm slung around a teenage Julien Cain. Beside them stood Rogers' wife and daughter, and another woman Casey didn't recognize—definitely not Rogers' ex-wife.

Casey glanced at Will, holding up the photo. "You need to see this," she said, voice tight.

Will stepped closer, frowning at the image. The puzzle was changing, and the pieces suddenly looked all wrong.

Captain Dan Rogers hadn't always been the man people whispered about in hallways. In his early days, he was the kind of cop rookies looked up to—ambitious, clean-cut, with an unshakeable sense of justice that seemed almost old-fashioned. He volunteered for the tough assignments, clocked long hours, and made a name for himself as someone who never bent the rules, not even for convenience.

But all that changed the year his daughter, Ivy Raine Rodgers, went away to college.

At first, there were only subtle signs—a missed call here, a cryptic text there. Dan chalked it up to growing pains and the distance every parent has to learn to bear. But then Ivy's name started surfacing in places it didn't belong: rumors of parties with older men, whispers about expensive gifts and friends with dangerous connections. By the time Dan understood the world she'd stumbled into—a glittering, hidden network of influencers, traffickers, and high-end escorts—it was already too late.

Ivy's overdose shattered whatever was left of his faith in the system he'd once defended. Her death wasn't just a tragedy; it was a fracture, splitting his life into a clean "before" and an irreparable "after." The justice he'd once believed in now felt hollow—just another mask for the ugly things people did in the dark.

And in the aftermath, something inside Dan Rogers shifted. The lines he'd spent his whole career upholding began to blur, and the man who'd never bent the rules slowly learned how to break them.

The man who offered to "help" clean up Ivy's mess was Steve—a name spoken in back rooms and buried in sealed indictments, a sadist with a silk tongue and a web of legitimate businesses to hide the darkness underneath. He operated quietly, moving people and secrets through a tangle of shell companies and encrypted forums on the dark web. Most people never knew his name. Dan Rogers knew it too well.

Steve approached Rogers in the days after Ivy's death, all sympathy, and subtle threats. He promised to make her record vanish, to keep her name out of the headlines, to spare the family whatever shreds of dignity remained. The price was simple, Steve said: Rogers would look the other way when certain names and shipments came up in local investigations. One compromise. One favor for another.

Dan told himself it was only this once—a debt owed to Ivy, nothing more. But once the bargain was struck, Steve never let go. Each time Dan looked the other way, each name he ignored, the chain tightened. The favors multiplied. The justifications wore thin.

And soon, there was no line left to cross—only a long, dark fall with Steve holding the other end of the rope.

It was a Tuesday afternoon when Rogers first saw Julien with Steve, their heads bent together over a burner phone outside a strip-mall coffee shop. Rogers didn't need to hear the conversation; the look in Steve's eyes—gleeful, predatory—told him enough. It wasn't long before Rogers learned the truth about his nephew: Julien had developed an appetite for college girls, for secret videos traded and sold in shadowy corners of the web. A taste for danger that mirrored the worst in Steve.

The discovery left Rogers gutted. Julien wasn't just a lost kid—he was his sister's son, Ivy's cousin. Family. Rogers felt the old tangle of duty and shame tighten around his throat. He tried to talk to Julien, to warn him, but the boy only laughed, flashing that empty, dangerous smile.

It got worse. Julien threatened to expose Rogers—his deals with Steve, the times he'd looked away, all the ways he'd tried to keep his family name clean by muddying his own hands. The kid had leverage, and he knew it.

Trapped, Rogers convinced himself he was protecting his sister by covering for Julien, shielding the family from disgrace. But as Julien's tastes grew darker—obsessions that bled into the killings, into the headlines—Rogers found himself caught, unable to pull free. Each attempt to shield his nephew only dragged him deeper into the mire, with Steve and Julien both pulling the strings.

Now, every move felt like a choice between damnation and betrayal. And Rogers knew, deep down, that sooner or later, one of them would drag him under for good.

Dan's Man Cave

Casey and Will continued their sweep of the building.

Halfway down the dividing wall between the man cave and the rest of the structure, a narrow door stood slightly ajar. Light flickered from beyond it—an unnatural glow spilling into the darker space like a pulse.

Will eased it open.

Inside, the room was alive with screens.

Several flat-panel televisions lined the far wall, all displaying live feeds of Rogers' house—different rooms, different angles, all current. To one side, a second bank of monitors showed still images and rotating feeds: Casey's apartment. The cameras Steve had shown her. Other women, unaware they were being watched, moving through their homes, parking garages, bedrooms.

This wasn't stored footage.

It was live.

Casey's stomach dropped.

To the right of the monitors stood a large metal cabinet—a server rack—its LEDs blinking in constant motion, lit up like a Christmas tree.

"Wow," Casey said quietly. "This is crazy."

The rest of the room was packed with listening and recording equipment. Microphones, receivers, storage devices. On a worktable sat the chest harness and body camera Steve had confessed to wearing during the assault on Kristen and Emily, laid out neatly, like tools returned to their place.

On the opposite side of the monitors was another door.

Will and Casey exchanged a look, raised their weapons, and moved through it.

The second room was empty of people—but not of purpose.

It was staged.

Cameras mounted on tripods surrounded the space. Microphones hung from exposed rafters. Ring lights stood positioned for full illumination. At the center of the room sat a bed covered in a red silk sheet, its four posts fitted with restraints for wrists and ankles. Leaning against the frame was a homemade spreader bar, heavy-duty, fitted with additional cuffs.

More restraints hung from the rafters. A swing. Everything placed with intention.

Along the far wall were shelves and hooks holding an array of devices—restraints, hoods, blindfolds, gags, whips, clamps—arranged like a grotesque display. Among them sat a propane blowtorch, painted white. Across its side, in careful lettering, were the words:

SIN REMOVER
CLEANSING FIRE

Will swallowed. "This isn't normal BDSM," he said quietly. "This is... something else. And he was watching us the whole time."

Opposite the wall stood a submission horse, fitted with restraints, and beside it a mechanical device—custom-built, unmistakable in its purpose. Will didn't look at it long.

"Sick fuck," was all he managed.

This was it.

This was where Wendi Baylor had been tortured and killed.

Will's mind snapped back to the photograph—the one sent directly to the department. Wendi alive. Julien Cain behind her, wearing the Ouroboros pendant and tattoo, positioned with deliberate care.

Was this the room?

Julien had stood here.

Dan Rogers had taken the picture.

Will took a step back, lowering his weapon. "We need to back out of this room right now. Don't touch anything." His voice was firm, procedural, locking emotion down where it couldn't interfere. "This is a crime scene. We call in the state forensic team."

Casey nodded, eyes still moving over the room, the screens, the evidence of how long they'd been watched.

They backed out slowly, leaving the door open just enough for the glow to spill into the hallway.

Behind them, the cameras kept rolling.

Casey and Will exit the room and return to the server and monitor room. Will asks Casey to hold the scene while he goes to the house to get one of the officers to call dispatch to get the state forensic team supervisor to call him. Neither one of them grabbed a radio in the hurried effort to execute the search warrant. While Will is heading to the house, Casey walks over to the recording devices on the table, picks up the chest harness and camera, and removes the SD card to inspect later as evidence.

Will came back into the warehouse office, the shock of fluorescent light and whirring computers almost jarring after the cold night outside. Casey was hunched over the keyboard, eyes darting over lists and files. As he approached, she clicked quickly through folders, her face tight with purpose.

"I found them," Casey said without turning. "The other three women. Steve kept names and contact info. These ladies... they're victims, Will. They're witnesses, too. We need to reach them quickly and let them know they're finally free of this horror show. Some random girls appear to have been drugged and filmed, and I didn't recognize any right off. They may be trapped in his web as well. I don't recognize any of them from missing persons, and one looks like a girl who works at the coffee shop. Most of the videos are from Steve's Warehouse, not many from here, except Wendi Baylor."

Will's voice cracked with urgency. "What about the files on my wife? My girls?" He moved toward the keyboard, reaching for the mouse.

Casey spun in the chair, catching his hand before he could touch the computer. "No," she said softly but firmly, placing her hand on his wrist. "Don't do this to yourself.

Don't tarnish the memory of your girls or your lovely bride. I won't let you."

Will stared at her, torn. "I have to know what's there. I need to be prepared for court, for what might come out, for what might retraumatize them. I need to see it before they take it away. They're the victims. I have to be ready."

He moved as if to sit, but Casey blocked him, pressing her body gently between him and the chair, taking his hands in hers. She looked up at him, her voice low and trembling. "Please, Will, stop. We don't have much time."

He pleaded, voice barely a whisper, "Please."

Casey gazed into his eyes—red, wet, desperate—needing to redirect, leaned up, brushing a kiss against his cheek, just at the corner of his mouth. "Will Anderson, I love you. I love your wife, your beautiful daughters, your smart-mouthed son, and your whole family. I trust you with every part of me. I'm asking you, just this once, trust me back. Don't look. There's nothing here your eyes need to see."

Before he could reply, two plainclothes officers called from the other room: "We've got Dan Rogers!"

Casey's grip lingered on Will's hands. "Let's go," she said, voice barely above a whisper. "Let's finish this."

Will and Casey hurried into the so-called "man cave" where two plainclothes officers stood by the door. "Where's Dan Rogers?" Will demanded.

One officer nodded toward the rear of the property. "I'll keep this building locked down, but you need to go out back. Sergeant Glenn Smith's waiting for you."

Will and Casey rounded the corner of the building and spotted Sergeant Smith with Officer Kelly White at the edge of the woods. Smith's flashlight beam cut through the trees, his expression grim.

"You're not going to believe this shit right here," Smith said, waving them over. "Follow me."

The four of them made their way through the brush to the mouth of a narrow trail. There, sprawled at the edge of the opening, was Dan Rogers, motionless, pistol still in hand, a ragged wound in his chest.

Smith crouched, shaking his head. "From the looks of it, he tripped running and shot himself. Not my call, though, I'll leave that to you experts. We found him face down and rolled him over."

Will knelt, inspecting the entry wound and the powder burns on Rogers' shirt. He stood up suddenly and, with a frustrated grunt, kicked a pinecone into the woods. The sting of justice denied was raw.

He turned to Casey, jaw clenched. "The bastard got off easy, and he doesn't even know it. Damn it, Casey. He was supposed to pay. For all he did to us, for what he did to you. It wasn't supposed to end like this for him."

Casey's gaze was cold but steady. "There's a special place in hell for him, and I can live with that. The bastard will never touch another soul." She let out a shaky breath, then offered a wry smile. "Let's go. I'm hungry."

They turned back toward the house, where the chaos of flashing lights and barking radios filled the night. A command post of vans and SUVs had appeared, evidence tents blooming like ghosts on the lawn. The state investigative unit was already sifting through the aftermath, bagging, tagging, and cataloguing what was left behind.

As Will and Casey walked back into the light, for a moment, the weight of the night lifted. The circle had closed, but the scars would remain.

The chaos slowly faded as dawn crept over the horizon, streaking the sky with gray and gold. By the time Will stepped outside, most of the flashing lights had dimmed, replaced by the steady rumble of generators and the low voices of investigators finishing their work.

Casey stood beside him, coffee in hand, watching as the last of the evidence bags were loaded into state vehicles. For the first time in what felt like years, there was no urgency to move, just the dull ache of exhaustion and the knowledge that the worst was finally over.

Family

Back at the Anderson house, the kitchen was warm with the scent of hot chocolate and the quiet hum of the refrigerator. Kristen sat at the table wrapped in one of Will's old flannel blankets, the fabric worn soft with years. Bracketed by Ellie and Emily, who leaned into her shoulder, clinging just enough to feel the steady rise and fall of her mother's breathing, while Billy stood close by, a quiet sentinel, his hand resting on the back of Kristen's chair like he could keep her anchored there by touch alone.

There were no speeches. No tidy words to sum up what they'd all been through. Instead, comfort lived in the little things—a mug of hot chocolate slid across the table, a hand squeezed under the blanket, a tear wiped away without comment.

Will stood in the doorway, letting the scene settle in his chest. The pain was still there, sharp in places, but it was dulled by something stronger—relief. Gratitude. The quiet, battered kind that comes only after you've stared down the worst and found your people still breathing on the other side.

He crossed the room and rested a steady hand on Kristen's shoulder. "We're safe," he said softly, almost afraid to break the moment. "He's gone. They're all gone."

311

Kristen's eyes lifted to his, rimmed red and shining in the dim kitchen light. "Are we really?" she asked, her voice barely above a whisper.

Will nodded, his gaze unwavering. "We are. And if there's anything left to fight..." He glanced at Emily, then at Billy, and tightened his grip just slightly. "...we'll fight it together. Always."

Billy's eyes met his father's for a long moment—no words, just a silent understanding. Whatever came next, they'd both be ready for it.

For the first time in days, the house felt like a home again. Not unscarred. Not untouched. But theirs—and safe.

Immunity Deal

Steve sat alone in the interrogation room, pale under the flickering light. His eyes darted to the door every few seconds, his foot tapping out a nervous rhythm on the linoleum.

When Kristen entered, she brought no warmth—just a manila folder and a stare cold enough to freeze steel. Her hair was pulled back, face bare, her movements sharp and economical.

She placed the folder on the table like a dealer laying down the final hand.

"Immunity," she said evenly. "You give us what we want, maybe you serve your time somewhere with walls... instead of razor wire."

Steve wet his lips. "You serious?"

Her silence was answer enough.

He swallowed. "It's Rodgers. Captain Dan Rodgers. He helped set it up... he's Julien's uncle."

Kristen gave one slow nod—then tore the folder in half and let the pieces drift across the table.

"We already knew."

His eyes widened.

"Julien gave him up three hours ago," she said. "Your servers are gone. Rodgers' place, it's done. And Rodgers himself? He's not coming back. Should've kept a better backup, Stevie. Julien spilled it all. He couldn't help himself, brags more than you. He said you and Rodgers were his lackies, his servants; he was the real master. He will spend the rest of his life behind bars or until he gets the needle if I have it my way. I really wish they would, for once, use the firing squad or even 'Old Sparky' still for him; that would be fitting."

She turned for the door, hand on the knob—then paused.

"Oh... one last thing. They already know who you are, what you've done. The men where you're headed?" Her voice lowered. "They have a way of... breaking the ones who think they're untouchable."

She turned, voice low, almost sweet.

"How do you like it?"

Steve blinked. "What?"

"You like it rough? Gentle? On your back? Or clinging to the mattress with tears in your eyes?"

He stared at her, stunned. She stepped closer, lowering her voice just enough.

"Your cellmate until trial is Randolph Joseph. Serial rapist. Likes soft, pretty white boys. Just like you."

His face drained of color.

"I hear he's hung like a horse," she added. "Hope you stretch."

Steve shifted in his chair, the color draining from his face.

Kristen leaned in just close enough for him to smell the faint scent of coffee on her breath. Her tone was almost casual.

"No need for a hammer when you've got a thermal detonator, Stevie. And I just armed it."

She straightened, opened the door, and left without looking back.

Steve didn't move. Couldn't.

Will was leaning against the hallway wall when Kristen stepped out of the interrogation room. She closed the door behind her with a slow, deliberate push, as if sealing a vault.

He raised an eyebrow. "That look on your face says you either got what we need... or committed a misdemeanor."

Kristen smirked. "Let's just say I armed the detonator."

Will tilted his head. "Detonator?"

She met his gaze, a glint of satisfaction in her eyes. "No need for a hammer when you've got a thermal detonator, Anderson. Steve's sitting in there right now wondering if it's already ticking."

Will blinked once, then let out a low whistle. "You know, you're terrifying when you're in a good mood."

Kristen's smirk deepened. "That's the point."

He pushed off the wall, falling in step beside her. "You're starting to scare me, sounding like Casey. Just remind me never to end up on your bad side."

Kristen glanced over at him, all mock innocence. "Oh, you wouldn't even see it coming."

Smoke and Ash

Casey had stopped by to check on her newly acquired extended family, asks Will to grab a bottle and join her out on his patio by the pool.

The stars are out. The pool water glows faint blue under the night lights. Will and Casey sit close on padded loungers, a bottle of Buffalo Trace bourbon between them, three fingers poured each. An Arturo Fuente Hemingway Short, her favorite top-shelf cigar, rests in Casey's hand, half-burned. She takes a slow drag and passes it to Will.

The bottle of Buffalo Trace bourbon sat half-drained between them, sweating in the soft heat of the Carolina night. Will leaned back in the patio chair, glass resting on his thigh, eyes following the lazy swirl of smoke rising from the thick cigar Casey brought with her.

She sat cross-legged, one boot kicked off, swirling her drink before taking a slow drag. She held the cigar between two fingers like she'd done it a thousand times.

"At Rogers' place, I erased it," she said, staring at the reflection of the moon in the pool. "All of it."

Will looked over, not speaking yet.

"Steve's backup phone. His cloud backups. Everything tied to Kristen? Gone. Nuked it all." She tapped ash into the tray, her voice calm, resolute. "We don't need those visuals out there. We've got enough to put him away six times over."

Will nodded once, lips pressed tight. He wasn't sure if it was relief or something else sitting heavy in his chest.

"I took care of the stuff from his house, too," Casey added. "Every file. His conquest girls. Wiped. Yours included."

That hit him. Will stared at his bourbon, then took a long drink. "You didn't have to do that."

Casey looked at him with tired but steady eyes. "Yeah, I did. You saved my life, Will. Pulled me out of that deal at my house before Julien could finish what he started."

She took another puff from the cigar and exhaled, the smoke curling toward the stars.

"And let me tell you something, nobody warns you about the damn awful itch when you grow back a full shave." She laughed bitterly. "It's like fire ants with razors, from front to back. How the hell do those fan girls do it?"

Will let out a chuckle, the first real one in days. "Kristen stopped complaining around day three. Switched to cotton underwear and hydration."

Casey smirked. "Smart girl. Me? I was about ready to dunk myself in a tub of oatmeal."

They clinked glasses, a quiet toast to survival and revenge.

Casey leans back, with boots kicked up on the stone edge of the pool, smoke curling into the stars.

Epilogue: Reflection

In the days that followed, the Andersons moved through their lives gingerly, like people learning to walk after a long illness. They leaned on each other, piecing things back together one hesitant step at a time. There were counseling appointments and late-night talks that began in tears and ended in exhausted, awkward laughter—an attempt to reclaim something like normalcy.

Emily scribbled in her journal each night, sometimes furiously, sometimes with trembling hands. Ellie buried herself in books and, with unexpected determination, started painting watercolors by the window. Billy laced up his sneakers before dawn, running until his breath came ragged and the horizon glowed with the first blush of morning. Kristen spent hours in the kitchen, baking bread she never quite finished, the scent lingering long after she'd left the room.

Casey checked in every day. Her wounds—physical and otherwise—were healing, soothed by the warmth of the family she'd chosen, and who, in turn, had chosen her.

There was comfort, too, in the knowledge that the rescued women were safe, and that other missing voices were being found—no longer hidden, no longer just victims, but survivors given a chance to begin again.

One evening, as the sun dipped behind the battered little house and shadows slowly stretched across the lawn, Will stood in the backyard. He felt the cool breeze, listened to the sound of his kids' laughter drifting through the screen door, and closed his eyes.

The darkness had passed. What remained was the memory of survival, a quiet, persistent hope. And from that, the fragile promise of a new beginning.

That night, Will and Casey sat shoulder to shoulder on the back steps, the old Anderson house spilling warm porchlight across the grass. A fresh bottle of Eagle Rare bourbon rested between them, their glasses sweating in the humid air. Out in the yard, fireflies blinked and hovered, slow and golden, as if time itself had decided to pause.

For a long while, neither said a word. After everything, silence felt like a gift—just the hush of crickets, the low murmur of distant laughter from inside, and the comfort of not having to explain themselves.

At last, Casey broke the quiet. "You think it'll ever go back to normal?"

Will didn't answer right away. He took a slow sip, watching the stars wheel overhead. "I don't know," he said finally, voice low and honest. "Maybe not the way it was. But maybe... something better. Something stronger."

Casey leaned into him, her head brushing his shoulder. "You did good, Will. You saved a lot of people."

A tired smile flickered on his face. "So did you. Couldn't have done any of it without you."

She gave him a playful nudge. "Damn right."

A soft breeze wandered through the yard. From the kitchen came the gentle clatter of dishes and the bright sound of Kristen and the kids laughing, alive and safe. The wounds would heal—maybe not all at once, but day by day. And what they'd built here, in all the darkness and light, would hold.

Suddenly, both their phones vibrated on the step between them, their peaceful bubble popping in an instant. The exact group text flashed across both screens.

Captain Monroe:

Anderson, Murphy, please report in ASAP. Body found at the 18th green of the Lakeview at Rocky Pointe Country Club.

Will and Casey's eyes met, the old spark of adrenaline already burning away the quiet. He tossed back the last of his bourbon, feeling the familiar shift as one life faded into the next.

Casey stood, rolling her shoulders, a wry smile on her lips. "Duty calls."

Will exhaled, setting down his glass. "Well. I guess the world's not done with us yet."

Casey stood, cracking a tired smile. "Come on, partner. Let's go see what's waiting at the eighteenth green at the Lakeview."

Will nodded, and together, they stepped out into the night—ready to face whatever waited in the dark.

About the Author

W. Mark Harrington draws on more than two decades of law enforcement experience in North and South Carolina, where he's encountered the kind of cases and characters that linger long after the file is closed. A lifelong fan of the "whodunit" tradition, Mark's storytelling is inspired by real crimes, firsthand accounts, and the stories cops swap over late-night coffee. His influences range from the hard-boiled mysteries of Raymond Chandler to the high-stakes thrillers of James Patterson, John Grisham, Michael Connelly, Jack Carr, Tom Clancy, and Stephen Hunter. When he's not writing, Mark is part of a close-knit family of five—each with an "M" name—who good-naturedly accuse him of gaming online when he's actually crafting his next twist-filled chapter. Demon of Oakhaven is his debut novel, introducing Detectives Will Anderson and Casey Murphy in a gripping new crime series.

Coming Soon: Book 2 in the
Will Anderson and Casey Murphy Series
Devil at Rocky Pointe
Available at your local retail bookstore and online at
Amazon.com

www.ingramcontent.com/pod-product-compliance
Lightning Source LLC
Chambersburg PA
CBHW011350010726
47494CB00008B/2249